A Good Rake Is Hard to Find

Manda Collins

St. Martin's Paperbacks

This is a work of fiction. All of the characters, organizations, and events portrayed in this novel are either products of the author's imagination or are used fictitiously.

A GOOD RAKE IS HARD TO FIND

Copyright © 2015 by Manda Collins.

All rights reserved.

For information address St. Martin's Press, 175 Fifth Avenue, New York, NY 10010.

ISBN: 978-1-250-06106-5

Printed in the United States of America

St. Martin's Paperbacks edition / April 2015

St. Martin's Paperbacks are published by St. Martin's Press, 175 Fifth Avenue, New York, NY 10010.

10 9 8 7 6 5 4 3 2 1

Also by Manda Collins

For Stephen, Tiny, Toast, and Charlie, who keep me company and offer distraction when needed while I'm slaving over a hot keyboard.

Acknowledgments

As always a slew of people helped get this book from idea to finished product. Thanks to my kick-ass agent, Holly Root, for hand-holding and serving as the voice of reason when my author's mania gets out of control; my insightful and clever editor, Holly Ingraham, whose suggestions always make me look at my prose in a new way and in turn make for a better book; to all the folks at St. Martin's Press including my publicist, Amy Goppert, the art, production, and sales departments, and all the folks who work behind the scenes to make sure my books make it into the hands of readers.

Thanks also to my Kiss & Thrill sisters: Carey, Rachel, Lena, Gwen, Krista, Sharon, Sarah, and Diana. And to Eloisa, Sharlene, Janga, Julianne, Santa, Hope, PJ, Ruth, Thea, Chrissy, Crystal, Flora, Gannon, Andrea, Buffy, Kim, Thea, and all the Duchesses for laughter, support, and general good cheer when I needed it most. I could not have made it through this past year without all of your friendship and support.

And finally thanks to my sister Jessie, and my menagerie, Stephen, Tiny, Toast, and Charlie, for keeping things going at home when I was buried under a heavy deadline.

Praise for Manda Collins's delectable Regency novels

WHY LORDS LOSE THEIR HEARTS

"This sweet and sensuous novel has an undercurrent of mystery that will keep readers riveted."

—*Publishers Weekly*

"Collins's tale blends intrigue and desire in a story that is an unusual and intriguing combination of chilling and sweet."   —*RT Book Reviews*

"A suspense-filled tale, *Why Lords Lose Their Hearts,* the third book in author Manda Collins's Wicked Widows trilogy, is a witty, sensual historical romance that will captivate readers from the very beginning. Filled with warmth, clever dialogue, engaging characters, sizzling chemistry, mystery, danger, surprising plot twists, tender romance, and true love, this story is a delight."

—*Romance Junkies*

"Fresh dialogue, suspense, revenge, a most unlikely villain, and of course, romance make *Why Lords Lose Their Hearts* a definite must-read!"

—*Reader to Reader Reviews*

WHY EARLS FALL IN LOVE

"With its shades of *I Know What You Did Last Summer* and strong gothic overtones, Collins's latest is a chill-seeker's delight. Along with the surprising climax, readers will thoroughly enjoy the well-crafted characters, the charming setting, and the romance that adds spice to the drama."   —*RT Book Reviews*

"Sparkling romance amid mystery." —*Publishers Weekly*

Prologue

Jonathan Craven was accounted to be the most skillful driver in England, but it didn't take much skill to know when he was being followed.

For one thing, the driver behind him wasn't doing anything to hide his presence behind Jonathan's curricle as it raced down the road from Basildon to Dartford.

He'd accepted the challenge of Sir Gerard Fincher, the leader of the Lords of Anarchy, the most controversial driving club in London—or perhaps even all of England—because he wanted to prove to the other man that it was possible to win a race without resorting to dirty tricks or finding some way to sabotage the other driver's equipage.

Of course, Gerard wasn't the one behind him now. Jonathan had managed to get a considerable lead over the other man when one of the club leader's own matched bays had pulled up lame just outside of town. It could happen to anyone, but now that he could hear the other carriage coming up behind him—and it was a large one given the sound of four horses pulling it—he wondered if Gerard hadn't sabotaged himself in order to give Jonathan the head start he thought he'd earned on his own.

A burst of nerves shot down his spine as he glanced back to see a plain black coach and four barreling down the macadamized road about a quarter of a mile behind. He could see no markings on the coach, and the driver was masked, something that was not customary except among highwaymen.

He might have suspected robbery was the object if not for the week leading up to this race. First he'd been set upon by thieves while he walked home from a club meeting. Thieves who had taken neither his expensive watch and fobs, nor his purse which was plump with his winnings at whist that evening.

Then, two nights later, he'd woken in the middle of the night to the sound of his casement window clicking shut. Since he himself had climbed down from said window using the trellis there many times in his misspent youth, he knew it was not inconceivable that someone had chosen the same route to break into his bedchamber. And when he threw off the covers to see if anything had been touched, he saw that his wardrobe was opened to reveal the safe he kept hidden there.

"Stand and deliver!" the masked man in the coach and four behind him shouted over the sound of their horses on the road.

"You must be a bold one to try this in broad daylight, man!" Jonathan shouted over his shoulder, but ignored the other driver's demand to stop. He knew instinctively that the moment he brought his curricle to a halt, he would regret it.

But despite his words, he knew that this stretch of the Dover Road was usually deserted at this time of day. Something he'd learned on the Anarchists' bimonthly treks from London to Dartford. Something any other member of the club would also have noticed, he thought with rising anger.

Despite the lightness and speed of the curricle, the four horses of the other man's coach boasted more power and, to Jonathan's alarm, the masked man was gaining on him.

"Pull over, Craven!" the man shouted as he maneuvered his vehicle to come alongside Jonathan's. "Pull over or there will be trouble."

The fact that the man knew his identity only solidified Jonathan's determination not to let this man any closer. For he knew in his gut that as soon as he did, he'd be dead. The Lords of Anarchy had killed before and there was nothing to stop them from killing now. Especially if it meant escaping the consequences of the crimes they'd been committing under the noses of the very people who trusted them.

"There is already trouble," he said, using the whip on his grays. Sorry, old fellows, he thought, disliking to hurt the horses, but it was literally a matter of life and death. And not just his. Many a horse was put down in the aftermath of a bad accident, and he was damned if he'd let these bastards slaughter his loyal team without a fight.

Despite his determination, however, the coach had managed to edge up beside the curricle, and to Jonathan's surprise the door of the passenger compartment opened and a glance back showed the small man was intent upon jumping into the tiger's seat that graced the back of his curricle.

Though he encouraged the horses in a low voice and used the whip with more frequency, he knew the two were already going as fast as they could. And still the coach hovered alongside him.

When the curricle bucked under the thrust of the small man's weight as he landed in the seat, he cursed aloud. For a moment he spared a thought for his sisters and father. What they would think when he turned up dead.

None of them had understood his addiction to speed. To them it was a desperate, dangerous pastime. One that endangered him every time he took to the reins. In vain had he explained that a carriage was only as safe as its driver. And as the best driver in town, the risk to him was minimal.

It had been, in the end, the men he drove with who proved to be the real danger. But he'd not been able to admit as much to Leonora or his father.

I'm sorry, Nora.

He felt the coach lurch as his unwanted passenger attempted to climb over the back of the curricle and into the seat beside him. Or, at least that's what he thought just before he felt the first blow.

He tried to hold the horses steady for their sake now as much as his own, but a second blow made it impossible for his hands to keep from clenching involuntarily. He was aware of the man landing on the cushion beside him and grabbing the reins, And he must have kept his other hand free, for Jonathan felt one more blow before he lost consciousness altogether.

A simple refrain flashed through his mind until he thought no more.

Sorry, Nora. Sorry, Nora. Sorry, Nora,

One

I'd like to know what the deuce Craven was thinking to get himself killed like that," Lord Frederick Lisle said from his favorite chair in the corner of Brooks's.

As was his custom, he had been the first of his friends to arrive, and therefore had his choice of seats. Freddy, as he was known to his friends, was a planner. It was rare that he came into a situation not already knowing every possible outcome. And social gatherings were no exception.

But he'd dashed well not planned on his friend Jonathan Craven dying unexpectedly. None of them had.

" 'The three horsemen' simply doesn't have the same ring to it," the Earl of Mainwaring groused into his brandy from the other side of the table. "Damned inconvenient of Craven to force that on us."

The third member of their party, the Duke of Trent, shrugged before taking a healthy drink. As a decorated soldier in the Napoleonic wars, Trent had become accustomed to friends dying. Or so Freddy surmised. Since Trent never said a damned thing about his time in the army, it was difficult to know either way.

It had been a month since Craven's death during a race between members of the driving club the Lords of

Anarchy. And, since Trent had been away on business, this was their first gathering since losing their friend.

"I just wasn't expecting it," Freddy said glumly, stretching his long legs out before him and crossing them at the ankle. "One doesn't expect someone one's own age to shuffle off this mortal coil. Or at least not someone like Jon. With the exception of his penchant for horses, he was the least reckless of all of us."

"It was those bloody Anarchists," Trent said, his green eyes narrow with anger. "Don't think I've had so much as a note from Jonny since he took up with them. I know you're a 'live and let live' sort of fellow, Freddy, but that lot is the very devil. The only reason the Home Office hasn't disbanded them for treason is because they're too bloody foolish to succeed at true anarchy."

"Aye," Mainwaring said, rubbing a hand over his chin where dark whiskers were already beginning to show despite it being only early evening. "The Lords of Anarchy are not nearly so well mannered as the Four Horse Club, that's for certain. A staid journey to Bedfont for supper twice a month isn't enough for Sir Gerard and his lot. If there's no risk in it for 'em, it's not worth doing."

Unlike the FHC, which drove in an orderly procession to their twice-monthly suppers, the Lords of Anarchy raced to their meetings in Dartford—a fourteen-mile drive from London. It was a dangerous prospect for anyone unlucky enough to venture onto the Dover Road on the first or fourteenth of the month.

"Live and let live, Trent," Freddy protested, his fair skin turning ruddy with annoyance. "Not live and let die. I might be an easygoing sort of fellow but I don't hold with just letting anything go without any sort of protest. I believe in the law, for God's sake."

"I'm glad to hear it," Trent responded without any hint

of apology. "For I've got a mind to look into the workings of that club and the circumstances behind Jon's death."

Mainwaring paused with his glass halfway to his lips. Putting it back down, he asked, "What do you mean, 'look into'? It's not as if Sir Gerard Fincher and his cronies will step aside and invite you to question the members of the club. Sounds like a job for the Runners if you ask me."

"Not the Runners," Freddy said thoughtfully. "There's no way Fincher would let his club members talk to a runner. And even if he did invite one into the group he'd be damned sure that none of them said anything about illegal happenings. A man like that rules with an iron fist. And there'd be retribution for anyone foolish enough to speak out of turn."

"Precisely," Trent said, leaning back in his chair and stretching his legs. "But if the club were to induct a new member, then it mightn't be too long before the inner circle lets down its guard. I rather imagine it's like any other organization of its type. The military being a similar example. They keep gossip, and discipline, in-house."

"And I suppose you're the one who will infiltrate this club?" Freddy asked, his brows raised in skepticism. It was all well and good for Trent to pose the idea, but the Anarchists were known to disdain the military almost as much as the working classes. There was no possible way for Trent to gain membership, his dukedom and fortune notwithstanding.

"No," Trent said with a speaking glance "You are, Frederick."

Freddy gaped. "Me?" Trent was known for his military strategy, but this was simple madness. "I might, in my younger days, have been a candidate for such a club. I know as well as anyone that I was a bit of a hellion before I went to France. But I'm trying to turn over a new leaf. I'm too old for all that devilry."

"But you've only been back for a couple of weeks," Mainwaring said thoughtfully. "You might have changed inside, but the rest of the world still sees the old Freddy who was up to every challenge. Besides, they will never take Trent with his military service."

"Et tu, Mainwaring?" Freddy said with disgust. "I suppose you wouldn't work because you're so damned lucky at cards you'd be run through before the week was out."

"I don't cheat," Mainwaring said through clenched teeth. It was a charge lobbed at the earl's head quite frequently by those who were unfortunate enough to sit across the card table from him. Which is why Freddy knew it would sting.

"And," the earl continued, "it's well-known that I am an indifferent driver at best."

Manwaring had a point there, Freddy thought morosely. His unusual childhood had prevented the earl from engaging in anything that might possibly be dangerous. As an adult he might be more of a risk-taker, but driving was still not one of his prime interests.

"He does have the right of it," Trent said unapologetically. "You're the only one of us who could possibly fit the club's requirements. You drive to an inch and you're known to be a hellion."

Really, Freddy reflected, all it took was a night out with friends to convince him that he was better off spending time with his dogs. "Stop calling me that," he said without much heat. The truth was that he *had* been a rake before he left for France. And a good while after. He'd had his reasons, but he hadn't had time enough back in England to supplant his reputation with a newer, more respectable one.

"Sorry, old fellow," Mainwaring said with a shrug. "But it's the truth. We know you're not up to your old tricks, but the rest of the world doesn't."

Freddy drank the rest of his brandy. It was a damnable thing to have his misdeeds from half a decade ago held up to scrutiny now, when he'd worked so hard to change. With a sigh, he sat up straighter in his chair and flexed his shoulders. "I suppose I could manage to charm myself into Sir Gerard Fincher's good graces. Repugnant though that would be."

The other men simply nodded. At least they were not going to gloat about their victory.

"I still don't know how Jonathan managed to spend any degree of time with Fincher," Mainwaring said with a shudder. "We were at school together. He was not a pleasant sort of chap. He was a prefect. And you know what it's like when a bully gets the smallest bit of power. Damned fellow made life hell for any number of chaps in my year. I was on another hall, thank the gods. Otherwise I'd have been a target for him as well."

"I don't think Jon was an Anarchist out of any real love for the members," Freddy said thoughtfully. "I think it was about the driving. He was always wanting to drive faster, more skillfully, farther distances. And they were, for all their bad behavior, the only group in England who offered that sort of competition for him."

"He dashed well wasn't going to find it with us," Trent said with a sigh. "I drive to get from one place to the next, but with Jon it was a passion."

"At least with us he might still be alive," Freddy said, looking into his now empty glass. "I'd never have countenanced driving that stretch of road in a curricle at that speed. Much less two abreast."

"There's no use complaining about what we could have done or should have done," Mainwaring said gruffly.

"It's over. He's gone. But if there's a way for one of us to find out if it was because of something the Anarchists did, then we've got to try. If not for Jon's sake then for our own."

"Aye," Freddy said with a nod. "I'll find out. Though it won't be easy. With a man like Fincher there's no way of knowing whether he's lying or not. I've seen him tell untruths with such sincerity that I almost believed it—and it was a tale I knew without doubt was a lie. He's always been that way. My father calls him colder than a north Yorkshire winter, and I know it to be the truth."

Mainwaring's dark brows drew together. "How do you know so much about Fincher? I thought he was just an acquaintance for all of us. But you sound like you've known him from childhood."

Freddy ran a restless hand over his chin. "The thing is," he admitted, "I've known Sir Gerald Fincher since we were in short coats. He's my cousin."

Mainwaring's eyes widened and Trent shook his head in exasperation.

"How long were you going to keep that bit of information from us?" Trent asked coolly.

"It's hardly a state secret," Freddy said with a shrug. "I told Jonathan when he decided to join the blasted club what sort of chap Gerry is. But he didn't care. It was all about the driving for him."

Mainwaring, the peacemaker, looked from one man to the other.

"We've all got family members we'd rather not claim, Trent," he said hastily. "I've always suspected my aunt Hazel of having Bonapartist leanings but it's hardly been something I wanted to shout from the rooftops."

"Of course we do." Trent's brow furrowed with frustration. "But if I thought your aunt Hazel was inducing Freddy to spy for the French, I'd do something about it."

"He was a grown man," Freddy protested. "I told him about Gerard and he chose to ignore me. I could hardly lock him in the cellar until the impulse passed."

He would have gone on, but a footman appeared beside their table at that moment looking decidedly uncomfortable.

"What is it, Ned?" Freddy asked, grateful for the interruption.

"My apologies, my lord," the young man said with a grimace, "but there is a situation at the door that demands your attention."

"The door?" Mainwaring echoed.

"The last time I saw a 'situation at the door,'" Trent said with a raised brow, "was when Pinky Byng's mistress showed up to throw his parting gift back in his face. I told him that garnets were too cheap for that one, but he didn't listen."

"I can assure you it's nothing like that," Freddy said with a laugh. "I always manage to make my mistresses think it's their idea to break it off with me rather than the other way around. Cheaper that way, my being a younger son and all."

Even so, he had a bad feeling about this. Some sixth sense told him that someone causing a scene at the door of Brooks's was not going to bring glad tidings of great joy.

And when he reached the door, followed close behind by Trent and Mainwaring who were not willing to miss such a diversion, he knew he was right.

"I might have known I'd find the three of you together," Miss Leonora Craven said, her generous red lips tight with annoyance. "Though you needn't have brought your little friends with you to the door for protection, Lord Frederick. I've no intention of harming your person no matter how you might deserve it for getting my brother killed."

Keenly aware of the curious glances they were getting from the club members who stood on the steps just behind her, Freddy turned to Ned. "I realize that ladies are not allowed in the club, Ned, but is there some small anteroom where we might be private for a few moments?"

It would do Leonora's reputation little good to be seen going into a room alone with the three of them, but then again, if her reputation was her first concern, she'd not have come to St. James Street at all.

"Of course, my lord." Ned ushered them to a door just off the hallway. "I'll bring some tea for the lady."

He didn't think Leonora would be there long enough for tea, but Freddy agreed, then shepherded her into the small sitting room, surprised, as he always was, by how tiny she seemed considering how large her personality could be.

The chamber was outfitted with a few club chairs, a settee, and a low table. Leonora stalked into the room, her dark head held high, while Freddy followed and took a place before the fire. Trent and Mainwaring, perhaps sensing that this was a private matter, had slipped away with Ned.

"Well, Nora," he said, once the door closed behind them, "you've got me here and made a hash of your reputation in the process. I hope it will be worth it."

Her green eyes flashed with anger, and Freddy couldn't help but notice the shadows beneath them. Her dark hair was just as glossy as ever, and framed her heart-shaped face in a halo of loose curls, one caressing her cheek like a kiss. But she looked thinner than the last time he'd seen her. The day she'd broken off their engagement and sent him on a reckless tear that ended with his leaving England for the freedoms of the Continent.

He'd expected their first meeting to be difficult, but to his surprise, much of the resentment he'd felt had dissipated in the years since they'd parted. It was true that she had not been particularly kind in breaking things off between them. Indeed, she'd never told him the true reason for it. Had tried to fob him off with some silly tale of being afraid of giving up control of her own life. It was something that had not once come up between them, so when she declared it to be why she was ending what had up to that point been a perfectly agreeable connection, he had been dumbfounded. And hurt that she would dismiss him without any more explanation than that.

Even so, in the intervening years, he'd had a great deal of time to think. And he'd come to realize that whatever her true reason for breaking things off, it had been something serious. Something that was more important to her than her own happiness. For they had been happy before she ended things.

And though he was not yet sanguine about what had happened, he was no longer consumed with bitterness over it.

Which did not mean he wasn't annoyed that she'd sought him out in Brooks's without a care for either of their reputations. It was the sort of reckless gesture he'd have been prone to in his wilder days, but now he was trying to mend his reputation. Having a woman pursue him to St. James Street was not going to help things.

Leonora, however, obviously did not care.

"You know as well as I do that my reputation is able to withstand more than that of the usual society lady thanks to my writing," she responded, waving off his concerns. "And besides that, in this instance, I wished to make a scene. I relish it, in fact."

"To what purpose?" Freddy demanded, growing tired of her taunts. "My reputation is already not what it should be. So if you're thinking to ruin me, you're missing the mark."

"Of course I know that," Leonora said, her eyes bright with emotion. "But I'm not all that concerned with such things at present. I want only justice for my brother. And I wish to know what you plan to do to make your cousin, to whom you introduced my impressionable brother, pay for Jonny's death."

Ah. That's where all this came from.

"I'm not sure what you mean, Miss Craven," he said with stiff formality, despite the fact that he and his friends had been discussing this very matter only moments ago.

"Oh, give over, my lord," she said sharply. "You know as well as I do that Jonathan's death was no accident. He was murdered by that vicious club and I can prove it."

Two

Seeking Freddy out in his club had seemed like a good idea at the time, but as she faced the whey-faced footman at the entrance to Brooks's, Leonora Craven, famous poetess, thought that she might better have waited to call on him at home in the morning. She was known for boldness in most things, but this might have been a bit too much.

When Freddy arrived, however, flanked by Mainwaring and Trent, looking not one bit the worse for wear since her brother's death, her anger crowded out any misgivings she might have. If nothing else her little stunt would cause talk, and the more talk there was about Lord Frederick "Freddy" Lisle, the better. It would make his entry into the Lords of Anarchy that much more believable.

At the moment, he looked dangerous enough to belong to the infamous driving club. His blue eyes flashed with anger and his finely chiseled jaw was clenched so tightly she thought he might lose a few teeth. His burnished light brown curls were mussed, but she knew from their time together that they were merely reverting to their natural state. She'd spent enough time with her fingers tangled in them to know their tendency to untidiness.

Blinking, she threw off the memory and realized he was talking.

"Do not be so loud," he hissed, looking to make sure the door was indeed closed. "If you go about making accusations like that you might find yourself with more to worry about than a damaged reputation. My cousin isn't exactly known for his forgiving nature."

"I don't care who hears me," Leonora said hotly. "If those men are responsible for Jonny's death then they deserve to have it known. And if you hadn't introduced my brother to those ruffians he'd still be alive now."

Ned, the footman, returned just then with the tea tray, which was also laden with biscuits and a few sandwiches. Despite her boldness, she kept silent while he left the tray.

Silently she took a seat and poured two steaming cups. One for herself and one for Frederick. To her surprise, her hands shook as she passed his cup. Clearly she was more rattled to be in his presence again than she'd expected.

Or it might be her recent lack of sleep. She'd not known the comfort of a full night's rest in weeks. Not since Jonny had been killed.

Not remarking on her obvious agitation, Freddy sipped from his cup then spoke. "What makes you think that Sir Gerard and his lot killed Jonny?"

His voice had lost its anger, and to Nora's dismay she felt tears welling up at the gentleness there. So long as she could keep her anger at the forefront of her mind, she could keep her finer feelings at bay, but kindness—especially from Freddy—made her feel exposed. Still, she was able to steel herself against the emotions after a few deep breaths. She had to remain calm for Jonny's sake.

"Last week I received a letter," she said, paying close

attention to her teacup rather than risking a glance at Freddy. "It was from Jonny. He'd had it sent by his solicitor in the event of his death."

She felt stillness fall over the little room. "What did it say?" he asked, his voice calm despite the waves of curiosity she sensed emanating from him.

"That he thought the club had found him out," Leonora said baldly. "That he'd hidden some important documents in the safe in his rooms. Documents that would make it clear just what the Lords of Anarchy were up to."

Freddy frowned. "Found him out about what?"

"I haven't a clue," Leonora said with a shake of her head. "He didn't explain. And when I looked in the safe in his bedchamber it was open, but empty."

"So either the documents were never there at all, or someone got into his bedchamber before you did," Freddy stated, his full attention on her.

"Or maybe he changed his mind," she offered. "Perhaps whatever it was about was resolved but he forgot to tell his solicitor not to send the letter."

"That's not like him," Freddy said. "You know how meticulous your brother is . . . was."

Leonora winced at the switch from present to past tense. "I know he was. It was just a possibility. I don't want to believe the worst."

"I don't suppose you could have misunderstood his letter?" Freddy asked with more diffidence than she'd have expected from him. "Perhaps misread something? Or jumped to the wrong conclusion?"

But she'd gone over the note again and again. She was convinced it was just as it seemed.

"I'm a poet," she stated. "Words are my livelihood. I know how to read, and to read between the lines. I didn't misunderstand." Opening her reticule, she removed a folded paper and handed it to him. "See for yourself if you wish."

He reached for the document, and when their hands touched, Leonora fought to keep her response from showing. The current of attraction between them hadn't dissolved along with the dissolution of their betrothal. It was discomfiting, but she would endure it. For Jonny's sake.

Apparently unaffected by her touch, Freddy scanned the letter. As he bowed his head to read, his hair glinted in the firelight. Leonora was reminded of just how handsome he was. Her sister was quite fond of pointing that out to her when bemoaning the fact that Leonora had let such a fine catch slip through her fingers. She herself only considered the matter in the dark of night when her bed seemed to mock her with its emptiness. Now was hardly the time for such reflections, however.

Oblivious to her thoughts, Freddy handed the letter back to her. "I suppose you think it was Sir Gerard and his cronies who stole the documents?"

"Who else could it have been?" Leonora asked, frustrated by the question. "They're the only ones who had any reason to want them. What they implicated the club in I have no idea, but it was obviously enough to prompt my brother to fear for his life."

"True enough," Freddy agreed, stretching his long legs out before him, his brow furrowed in thought. "And who's to say that Jonny didn't trust the wrong club member with his suspicions. It's very possible that whoever he confided in told Gerard."

But Leonora balked at the idea. "It's possible, I suppose. But it doesn't make much sense. Why would he leave that letter for me, otherwise? If he could trust someone in the club, there would be no need to rely on me. And we both know what Jonny thought of my involvement in anything having to do with what he considered men's business. He sent that letter to me because I was the only one he knew he could trust."

"He doubtless thought you'd come to me," Freddy said with a shrug. And perhaps seeing her stiffen, he held out a staying hand. "Now, don't get your back up. I am not saying you should have done, but that Jonny would certainly expect you to. I don't think he ever really believed that we were serious about breaking things off between us."

"Silly clod," she said with affection. "He was always more romantic than either I or Helen was."

"I think he fell in love five times the first week we were up at Oxford," Freddy said with a grin. "I think he was always in search of the perfect woman."

"Much to the dismay of whoever happened to be on his arm at the time." Leonora shook her head at the memory.

For a moment it was as if they'd never been apart. There was an easy give and take to their interactions that Leonora found just as seductive as Freddy's good looks. She'd always thought him handsome. And that had only increased with time. When he'd left for France, he'd still been a boy. But now, with his wide shoulders and solid strength, he was a man. And she felt the pull of an attraction so fierce now it left her almost breathless.

"So, if he was hoping you'd come to me for help with this matter," Freddy said, apparently unfazed by the current between them, "then is it possible that there were no documents? That he was trying to lead us on a wild-goose chase simply to throw us together?"

But Leonora shook her head. "I don't think so. It's not as if he planned his own death to bring us together. Someone wanted him silenced. And it was someone in that club. I'm sure of it."

"It would have to be," Freddy said, rising to pace

before the fireplace. "No one else was closely involved in the race from London to Dartford. And they're the only ones who had reason to want him dead."

Leonora nodded, relieved they were in agreement. "It's the only explanation that makes sense," she said. "He might possibly have crashed on his own. It happens. But the involvement of the letter and the missing documents say otherwise."

"If it weren't," Freddy said, "there would be no reason to get rid of him." Then, as if hearing his own words, he winced. "I did not mean that as crudely as it sounded."

But Leonora shook her head. "I've been thinking of it in very similar terms. After all, the way Jonny died was very much akin to a coachman tossing a parcel of refuse onto the side of the road."

Jonathan had been thrown from his curricle during a race to which he'd challenged the club's leader. Since Jonny had been in the lead at the time, and had been on a particularly deserted stretch of the Dover Road, no one had seen the accident that killed him. Or at least, no one admitted to seeing him. The number of blows on her brother's body, especially his head, and the absence of his curricle, which the first men on the scene had claimed must have been stolen, sparked Leonora's suspicions immediately. With no way to see what sort of damage had been done to the vehicle, it was impossible to know just how the accident had happened. Or if it had been an accident at all.

She closed her eyes as she thought about how terrifying her brother's last moments must have been, and when she opened them, it was to see Freddy kneeling beside her chair.

"I am sorry, Nora," he said softly, taking her gloved hand in his. "I don't think I've been able to truly convey my sympathies to you. I know how much you loved him.

In spite of his disapproval of your stance on the rights of women."

Freddy, she reflected, was one of the few people who knew about her brother's distaste for her rabble-rousing as he called it. And he knew how much Jonathan's dislike for her stance had hurt her. Whereas as children they'd been quite close, once Nora began to speak out about how unjust women's lot was under the law, a distance had sprung up between brother and sister that had never been fully reversed before he died.

That uneasiness between them was something she'd regret for the rest of her life.

"I know you loved him, too," she whispered, clinging to Freddy's hand despite her earlier frustration with him. One of the most unbearable aspects of Jonathan's loss had been the inability to speak about her sorrow with someone who understood how things had truly been between them.

Her sister, Helen, was also devastated by Jonny's death, but she was busy with her own family now and had been unaware of how things stood between her siblings.

"And that you had no idea what would happen when you introduced him to your cousin. How can you have?" They'd been fresh out of university and eager for every adventure. And neither Jonathan nor his friends could have imagined how getting involved with Sir Gerard Fincher would change things.

"Jon was always one to go his own way," Freddy said gravely. "For all that we were friends, the rest of us were never as interested in driving and coaching as he was. We were poor competition for him, so he went to a place where he didn't have to hold back. Where he could push his horses to the limit with the fastest rig he could get. It wasn't enough to drive well for Jon. He had to be the best and the fastest. And for that he needed competition. Something none of us was able to offer him."

"I suppose," she said sadly. She supposed she could understand it to a degree. After all, she enjoyed spending time with her fellow poets. She didn't befriend them exclusively, but there was a certain level of conversation that could only be had with others who thought as deeply as she did about words and rhythm and meter and meaning. And as for competition, she supposed it was something akin to her annoyance when one of her more sophisticated poems was published alongside the amateurish rhymes of a man with more influence than talent.

"But it's difficult not to be angry with him for risking his life," she said, appreciating the sympathy in Freddy's blue eyes. And the strength of him there beside her. As if it were possible for her to gain fortitude from his mere proximity.

"And," she said, admitting her true reason for being so angry with her brother, "for not telling me about the business with the Anarchists before he got himself killed."

"Do not think you are alone in your anger," Freddy said, taking her other hand. "Trent and Mainwaring and I gathered here tonight to talk for a number of reasons. Our annoyance with Jon for getting himself killed chief among them."

She looked up and saw from the fire in his eyes that he was telling the truth. "Until I arrived to ruin things, you mean."

"I didn't say that," he said with a smile, for a moment lightening the seriousness that had lain heavy over them for the past quarter hour. He quirked his head a little and raised a single brow. "But you do like to make an entrance, don't you, Nora?"

She felt her cheeks flush, something she only ever experienced in Freddy's company. "I couldn't sleep," she said softly. "And I simply had to speak to you tonight. Whatever the consequences."

"How long?" Freddy asked, all seriousness. Her inability to sleep was something she'd been forced to confide in him back when they'd been engaged. Mostly because it had been impossible for him not to notice the shadows beneath her eyes when she was in the grips of a particularly long stretch of wakefulness.

It had been something she struggled with since her early teens. It often came with intense creativity, which was fortuitous for her writing, but also with a price.

"Only a few days," she admitted. "I had finally managed to get things under control a few months ago. But it was impossible to rest once I learned of his death. Then I began writing a series of verse about it. About him. And despite my better judgment, I let myself get caught up in the writing, and stayed up all night. And of course it was impossible to close my eyes last night."

"And so here you are tonight," he said with a frown. "You must take better care of yourself, Leonora." He reached out and stroked a thumb over her cheek. "You will make yourself ill."

"It's difficult to care," she admitted with a shrug. "Not when Jonny is gone. And his killer runs free."

"Well, I care," Freddy said firmly, and his words sent a pang of loneliness coursing through her so sharp she almost cried out. How long had it been since she'd felt that sort of focused attention on her well-being?

Her father loved her. And so did Helen. But there was something about having someone to call your very own. Someone who focused his attention on pleasing you.

If she weren't careful, Leonora thought, she'd find herself falling under Freddy's spell, just as she had five years ago. And that would be a terrible thing for both of them.

Because there was no possible way for them to be together without her causing him a lifetime of regret. And she was determined that he, at least, should have everything in life he wished for.

She'd learned long ago that such happy-ever-afters would never be her own lot.

"So what will it take to make you return home and for some laudanum to help you sleep?" he asked, his voice tinged with a mix of affection and exasperation.

She despised laudanum, which Freddy well knew. It had been one of their biggest points of contention during their engagement. He simply didn't understand why she refused to use the one thing that gave her the rest she needed. It was difficult to explain to someone like Freddy, who seemed able to simply close his eyes and drift off at the drop of a hat.

But Leonora had seen what daily doses of laudanum could do to a person. And once one began using it, it became nigh impossible to stop. She refused to become dependent on something that made her feel as if her mind were wrapped in fog as thick as a London sky in winter.

Even so, she was exhausted enough—and desperate enough—at this point to agree to his request. If she were going to concentrate on bringing down Sir Gerard Fincher, she had to get some rest.

"So long as you agree to help me prove that the Lords of Anarchy are responsible for Jonathan's death," she told him, "I'll agree to just about anything."

The flare of heat in his blue eyes gave her some idea of the tenor of the "anything" he imagined. But just as quickly it was gone, and Freddy was rising and offering her his hand.

"Then it's a deal," he said, as she rose wearily from the club chair. "I will help you prove my cousin was responsible for your brother's death, and you will get some rest."

Now that she'd secured his agreement, however, Leonora knew she would be able to sleep without drugs tonight. She felt her body relax for the first time since she'd learned of her brother's death.

She nodded, and stifled a yawn, but before she could turn to leave, Freddy stayed her with a hand on her arm. "I'm afraid I have another request that you might not be so sanguine about once you hear it."

Leonora shrugged, her body too exhausted to cause an alarm. "You may as well try me now while I'm too sleepy to refuse."

"You won't like it," he said seriously. "But I think that the best way for the two of us to investigate the Lords of Anarchy will be together."

"Well, of course," she agreed. "I'm hardly going to let you investigate things without keeping me apprised of them. And I'll naturally wish to be included in some of the investigation."

"That's not what I'm talking about, Nora," he said with a sigh. "I mean that we should conduct this investigation as an *engaged* couple."

Three

"Engaged?" Leonora asked, her mouth hanging open. "I . . . you mean . . . to be married? But why? What purpose will it serve?"

He'd known it would be a difficult prospect to convince her, but as soon as the notion came to him, it had been impossible to dislodge from his mind. It would be difficult for both of them, but he feared it was the only way his cousin could be thoroughly routed.

"Yes, to be married," he explained as she frowned up at him, that errant curl by her ears tempting him, like a beckoning finger, to reach out and caress the cheek where it rested. "Not a true engagement, of course. But one that is real enough to seem valid in the eyes of the Lords of Anarchy at least."

If he'd supposed she would leap at the chance to have her name linked with his again, he was doomed to disappointment.

"And what sort of proof will the Anarchists need for this betrothal you propose to seem valid?" she asked with a moue of distaste. "The sight of you throwing me over your shoulder and carrying me off to your lair? Or maybe I shall need to compete in a driving challenge of some sort. Though they do not allow ladies in their club, I have a feeling they hypocritically would prefer that ladies were excellent drivers."

"Don't be glib, Leonora," he chided, though he rather agreed with her assessment. "It doesn't suit you."

"I will be as glib as I wish, Freddy," she snapped, dropping back into the club chair with a flounce, as if her legs would no longer hold her up. "I came here tonight to convince you to investigate Jonny's murder, not to embark upon yet another foolish engagement with you. If I wanted to be married I'd have done so by now."

There was a vehemence in her tone that stirred some vestige of the hurt and anger he'd felt when she broke things off with him. What, he wondered, was so objectionable to marriage? He had supposed it was marriage to himself that she found abhorrent but it seemed now that she'd developed an aversion to the institution itself.

Realizing that his plan was going to require more than a quick conversation, Freddy took the seat opposite hers. He wished he'd requested a bottle of brandy at the same time Ned had brought the tea. He wasn't sure about Leonora, but he could certainly use a bit of liquid courage for this conversation.

"It isn't meant to be an actual marriage, Nora," he said with what he considered to be admirable calm. "It's a ruse. Unless, that is, you do not wish to be a part of this investigation. Which is all the same to me really. I generally prefer to work alone. And if I'm not concerned about you I'll be able to more fully participate in the activities of the club." He let his words sink in for a moment so that she understood just what he meant by "activities."

But Leonora refused to be distracted by the mention of the lascivious nature of some of the club's meetings. "But why?" she demanded. "What purpose would it serve for your cousin to believe we're betrothed? If you mean to become a member yourself it's not necessary. There is no rule that says club members need to be wed. Or even betrothed."

"It is rumored that my cousin's wife holds just as much sway over the female companions of club members as he does over the members themselves," he explained. "And if my own knowledge of their marriage is accurate, Lady Melisande Fincher is nearly as ruthless as Gerard."

She was silent, thinking no doubt of the repercussions of a false betrothal. Perhaps remembering just how painful it had been when she ended their very real betrothal five years ago.

Finally, when he'd almost given up hope of a response, she said, "I suppose there is some merit to your absurd notion. If Melisande is as involved in club matters as you say, then someone will need to get close to her. To learn what she knows about my brother's death."

Though he felt a surge of relief at her acquiescence, Freddy nodded soberly. "I think it's imperative that we put about word of our betrothal at once. I realize you are still in mourning, so we will simply say that the wedding will be a quiet family affair."

He had a feeling he'd soon be fending off questions from his mother over the unusual circumstances of the match, but that could wait. For now all that mattered was making his cousin believe that the betrothal was a real one.

"I'll get the notice out to the papers first thing tomorrow," he continued, noting that she'd once more lapsed into a thoughtful silence. "I suppose I should visit your father tomorrow, as well. I wonder if he'll be more inclined to shake my hand or put a bullet in me. I'm thinking hand shaking considering just how difficult you've been these years since our last betrothal. The poor man is probably desperate to get you off his hands."

"I fear you are unduly optimistic," she said with a shake of her head. "Papa was none too happy with the way things worked out between us before. He's likely to refuse your request out of hand."

But he could tell from the quirk of her brow that she was likely exaggerating. He'd always been a favorite with Joseph Craven, whose lack of a title belied a superb lineage and wealth that rivaled that of the most celebrated families in England.

"We'll see," he said with a shrug. If Mr. Craven did cut up rough, Freddy was not above explaining the gist of their plan (downplaying the risk to Leonora, of course) to persuade him. But he'd cross that bridge when he came to it. "Now, shall we leave? There are quite a few things I need to do before we announce our betrothal to the world."

"And there is the matter of worming your way into Sir Gerard Fincher's good graces," she added, rising from her chair. "Though I suppose it shouldn't be so very difficult considering the man is your cousin."

"You'd be surprised," Freddy said, offering her his arm. "If you will recall, Gerry and I have never been on the best of terms."

"Oh, I remember," Leonora said, drawing the hood of her cloak up over her head, its deep blue color accentuating the shadows beneath her eyes. Once again, Freddy found himself wanting to bundle her up and ensure that she got the rest she needed. But it had been his hovering that he suspected led her to break off their first engagement. And he was damned if he'd let her break this false one, too.

"I thought perhaps you'd enlist your papa or one of your brothers to aid you," she continued, allowing him to guide her to the door of the little antechamber where they'd been talking. "After all, there is nothing more convincing than a word from a well-placed relation to smooth the way. At least it has been my experience."

It wasn't a bad idea, Freddy thought as they wended their way along the servants' passage to the back door of Brooks's, where she might escape the scrutiny of curious club members coming into the club for the night.

He had thought he'd need to drive her home in his own carriage, but as soon as they stepped out he saw one of her father's carriages was waiting in the mews behind the club.

Silently, they crossed the narrow street, and with a nod to the coachman who was giving him a quizzical look, he handed her up into the carriage. Then, to Leonora's astonishment he climbed up into the carriage after her.

"What are you doing?" she hissed, as he gave a rap on the roof to indicate to the driver that they should depart.

"I am escorting you home, Leonora," he responded solemnly. "You might have embarked upon your hare-brained scheme to infiltrate Brooks's without an escort, but I'm certainly not going to let you drive down St. James Street alone. Besides, you look so exhausted I thought you might not be able to make it to the door of your father's house."

"How flattering, sir," she said with mock gratitude. "I vow, next you'll be telling me you question my ability to put myself to bed and will offer to carry me in."

Her words hung in the air, like a gauntlet thrown down before him. For a breath he considered what the scenario she painted would be like. He could picture lifting her into his arms and carrying her up the grand staircase of her house, and lowering her to the smooth counter-pane (her clothing and his having magically vanished in the process).

The air between them snapped with awareness. Their

gazes held for a moment before she glanced down. He was suddenly annoyed by the darkness of the carriage interior. He wanted to see what tale her eyes told about her true feelings.

But as he'd expected, she pretended as if nothing had happened.

Just as well.

When she said nothing, he said, "I feel sure your father would be less than pleased if I were to cause a disturbance in the house at this hour."

And just like that the moment was gone.

"Doubtless you are right," she said, a hint of relief in her tone.

Then she went on. "I am grateful for your help, Freddy," she said solemnly. "If you'd refused I'd have found a way to get myself into the club regardless, but I will feel more confident knowing you're there, too. There is something about your cousin I cannot like. And I would much rather not place myself in his hands, if it's at all possible."

The idea of her anywhere near his cousin sent a chill through him, but Freddy merely nodded. "Jonny was my friend. And whether you believe it or not, Trent, Mainwaring, and I were discussing ways to prove the Lords of Anarchy were somehow responsible for your brother's death before you arrived."

She looked skeptical, but did not gainsay him. Instead she asked, "What had you decided?"

"Only that I should find a way to join the club," Freddy admitted. "We hadn't got much farther before Ned came to tell me you'd arrived. Or talked your way inside, as the case may be."

"So it's quite a good thing that I came when I did, isn't it?" Leonora asked with a flash of teeth. "Otherwise you might never have come up with a viable plan."

It was rather a whitewashed vision of her arrival's impact on his plans, but Freddy was willing to concede the point. After all, her intrusion had given him a more viable plan to get into his cousin's club than just "Item One: Convince Gerry to let me in."

By this time the carriage began to slow, and finally rolled to a stop. Freddy didn't wait for the coachman to open the door, but opened it himself and jumped down to the street.

Instead of handing Leonora down the stairs, he reached inside, took her by the waist and lifted her lightly down. It was no accident that her lithe curves brushed against the front of his body as he lowered her.

When she was on her feet, he looked down into her face, a pale oval in the moonlight. "Good night, Leonora," he said softly. "I'll be by in the morning to speak with your father."

"I . . ." She seemed to struggle with something, but then must have decided against whatever she'd been about to say. "Good night, Freddy."

Then, before he could kiss her, as she doubtless knew he'd intended, she wrenched herself away and hurried up the steps to the door of Craven House.

Leaving Freddy to stare after her before he turned and walked the short distance to his own house in Berkeley Square.

The following morning, Leonora found her father in his library discussing estate business with his private secretary, Mr. Soames.

Though Joseph Craven held no title, he was a gentleman of some considerable wealth, and his estate in Hampshire was known to be one of the finest in England. It had been one of his fondest wishes to one day hand his property down to his son, but that wish had died along with Jonathan a few weeks earlier. Now when the elder Craven died, the estate would pass into the hands of a distant cousin, and if his prior visits were any indication, Leonora would not find life under Cousin Humphrey's roof to be as liberal as life with her father. And though she knew her sister would welcome her, she had no wish to become a burden.

In fact, only a few days before, Papa had broached the topic of betrothals to her, something he'd not mentioned since her engagement to Freddy had come to an end all those years ago. Leonora had assured her father that her attitude toward the matrimonial state was unchanged, despite the threat of Cousin Humphry, and that it was likely to remain so.

What would he say when Freddy showed up on his doorstep asking for her hand once again? Doubtless he'd think the poor fellow had lost his wits.

Leonora certainly felt as if *she* had.

But when Freddy had broached the idea last evening in Brooks's—and really, what on earth had possessed her to barge into the gentleman's club like that without a by-your-leave? She'd done some foolish things in the grips of insomnia before but that was the most outrageous by far.

The betrothal, however, in the light of day, while unusual, did seem like a rather effective means for gaining information about Sir Gerard Fincher. Her brother had mentioned more than once just how much influence that lady wielded on her husband. And indeed over all the members of the club. Despite being a woman, Melisande was quite powerful in her own way. And Leonora had long suspected she had some sort of hold over her brother.

Jonny had not been ready to marry—far from it—but he had escorted ladies to various fashionable entertainments solely for the sake of winning Lady Melisande

Fincher's approval. "It's not as if I'm marrying the chits, Nora," he'd told her once when she questioned the other woman's intrusion into his social life. "Besides, I mean to be the leader of the Anarchists one day. Any bit I can do to win the approval of Sir Gerard Fincher and his lady, I'll do."

As for Leonora, she felt a bit of trepidation about the notion of gaining an entrance into the club with a reputation for every sort of sin, from the anarchism of its name, to womanizing. But she was willing to risk everything if it meant finding out who had killed her brother. If only for her father's sake.

It had been a few weeks since they'd received the news, and since then she'd seen her father sink deeper and deeper into depression. Though he'd been confined to a wheeled chair since she was a child, Leonora had always thought of her father as a robust and commanding figure. Unfortunately, he was wont to suffer from dark moods from time to time. And Jonny's death had sent him into a depression that showed no signs of abating. She had to do something to assuage his grief.

And if Freddy was able to help her get the answers she needed, then she might consider telling him the painful secret that had kept her from going through with their marriage five years ago. She could not marry him, of course. It was too late for that. But it might ease his frustration to know her decision had nothing whatsoever to do with him. Or rather, not something he'd done.

But that was something to think about on another day. Today was for persuading her father that this pretend betrothal between them was real. A sort of situational folly that looked quite real from a distance, but upon closer inspection was hollow.

"My dear daughter," Joseph Craven said when she

stepped into his den. "What brings you here so bright and early? I thought you would be writing by now."

Leonora usually spent mornings after breakfast in her own sitting room composing verses or writing essays for various ladies' publications where her opinion had become quite popular among readers.

Whereas her father liked to spend his mornings in his study poring over business documents and instructing his secretary about various matters relating to the running of the many Craven business interests. Along with the farm at the Hampshire estate, there was also a textile factory in Manchester and various other investments. The snobs might turn up their noses at any gentleman who was involved in trade, but it was an open secret that most men of the best families dabbled in all sorts of activities that had been eschewed by the generation before them.

As Mr. Craven derived much satisfaction from his tangles as he referred to them, Leonora had no objections. Since her father had been supportive of her ventures into the world of poetry and literature, it would have been hypocritical of her to do so.

Stepping fully into the room and walking behind his desk to kiss him on the cheek, she said, "Must I have a reason to visit my dear papa?" she asked once Mr. Soames, the secretary, had left the room. "Why, you make it sound as if I follow a schedule with the regularity of a clock."

"Hardly, my dear," he said with a fond smile. "You are nothing if not unpredictable."

Despite his hearty tone, she knew he was still in the grips of the darkness that had consumed him since Jonny's death. Sometimes it was the pain—his constant companion since he'd broken both legs in a riding accident when Leonora was a child—that brought his moods down, but this time it was all thanks to the loss of his only son.

Still, this morning he seemed more like himself than he had in some time, for which Leonora was grateful.

"I prefer to call it spontaneity," she said with a grin, before sinking into the chair across from his desk. "And speaking of spontaneity, I have news that might forever cement my reputation for it once all is revealed."

"Oh, dear," her father said, leaning back in his chair to steeple his hands together before him. "Let me guess . . ." He furrowed his brow in thought before saying, "You are embarking upon an expedition to Egypt."

It was something she'd threatened more than once, but Leonora had never quite decided to take the plunge. For one thing she got seasick quite dreadfully, which she'd learned to her dismay the one time she'd tried to cross the Channel to visit Paris. Unfortunately she'd become so ill that the captain had been convinced to turn back to England on her behalf thanks to a hefty bribe from her father.

"A good guess," she acknowledged with a laugh. "Though you know as well as I do that the journey would likely do me in."

"That is true," he agreed with a wry smile. "Unfortunately you inherited your mama's queasy stomach when it comes to sea travel. Thank goodness travel was never one of her great ambitions."

Mathilda Craven had been a great homebody, by all the accounts Leonora had heard of her. Since she'd been two when her mother died, Leonora had no memories of her. But she'd always enjoyed hearing her father tell stories of their life together, and even of the tales Mathilda had told him before she died. Unlike some households that seemed to erase all traces of the dead loved one from the home, Joseph Craven had done his utmost to ensure that his wife's memory was kept alive in his children's memories.

"Too true," Leonora agreed. "And before you guess again, I think you will be hard-pressed to ever guess the news I've got to tell you."

Her father's brow furrowed. "Really? Something that unexpected? Then you must tell me, by all means."

She took a deep breath, but before she could say anything a knock sounded on the door.

"Apologies, Mr. Craven, sir," the butler, Greentree, intoned, "but his lordship insisted on seeing you immediately on a matter of some importance."

And before she could turn, Leonora knew who she'd see standing behind her.

"I beg your pardon, Mr. Craven," Freddy said, stepping forward and offering a slight bow to Leonora's father, "but I did rather insist."

Seeing Leonora, he feigned surprise. "Miss Craven," he said with a gasp. "I see you have beaten me to it. I did not think you could possibly be as impatient as I am to see this thing between us formalized but I see I was wrong." Turning to Mr. Craven, he laughed. "I'll wager you were quite shocked when Leonora told you our news, weren't you, sir? I must admit I was rather shocked myself when I discovered that our old feelings were unchanged. But I suppose I've never really stopped—"

He was cut short by Joseph Craven. "What are you prattling on about, Lord Frederick?" the older man barked. He'd never approved of nicknames, least of all Freddy's, Leonora reflected. "Are you telling me that my daughter has been foolish enough to enter into yet another betrothal to you? Is that what you're telling me?"

Seeing that her father was growing rather incensed, Leonora stood up and slipped an arm through Freddy's. She'd thought he might be a bit upset at the news, but she hadn't supposed he'd become so angry. "Papa, you must see that I've never stopped loving Freddy," she said, crossing her fingers behind her back at the fib. "And you will recall that just the other day you were lamenting the fact that I have chosen not to marry."

"Yes, but that was marriage to someone who hadn't already broken your heart," Craven said bluntly. "When I think of how distraught you became the last time, all because this fellow . . . this . . . this scoundrel was unfaithful! His very presence in my home is enough to make my blood boil. He's lucky I don't hold with dueling or he'd be six feet underground by now."

At her father's words, Leonora felt Freddy stiffen beside her. "I was . . ." He turned to her, his eyes bright with anger. "What did you tell him about the reasons for your breaking things off?"

Leonora felt her cheeks redden. "I . . . that is to say . . . I had to have a good reason to break things off, you see. And there was that evening I saw you at Vauxhall . . ."

"She. Was. My. Cousin," Freddy said through clenched teeth. "And we were only talking. Good God, Leonora, no wonder your brother refused to speak to me for a full year afterward. I thought it was because he thought I should have married you anyway."

"Oh no, he would have never spoken to you again if I hadn't broken down and told him the truth. That I was simply not ready for marriage, that I needed time to devote to my writing." She looked intently into his eyes, communicating that she needed him to go along with her explanation.

Daring him to disagree.

Four

For a brief moment, Freddy wavered. His desire to know what *had* made her break their engagement warring with the need to persuade Mr. Craven that this new betrothal was the real thing.

It was a small portrait of Jonathan Craven, hanging on the wall behind his father, that decided the thing for Freddy. Whatever hurt he felt over Leonora's rejection five years ago, he was here now because they'd agreed to find out the truth of why Jonny had been murdered and who had done it. And pressing Leonora for an answer now would jeopardize their plan.

And, when it came down to it, he wasn't sure her true reasons mattered at this point. It might do so if he were foolish enough to fall in love with her again. But despite the inescapable pull between them, he was determined that all he would allow himself to feel this time around was affection.

There was some danger that pretending to a betrothal would lead to an actual marriage, but even if that happened, he would never allow her to have the kind of sway over him that she'd once had.

He would remain detached. Despite the way desire

and affection coursed through him whenever he was in her company.

"So this is why you wouldn't let me tell anyone?" Craven asked, looking from one of them to the other. "And Lord Frederick did not break your heart?"

"Well, there was that night at Vaux—" Leonora began, but stopped when Freddy growled. "All right, no, Father, he did not break my heart. In fact, I rather think that I broke his."

"I'd hardly say that is the case," Freddy protested. "I've managed rather well on my own after all, and there were those years on the Continent—"

But this time it was Mr. Craven who growled.

"That is to say," Freddy amended, "I daresay my heart was broken. Never been rejected by a lady before. Certainly not one I'd asked to marry me. Indeed, I'd not have asked her again if it weren't for—"

At a cough from Leonora he broke off.

"That is to say," he continued, "I am quite pleased she's agreed to have me."

"You are both quite mad," Joseph Craven said, looking from his daughter to Freddy then back again. "Do you mean to tell me that you are embarking upon another betrothal? After all of this mayhem?"

"Papa!" Leonora beamed. "How on earth did you guess?"

Ignoring her, Freddy said, "Sir, I realize that this display doesn't give you the best impression of my ability to take care of your daughter, but I can assure you that I am ten times the fellow I was all those years ago. Indeed, I have managed to amass a bit of wealth and—"

"I cannot forbid the match because Leonora is of age," Craven said, pulling out his handkerchief and wiping his brow with it. "But I hope you know what you're getting yourself into, Freddy."

At her father's use of Freddy's nickname, Leonora knew just how shocked her father had been by their revelation.

"Oh, I have some idea, sir," Freddy replied, gripping Leonora's arm against his side. She tried to extricate herself but he held fast. "Indeed, I should like to have a word with her right now, so that we can make plans for the wedding."

"A short engagement?" Mr. Craven asked with what looked suspiciously like wicked humor to his daughter.

"Oh, quite," Freddy replied, dragging Leonora through the doorway. "The shorter the better."

Before Lenora could object, he shut the door behind them.

As soon as they were in the hall, away from her father's all too watchful eye, Leonora wanted nothing more than to flee the angry man at her side for the comfort of her sitting room, where she was mistress of her domain.

"A dalliance?" Freddy demanded once they were well past the door to her father's study. Turning, he pointed to a small parlor, indicating that they should go there at once.

Fighting her childish desire to refuse him, Leonora walked, head held high, into the cozy room. Despite the unseasonably warm spring, a fire had been lit in the room, for which she was grateful since she'd turned suddenly cold.

"I had to tell them something," she said once he'd closed the door. "The true reason was mine and I relished telling my family the truth almost as much as telling you. Which was not at all."

She could tell by his clenched jaw that her words frustrated him. And though she understood why, keeping the secret of her inability to bear children was something she could never reveal to him. Not if she didn't wish to tell him the reason she was so broken. And it was that circumstance that had started this whole mad deception, that was so shameful that she was willing to go to her grave with its secret.

Not to mention the fact that none of it was relevant now that their betrothal was a false one. If she thought there were any danger that their ruse would lead to a true engagement, or worse, marriage, she would put an end to this whole farce without a backward glance.

In the quiet of the tiny sitting room, however, she revealed none of this. Only waited for him to say something—anything—to break the silence between them.

Finally, he sighed, and thrust a hand through his light brown curls, which were already showing signs of the unruliness that so plagued him.

"I don't understand why you cannot simply tell me why you refused," he said tightly, clearly more overset about that matter than she'd hoped. "It isn't as if anything is at stake now. After all, we've both agreed that this betrothal is to be dissolved as soon as we bring my cousin to justice."

For a moment, she considered revealing all. What a relief it would be to unburden herself of the shame she'd kept hidden within her for nearly ten years now. Perhaps Freddy's response would be easier to endure than she'd imagined. Perhaps he would feel compassion for the wild fifteen-year-old she'd once been. Who risked everything and lost it all.

He'd not been a saint—when she met him, and over these past years he'd spent gadding about the Continent. But there was something within her that kept her from speaking the words that would reveal her shame to him. It was too much to risk, she realized. Especially now that they had agreed to prove Sir Gerard Fincher had some role in Jonathan's death.

She'd kept the secret in the past for her own sake. And for Freddy's. But now, she kept it for Jonny's.

Perhaps once this was all finished, after Jonny had been avenged, and once their second betrothal had been set aside as they agreed, then she would reveal her sad tale to him.

But not before. Not with so much at stake.

"I know it is irksome for you," she said with a coolness she did not feel, "but there is truly nothing I can do about that. Our focus now should be on revealing your cousin's perfidy. Not trading secrets like schoolgirls."

If her insult hit home, he didn't show it. Just glared at her for a moment. As if by looking hard enough he could discern what it was she was so reluctant to reveal to him.

Finally, he shrugged, and shook his head slightly, as if clearing it.

"I will make you tell me before this is all over," he said intently. And for a moment Leonora felt that jolt between them. The connection that could be severed neither by time nor space.

"Perhaps." She nodded. "But until then, I request that you do not press me on this. It distracts both of us from our true goal here. Do not forget that this is all for Jonathan's sake."

"Of course it is," he agreed blandly. "I give you my word that I will not ask again. Not unless you bring it up."

Seeing that he was sincere, she allowed her body to relax the slightest bit.

"Good," she said firmly, lowering herself onto the settee that was set at an angle to the corner. "Now, what is our next move? I assume you've sent the notice to the papers?"

Pacing a little to lean his shoulders against the mantel, Freddy crossed his arms over his chest. "I did," he said. "First thing this morning. And I believe it's time for us to move on to phase two."

She paused in the act of smoothing her hair—a nervous habit she'd not been able to eradicate no matter how many times her past governesses had chided. "What is phase two?" she asked, hoping the answer was not something she would find objectionable. She'd already created too much tension between them, but if this was something she felt strongly about she'd need to tell him.

"My cousin is having a dinner party cum Lords of Anarchy meeting tomorrow evening at his home in Half Moon Street. And I intend to wrangle an invitation for both of us to attend. To announce our betrothal there."

A party? Leonora felt an objection rise in her throat. "I cannot attend a party. My brother was killed only a few weeks ago. I have mourning clothes, but I cannot be seen making merry. Even if it means turning down an invitation into the lion's den."

"No need to worry," Freddy said soothingly, and her response to his tone told her just how rattled she'd been at the proposition of dishonoring Jonny's memory. "It is not a dancing party. And aside from that it is a private party. Even the high sticklers will not be able to find fault with your attending a dinner held in your brother's honor."

"It's in Jonathan's honor?" she asked, diverted by the notion. "I am torn between gratitude and revulsion. What kind of monster honors the very man he killed?"

"Well," he said with a shrug, "it is merely our own suspicions that say Gerard is responsible for Jonathan's accident. So to the rest of the world it is merely a tribute to a fellow club member who was lost in an accident pursuing the sport he loved best."

He continued. "It is also an opportunity for both of us to get the lay of the land. To begin our inroads into the club itself. My cousin has been after me to join for some years now, and I have a strong feeling that he will be unable to resist parading you before the other members. Especially if he's the one who killed your brother. He's the sort who liked to torture flies as a child. Having you there, oblivious—at least in his own mind—to the truth of things, will be a delightful joke to him."

Leonora shuddered. Again grateful for the fire.

"I suppose that makes sense," she said with a frown. "The more I learn about your cousin, however, the less I like him."

Freddy laughed. "You're not alone in that," he agreed. "But just remember that we will have the last word on this. And imagine how satisfying it will feel to finally bring him to justice."

"Oh, I will," she said with a grin. "Most assuredly."

Freddy left the Craven town house with the intention of seeking out Mainwaring and Trent to discuss their next move in the plan to infiltrate the Lords of Anarchy. He had not gone far, however, when a highly polished open carriage sporting a pair of the most perfectly matched bays he'd ever seen came round the corner of Half Moon Street.

Slowing his mount, Hector, he was unsurprised to find his cousin Gerard himself handling the reins.

"Well met, Lord Frederick," Sir Gerard Fincher said, inclining his head in a manner that reminded Freddy of an emperor greeting his subjects. "I've not seen you since your return from the Continent."

"Indeed, cousin," Freddy agreed, then sweeping off his beaver hat, he nodded to his cousin's female companion. A companion who was most decidedly not his cousin's wife. "Mrs. Chater, you are looking lovely as always."

The dimpled matron, whose husband was a member of the club, was well known around town as his cousin's mistress, though Freddy was rather surprised that Gerard risked his wife's wrath so openly. Melisande had always struck him as rather frightening when crossed.

The Honorable Henry Chater, Mrs. Chater's husband, however, was rumored to be quite sanguine with the arrangement. Something Freddy found difficult to understand.

"Thank you, my lord," his cousin's mistress simpered. "You are too kind."

"I hope you are finding London to be much as you left it," Sir Gerard said. "Though I like to think we have made it more entertaining in your absence."

That was one way of putting it, Freddy thought. Aloud he said, "Indeed, I have heard much said about your driving club. It sounds like just the sort of thing I'd like to participate in. Though I doubt I'd be able to match you with the reins. You always were more of a dab hand than I ever was."

The flattery hit its mark, and Freddy was pleased to note the flash of satisfaction in his cousin's eyes at the compliment. "You are too kind," Fincher said with a wolfish grin. "We did have fun in the old days when we were learning the whip, didn't we?"

"We did," Freddy confirmed with an answering smile. "But you were always the more skilled driver."

It was just the right thing to say, for Sir Gerard smiled with genuine pleasure. He'd always been a proud one, Freddy reflected. Even when they were boys. Good to know some things hadn't changed. It would make his mission easier if he could rely upon Gerry's self-love to manipulate him.

"You flatter me, cousin," Fincher said, inclining his head. "I happen to know that a pair of sweet bays are going to be on the block at Tatt's this week, if you're interested. I know the owner. Has to sell them to pay his gaming debts, poor fellow. I think they'll be just the thing. He might even include the rig with them too if you offer him enough."

But Freddy wasn't quite ready to spend a great deal of money on a carriage he had no use for. His brother Archer, who was currently in the country with his new wife, had offered to let Freddy borrow his own curricle and chaise and four when he needed them. That would do well enough for Freddy. It wouldn't hurt to let Gerard think he wasn't quite able to afford a new rig.

"That would be capital," he said, masking his annoyance with a grin. "But I've made other arrangements. Though I appreciate the offer."

Fincher looked thoughtful for a moment, then as if deciding upon something, continued, "I think you'd be a welcome addition to the club, cousin. I don't know why I didn't think of it before. We have a recent opening, as I'm sure you know. Poor old Craven."

Freddy felt himself tense at the mention of Jonathan. He hadn't expected Fincher to mention it so openly. "Jonathan Craven?" he asked, with a frown. "Was he a member? I heard about his death of course. We were friends, you know."

"Yes, indeed," Fincher replied smoothly, "he was a member, poor chap. It was terrible what happened to him. Nothing to do with the club, you understand. But terrible."

That his cousin was denying that Jonathan's death had anything to do with the club—and by extension, himself— took Freddy aback somewhat. But he was careful to hide his surprise. "Indeed. I am relieved to hear it. Though you must know that there is talk about the club being involved.

I will, of course, do my best to quell the rumors when I hear them."

"I would be grateful," Fincher said with an angry frown. "Though I could wish that people were not so eager to spread lies. I've even heard that some people blame me, personally, for Craven's accident. As if I have any control over a man's horses when he's miles away. It's pure lunacy."

"It is the way of the world, my dear Sir Gerard," Mrs. Chater said with a sympathetic pat on his hand. "People will talk when they are jealous. You know that as well as I. You are simply too powerful for them to resist."

Despite the widow's blandishments, Gerard was obviously still gripped by anger. There was an uncomfortable silence while he got hold of his temper. Finally, after a breath he said, "We are having a small soiree tomorrow evening, Frederick, and I'd like for you to come. A small affair to celebrate Jonathan's life. I will have Melisande send round an invitation for you. If I had thought of it I'd have invited you sooner."

Freddy was careful not to show his triumph at the invitation. He hadn't even needed to ask. "I would be delighted to attend. Thank you." And though he disliked the notion of Leonora even breathing the same air as his cousin, mindful of his promise to her, he added, "And might I also secure an invitation for my betrothed?"

Once more, Sir Gerard's eyes widened in surprise. "Never say, some winsome lady has snared the elusive Lord Frederick Lisle in the parson's mousetrap," the other man said with shock. "I daresay she is some Continental beauty you brought back with you from Paris."

"Indeed not," Freddy said with what he hoped was a wolfish grin. "She is someone I have known for quite some time. Miss Leonora Craven and I have decided to give it another go."

Mrs. Chater gasped. "The bluestocking? And you, my lord? I should never have guessed it." Her eyes traveled the length of his body in a boldly assessing way. "I wonder if she'll know what to do with you."

Before Freddy could respond, Gerard patted his mistress's hand, though her wince revealed it might have been a bit rougher than it seemed. "My cousin and Miss Craven were betrothed once before, Mrs. Chater. Many years ago. It was not common knowledge, of course. But Freddy and Miss Craven's brother, the fellow who just died, were great friends."

Something in his cousin's tone sent a chill up Freddy's spine. But unlike earlier, he didn't make the mistake of revealing his feelings openly. His eyes, now hooded, were watchful.

"It's quite true, Mrs. Chater," Freddy said, pretending to ignore his cousin's scrutiny with a sheepish smile. "The lady decided to break things off before the marriage, of course, or we'd even now be wed. She went her way and I went mine. Then, when I returned to London, I went to see her to offer my condolences and we found that our affection for one another had returned, and only this morning she agreed to be my wife. The announcement will be in the papers before the end of the week."

"Perhaps you should spirit the lady off to Gretna this time, Freddy," Sir Gerard said with a cruel laugh, "just to ensure that she goes through with the thing." His tone indicated that he would not be so foolish as to let a lady leave him before the wedding.

"There is little danger of that this time," Freddy retorted coolly. "I was the one at fault before, and I have no intention of making the same mistake twice."

"I am pleased to hear it, cousin," Gerard said in a tone that did not seem convinced. "I will also have Melisande send an invitation to Miss Craven. I am pleased to hear she is out in company again. I believe she was quite seriously touched by her brother's death."

"Of course she was, Sir Gerard," Mrs. Chater said firmly. "Any sister of worth would be quite upset. I will do whatever I can to welcome her to the gathering."

If Freddy thought it odd that his cousin's mistress spoke as if she were to host the soiree instead of Melisande Fincher, however, it was impossible to say anything without offending the lady. And Gerard didn't seem to think there was anything odd about it. "I know the members of the club in attendance will be pleased to see her," he said with a nod. "Now, if you will excuse me, my horses are a bit restless."

As they stood there, the bays had become increasingly restive, though Sir Gerard had managed to keep them under control while they chatted. Now, however, they were pawing the ground and snorting, as if the enforced inactivity were the equine equivalent of a cage.

Freddy saluted his cousin with his whip, and drew his own mount to the side so that his cousin could steer his horses away from the curb and into the cobblestone street. "See you tomorrow evening," Sir Gerard said, before allowing his horses to have their heads a bit.

Lost in thought, Freddy steered Hector in the opposite direction, headed for White's where he was supposed to meet with Mainwaring and Trent. He'd thought it would be more difficult to inveigle an invitation from his cousin. The fact that it had been easier than expected made him a bit wary about the whole thing. There was something odd about the ease with which Sir Gerard had welcomed him into his circle. Even so, Freddy was not about to turn down the invitation. He needed to get inside the Lords of Anarchy, and if a family connection paved the way for him to do it, then so be it.

He'd simply have to be careful about taking his cousin's words at face value.

And make doubly sure that Leonora knew to do so, too.

Five

"Married?" Miss Ophelia Dantry demanded later that afternoon when Leonora divulged the news of her engagement to her two closest friends. "Why on earth would you agree to such a thing, Leonora? You have so much autonomy now without being bothered with the burden of a husband."

"Not everyone is as opposed to the married state as you are, Fee," Lady Hermione Upperton said with a roll of her eyes. "To hear you tell it, marriage is a prison for any woman who enters into it. Regardless of the amiability of her husband."

"Since the marriage will never take place," Leonora assured her friends, "then the matter is neither here nor there. It is merely a ruse to ensure that I am able to gain entrance to the world of the Lords of Anarchy. Though I can assure you both that even if I had to marry Lord Frederick Lisle to find out who killed my brother, I would do it."

She and Freddy had agreed to keep their pact a secret, but she trusted her friends implicitly. "But Frederick?" Ophelia demanded. "After he treated you so abominably the last time you were betrothed?"

The three ladies had been friends since attending the

same finishing school the year they made their debuts in society. Now, some five years later, all three were considered to be firmly on the shelf by most hostesses of the *ton,* but none of them minded. Ophelia had learned first-hand how miserable marriage could be from her mother's unhappy union to her father and was determined to escape the state herself. Hermione had yet to find a gentleman who was comfortable with a lady who was more nimble with the reins than he was. And though Leonora said it was because of her aversion to being ordered about by another man, her true reason was the same that had kept her from marrying Freddy before. Her inability to bear children.

Despite her own misgivings about her temporary arrangement with Freddy, though, Leonora was not quite willing to let Ophelia question it. "I have made my decision, Ophelia," she said firmly. "I know your feelings on the matter of marriage. I even agree with you on many points, but despite what you think of him, Frederick is an honorable man. What happened between us before was entirely my own fault. No matter what you might have heard."

"We are simply worried for you, Nora," Hermione said with a speaking look in Ophelia's direction that Leonora could not help seeing. "The last time the two of you broke things off you were not yourself for . . . some time."

She left unspoken the fact that Leonora had come close to such soul-crushing despair that her friends had feared for her life. For a moment Leonora wanted more than anything to confide her grief to her two greatest friends in the world. But though she knew they would be the last people to find her wanting, it was her own shame that kept her silent on the matter.

"I do know, my dears," she said now, taking her

friends' hands in her own. "And do not for one moment think that I am not appreciative of your concern. But you must allow me to do what I think right. And in this case, that means this alliance with Freddy."

"I suppose you know what is best," Ophelia groused, though it was clear from her expression that she wasn't so sure. "I do wish you'd have chosen someone else for this ruse, however. He's so very high-handed."

"Though quite handsome," Hermione said with a giggle. "I always thought so. And he can be quite amusing, even you must admit, Fee."

"Amusement will be the furthest thing from my mind, I'm afraid," Leonora said, relieved that her friends seemed to be reconciled to the situation. She would do what she must, but it would be easier to embark upon the investigation into her brother's death knowing that she had the support of her dearest friends. "As you know, Jonathan was one of Freddy's oldest friends, and he is just as convinced as I am that the Lords of Anarchy had something to do with Jonny's death."

"If they were the least bit willing to behave like civilized creatures and allow ladies into their ranks," Hermione said, pouring herself another cup of tea, "then I might have investigated things a bit, as well."

"I doubt sincerely that they would be willing to change their name to the Lords and Ladies of Anarchy," Ophelia said wryly. "And honestly, I am shocked that the crown has allowed them to go about calling themselves the Lords of Anarchy given how unsettled things still are over what happened in France only a matter of years ago. England might not be as ripe for revolution as France was, but it must give the government pause to have a group that uses the term 'anarchist,' even in jest, to walk the streets."

"If the members weren't all quite happy enjoying the

benefits of coming from the finest families in England, I think you'd be right," Leonora said with a sigh. "But despite the name they seem more likely to wage war on a keg of ale than the crown."

"True enough," Hermione agreed. "I daresay the prince recalls his own cronies' days with the Four Horse Club with fondness. Now there was a group of true driving aficionados. And they allowed ladies into their midst."

"I am quite familiar with the FHC," Leonora said with a smile. "Between you and Jonny I believe I could recite their history from memory."

"Please don't," Ophelia said with a moue of distaste. "If I have to hear the Tommy Ounslow rhyme again I will expire right here at the tea table."

"Ha-ha," Hermione said, frowning. To Leonora she said, "Tell us how you and Freddy mean to go about your investigation."

Grateful that her friends had chosen not to engage in the quarrel that seemed to hover just beneath the surface, Leonora said, "Well, Freddy and I will announce our betrothal in the papers, and in the meantime he will do what he can to gain the confidence of his cousin Sir Gerard Fincher."

"Better him than you," Hermione said fiercely. "Despite my desire to gain entry into the Lords of Anarchy, I cannot like Sir Gerard in the least. He always seems to be agreeable, but the smile never reaches his eyes."

"His wife is nearly as cold," Leonora said with shiver. "And unfortunately it's she I'll need to befriend if I'm to gain any information about Jonny's last days within the group. She was quite fond of him from what I recall of his stories of the goings-on within the club. He always spoke of her kindly, at least. And he told me how she took his side against her husband once."

"They tend not to move in our circles, though," Ophelia

said. "I do know that she is quite fond of her little dog. I have seen her with him in the park any number of times. I wonder if that might be a way for you to befriend her, Leonora."

"Moppet does enjoy a walk in the park from time to time," Leonora said thoughtfully, referring to her father's spaniel, who spent most of his time lazing by the fire. She wasn't sure if he did enjoy the park, but before the week was out, she vowed, she would learn the answer. "An excellent idea, Fee. I will simply have to take him there."

Before her friends could respond, Leonora's maid appeared in the doorway. "An invitation has arrived, miss. By special messenger."

While Ophelia and Hermione looked on, Leonora unfolded the missive to read it.

"Well?" Hermione demanded. "What is it?"

"An invitation to a small gathering at the home of Sir Gerard and Lady Fincher tomorrow evening," Leonora said with a grin. "It seems, ladies, that I have chosen the right companion for my investigation. In less than four hours, Freddy has managed to get us an invitation into the lion's den."

It remained to be seen, however, whether the creature would bare his teeth.

Leonora rather thought he would.

As soon as her friends left, Leonora, feeling restless, wandered upstairs. Rather than stopping to enter her own rooms, she continued down the hallway toward the wing that housed her brother's rooms.

An intensely private person, Jonathan had never once invited his sister into his bedchamber, though as a girl in the schoolroom she'd once picked the lock and explored it on her own. To her disappointment she'd found nothing more scandalous than a packet of cheroots. But she couldn't inform her father of her findings for fear of revealing how she'd discovered them.

Now that he was gone, however, Leonora had spent quite a bit of time there. Trying to get closer somehow to the brother she'd lost.

With the knowledge of Jonny's death heavy on her heart, Leonora turned the knob of the door and was once again sad to find it unlocked. Now that Jonny was gone there was no one to guard his room from prying eyes. It was another sad reminder that he was not coming back, no matter how she wished it.

Her gown rustled against the carpets as she stepped inside and closed the door behind her. Jonny's valet, Chesterton, had left only a few days after his master's death, and the rooms had not been tidied in his absence. Hurrying to the window, Leonora opened the heavy drapes, letting the wan afternoon sunlight into the darkened chamber. What she saw, however, provoked a gasp.

Someone had ransacked the room.

Everywhere she looked, drawers hung open, their contents spilling out over the edges onto the floor. Jonathan's writing desk, which Leonora knew from her earlier explorations of the room had been kept in regimented order, now looked as if it had been assailed by a strong wind. Papers and wax and seals and letters which had all been kept in their own little cubbies were scattered across the desk's surface and over the floor. A bottle of ink had been carelessly flung aside, its contents having dripped onto the carpet below, now nearly dried.

Whoever had done this must have done it recently, Leonora thought, a chill running through her. Both she and her father had paid visits to the chamber on learning of his death—as if some vestige of him remained there to whom they might say their good-byes.

And when Leonora received the letter posted to her

by her brother's solicitor, she'd come here to search for the documents in the safe. The safe which was now missing from the wardrobe where it had been hidden.

She'd wondered if the room had been searched thoroughly when the documents were stolen, though that time it had been pristine except for the open wardrobe. Now, however, it was in shambles.

Had the same person who'd taken the documents come back looking for more? And if so, what? Jonathan's letter had implied that the items in the safe were all he kept of import in his bedchamber. But the second search indicated otherwise.

Collapsing into a wing chair before the fire, Leonora scanned the chamber, her mind exploring the ramifications of her discovery.

Her suspicion thus far had been that the Lords of Anarchy had arranged for Jonathan to be killed during his ill-considered race. But she'd not had any notion of what the reason might be. Aside, that is, from his note mentioning that he knew something incriminating about Sir Gerard Fincher.

The fact that someone had come looking again seemed to indicate that there was more than one person involved in the secret he'd uncovered. And, perhaps, that some other item or paper was missing that the mysterious intruder suspected Jonathan of having stolen.

A quick glance had revealed that her brother's collection of jeweled stickpins remained intact, though they'd been scattered across the carpet before the wardrobe where their case had been kept. So, it was clearly not money the culprit was after.

The thoroughness of the disarray seemed to indicate to Leonora that whoever had done the searching had not discovered what he was looking for. Otherwise, he'd have stopped as soon as he'd found it. Wouldn't he?

"Jonny," she said aloud, shaking her head in bewilderment. "What were you involved with?"

Whatever it was, she thought, rising with a renewed sense of determination, she meant to find out.

She briefly considered asking one of the maids to come assist her in putting the room back together, but something stopped her. And moving from mess to mess, she tidied the room of a brother who would never come through the doorway again.

She was placing the books that had been dumped out of their neatly arranged rows on the built-in bookcase, when her hand brushed against a protrusion along the underside of the second shelf. Curious, she ran her fingers along the wood and with her heartbeat quickening she realized it was a lever. With shaking fingers, she pulled the metal arm toward her and, with a click, a recess was revealed in the back of the shelf.

Not stopping to consider the consequences of putting her hand into a darkened cubby, Lenora reached in and pulled out what looked to be a journal, and a faded length of crimson ribbon.

This was it, she thought, glancing around the empty room, as if someone were there to take the hidden treasure from her. This was what the intruder had been looking for. She knew it with every bit of her heart.

And, because some part of her felt unsafe in her brother's recently searched rooms, she hurried out, shutting the door firmly behind her.

Once she'd reached her own bedchamber, she was relieved to find her maid was elsewhere. Carrying her prize to the chair before the window, she opened the leather-bound volume and saw the first page was inscribed with her brother's name, in his own hand. It was dated April, two years previously.

Her breath coming faster, she began to read.

* * *

"That was fast work," Mainwaring said with a wry grin as he and Freddy drove through the park in the curricle Freddy had borrowed from his brother Archer, who was in the country with his very pregnant new wife. "I sincerely thought Miss Craven would have nothing to do with you. It is a testament to your charm that I have been proved wrong."

"More a testament to her own desperation to know more about the Lords of Anarchy, I'd say," Freddy replied as he expertly steered them along the path. A jaunt in the park was something akin to riding a racehorse on a country amble, but though Freddy was comfortable enough behind the reins, Mainwaring was not fond of speed or daring when it came to transportation. So in a nod to the other man's preferences, Freddy was tooling them around the park. "She was none too happy about the engagement, but was convinced of its necessity for her to gain access to Sir Gerard and his coterie of followers."

"It shows the lady's strength of character," Mainwaring said with a nod. "That a lady would be willing to risk future marriage prospects—which could mean the difference between a comfortable life and a life of indentured servitude as a poor relation—is admirable."

"Don't ever let her hear you say that," Freddy said with a frown. "Leonora has some very strong ideas about ladies and marriage and such. She'll have flayed you alive before you even realize she's made the first cut."

Mainwaring chuckled. "Don't be absurd, she's a lady, not a mercenary."

"True enough," Freddy said with a laugh. "But I promise you she will not take it kindly if you go spouting your views about proper ladies."

Mainwaring tipped his hat at a barouche carrying three young ladies whom Freddy did not know. He was going to have to ask Leonora to school him on the makeup of the *ton* since his return from the Continent.

"Miss Fotheringay, Lady Felicity Mount, and Lady Alice Needham," Mainwaring supplied as they passed the other carriage. "As silly a group of chits as you'll ever meet, but pretty enough."

"I should have known you'd have wrangled introductions to all the ladies fresh from the schoolroom, Mainwaring," Freddy said, rolling his eyes. Mainwaring had always been quick to discover the names of all the eligible beauties in a room. Why shouldn't he be able to do the same with the whole of the *ton*?

"There's nothing wrong with knowing one's enemies," Mainwaring said unrepentantly. "And those three are particularly dangerous, as they've been on the town for a couple of years now without bringing anyone up to scratch. I shouldn't be surprised if one of them traps some unlucky fellow into an engagement before the season is out. Or, if not them, then their desperate mamas. For I'm not sure the girls are clever enough for it."

"You really are heartless, aren't you?" Freddy asked with mock disapproval. "How can you deprive those poor girls of the honor of becoming the next Lady Mainwaring? It's positively cold of you."

"I don't see you offering yourself as the sacrificial lamb for slaughter," his companion said without remorse.

"That is because I've already convinced a clever young lady to be my bride," Freddy said, grinning. "Even if it is a false engagement for the time being, it protects me from the dangers of being a single man amid all these husband huntresses."

Mainwaring shook his head. "Back to Miss Craven. What do you intend to do when the two of you attend your cousin's soiree tomorrow evening? You can hardly search his house, or interview the other members of the club under Sir Gerard's very nose. And I shouldn't think that Miss Craven, for all her cleverness, will come right out and ask the fellow whether he murdered her brother."

"Hardly," Freddy returned, his expression sobering. "I am hoping that once Gerard introduces me as the replacement for Jonathan Craven in the club, I'll be able to determine if any of the other club members are feeling the least bit uneasy about Craven's death. After all, they were likely his friends as well as Gerard's. It simply remains to be seen if they are more fearful of Gerard or loyal to Jonny. Unfortunately I suspect that fear of Gerard will win out."

"Gerard is alive to threaten them," Mainwaring agreed. "And it's likely that whatever loyalty they felt for Jonathan died with him. A bird in the hand—or is that the devil you know? Whatever the axiom, Gerard is alive and capable of murder. Jonny is not."

"Precisely," Freddy agreed. "Which is why I'll need to be subtle about my inquiries. The last thing I want is for my cousin to suspect right off the mark that my reasons for joining his club have anything to do with Jonathan's death."

"Have you discussed this with Leonora?" Mainwaring asked, as they left the park and headed back toward Mayfair. "I seem to recall that subtlety is not her most admirable trait."

Freddy winced. "Not quite yet. I'm still working on my strategy. One cannot simply tell her what to do. In addition to her forthrightness, she also is as stubborn as a mule."

"Better you than me, old fellow," Mainwaring said with a grin. "Better you than me."

Six

The next morning, Leonora sat down at the breakfast table, unable to stifle a yawn.

"Not sleeping well, my dear?" her father asked, biting into a piece of toast. "Perhaps you should have Mrs. Thompson mix you up one of her tisanes. They always seemed to help your mama."

Leonora cursed inwardly at her inability to hide her sleep deprivation. She'd been up most of the night reading her brother's journal. And unfortunately, its contents, while fascinating, had not contained the revelation about the reason for his death that she'd hoped to discover. Though there had been something she wished to show to Freddy as soon as she could.

"I'll do that, Papa," she said aloud, accepting the cup of tea the footman had just poured for her. "Though perhaps I will wait and see if I can sleep without it tonight. After the gathering at Sir Gerard Fincher's home this evening, I have little doubt I'll be exhausted."

Her father's salt-and-pepper brows drew together, and he set down the newspaper he'd been perusing. "Sir Gerard Fincher?" he asked, his displeasure evident. "You're going to a social evening at that blackguard's home? Why is this the first I've heard of it?"

"It's not as if I've been in the habit of telling you about my every social engagement, Papa," Leonora said with a frown of her own. "You'd find that just as tedious as I would."

She'd always exercised more autonomy than most unmarried young ladies she knew, but Leonora thought that had been because she'd displayed more maturity than most young ladies of her acquaintance. That and the fact that her aunt Hortense, who most often acted as her companion, was of the opinion that ladies should be afforded more and not less freedom where decisions about their social activities were concerned. Without her aunt's influence, Leonora doubted very much that she'd have embarked on her career as a poet. She'd certainly never have started her weekly salons.

"That is true," her father responded, still looking peeved, "but I had thought that you would have more sense than to visit the de facto home of the driving club I hold responsible for your brother's death. Sir Gerard Fincher might not have been driving the carriage that killed your brother, Leonora, but it was his club's recklessness, and the sense of competition it fostered, that was responsible for Jonathan's death. Just as surely as if Sir Gerard had shot him with a pistol."

Though she'd considered her father's disapproval when embarking upon her faux betrothal with Freddy, Leonora had not considered that Mr. Craven would have anything to say about her moving in the same circles as Sir Gerard. She'd been shortsighted she knew now. And would need to tell him at least a partial truth in order to stop him from forbidding her to attend that evening's party at Sir Gerard's home.

"I quite agree, Papa," she said with candor. "I believe that the Lords of Anarchy are responsible for Jonny's death, too. Which is why I simply must attend this party at Sir Gerard's house tonight."

Her mind racing as she considered her story, she went on, "Jonny was my twin. And we were closer than most siblings. I simply must understand what it was that led him to join that infernal club. It's the one piece of the puzzle that I don't understand. Because I know Jonny was not easily led. There must have been some reason for him to become involved with those men. And I shan't be able to rest until I know what that reason was."

Mr. Craven's look of disapproval turned to one of surprise. "Is that what is keeping you awake at night, my dear? I must confess, it hadn't occurred to me that you would wish to speak to Sir Gerard, else I'd have had the fellow brought round immediately. Much as it would pain me to do so."

"But that's just it, Papa," Leonora went on. "I need to speak to him in his own home. On his own ground, so to speak. Because he'll be more likely to tell me the truth there. At least that is what I hope."

"And you have asked Lord Frederick to accompany you," Mr. Craven said, understanding dawning in his eyes. "I must admit that I do feel better knowing you will be escorted by someone I trust. So long as he is with you, I know that Freddy will not let anything untoward happen to you."

"Exactly, Papa." She nodded. "And because Freddy is Sir Gerard's cousin, I think the man will be more likely to tell me the truth. I simply must know what it was about the club's activities that led Jonny to risk his life like that. Even if it is only to learn that he was indebted to someone and needed to win the race for that reason, it will be a reason." And to her surprise, Leonora realized that she was telling the truth. She might be hiding her pact with

Freddy to investigate the reason for Jonny's murder, but she did want those answers for herself. So that she could have some reason to attach to what seemed at this point to be a senseless loss of life.

Mr. Craven, his eyes still troubled, nodded. "I understand, my dear. If you really feel you must visit the home of that vile man, then I shan't stop you. So long as you bring Lord Frederick with you. But I would also like for you to take your aunt Hortense along, as well."

Leonora bit back a groan. She'd been so close, she thought. "But surely it will be unexceptional for me to attend an evening entertainment with my betrothed," Leonora protested aloud. "And as you know, Aunt Hortense does not enjoy soirees. She dislikes that they seem to have no purpose other than seeing and being seen."

"Well, your aunt will simply be forced to swallow her dislike for one evening," Mr. Craven said wryly, "because without her you will not be allowed to attend at all."

"Yes, Papa," Leonora said with a sigh.

Her father might be liberal about a great many things when it came to her comings and goings, but she knew from experience that once he set his mind to something, he would not be moved.

Now, she thought, she'd best brace herself to break the news to Freddy.

"I cannot imagine why you would choose to attend a party at the home of Sir Gerard Fincher of all people, Leonora," Aunt Hortense huffed from her perch beside Leonora's dressing table.

Since she had come to think of herself as independent, Leonora had been annoyed at her father for suggesting a chaperone for their visit to the Fincher house, but she supposed if they were to pass within the driving club as authentically engaged, she'd need to follow the proprieties. At least Aunt Hortense was the least demanding of her aunts. A spinster who had spent much of her adult life doing as she pleased, Hortense Craven was a follower of Miss Wollstonecraft, and it had been she who introduced Leonora to the philosophical works of that lady. As such, she was hardly one to consider such foolishness as propriety to be worth her notice. Even so, she had agreed to accompany Leonora each time her niece requested her chaperonage. Which had more to do with Aunt Hortense's soft spot for her family than any innate wish to thumb her nose at society.

Hortense was also quite fond of a good dance, and was quite fond of cards, so Leonora had little doubt that she would make good use of the Finchers' card room.

"I've already told you, aunt," Leonora said, exchanging a look with her aunt in the pier glass. "I wish to know more about the people with whom Jonathan spent his last days. And as the Finchers—as well as the entire Lords of Anarchy club—were my brother's last companions, then that is where I wish to go."

"But so hard on the heels of your engagement, my dear," Aunt Hortense sniffed. "Lord Frederick Lisle is a handsome devil, make no mistake, but are you sure you can trust him? With your hand, I mean? After all, he is a man, and history has taught us both that they can make a mess of things when they are left in charge."

"I am hardly agreeing to let him enslave me, Aunt Hortense," Leonora said wryly, as her maid inserted the last pin into her intricate coiffure. "If I thought him capable of such a thing I'd not embark upon an engagement at all. But I do not, thank heavens. And I think we will rub along rather well together."

"I know, dearest," the older woman said with a shake of her graying hair. "I simply don't know how to feel that my dear niece has agreed to marry the very same man who broke her heart years ago. It goes against every protective instinct in me to step aside like that."

"And do not think I don't appreciate it," Leonora said with a laugh as she rose and twirled a bit before the glass. "Will I do?"

"Very well indeed, my dear niece," Aunt Hortense said with a grin. "And if you mean to catch more flies with honey than with vinegar, then you have already passed the first test. For I do not see how any man there will be able to resist you. Young Lisle will have his work cut out for himself, that is certain."

The two ladies retrieved their wraps and were nearing the ground floor on the staircase, when a knock on the main door sounded. Just as they stepped down, the butler opened the door to greet Freddy.

"Evening, Greentree," Freddy said with a slight bow. "I'm here to . . . ah." He turned to face Leonora and Hortense. "Ladies, you are both looking ravishing tonight. I shall be the envy of every man there."

"You always were a silver-tongued devil, Lord Frederick," Hortense said with a blush as Freddy bowed over her hand. "But do not expect me to fall for your charms, young man.

"But then why should I?" she continued, not letting either Leonora or Freddy get a word in. "For it's as plain as a pikestaff that you have fallen under my niece's spell once more. At last." She added in a stage whisper, "I don't mind telling you that the gel has been near impossible to live with since the two of you broke things off."

"Aunt Hortense," Leonora said sharply, "that is quite enough, though I do appreciate the sentiment. You needn't have worried, however. For Freddy has rescued me from that old life. Haven't you, my lord?"

Freddy's brow furrowed as he looked from one lady to the other. "Are you quite sure you're recovered, my dear?" he said with a small smile. "For I shouldn't mind in the least to spend the evening here playing whist for pennies with your aunt."

"Pennies?" Hortense snorted. "I should like to see you play for guineas at the very least. Young cardsharp, thinking you might best me. I should have known you were a wrong 'un the moment I saw you."

"Lovely as all this bickering is," Leonora said, nodding to the butler that he should help them leave. "I think it's time we get on with things. I believe the card rooms fill up quickly at these affairs, and traffic will be difficult this evening."

Freddy exchanged a speaking glance with her, but merely nodded as he helped her into her wrap, and to Leonora's distraction, he slid his thumb quite gently down her neck.

"You are correct, as usual, my dear," Hortense said with a simpering smile. "And I suppose it's none of my business if you marry the fellow or not. It's a pleasure of course to see you again, Lord Frederick, but I simply cannot imagine her father will allow it. My brother is quite protective of my niece."

With that, Freddy escorted them down the stairs and to his waiting carriage, which looked to be quite polished and new. Freddy, Leonora reflected, had wasted no time in rigging himself out with an open barouche. It wasn't the sort of thing driven by the Lords of Anarchy, but it was definitely impressive. Whether Sir Gerard Fincher and his crew would wish to drive it, Leonora couldn't say.

As if reading her thoughts, Freddy said brightly, "This handsome carriage is on loan from my brother Archer. He and his lady are in the country awaiting the birth of their first child. He was kind enough to leave word with his servants that his town carriages were at my disposal."

"That must be exciting," Leonora said with a pang of sadness for the children she'd never have. What must it be like for Archer's wife, Perdita, now? She could not imagine a happier scene than one of new parents cradling their sweet baby.

"It is," Freddy said, leading both ladies to where the steps had been lowered at the carriage door. "This will be my parents' first grandchild as well so the entire Lisle family is on tenterhooks. My brothers and I are already vying for the position of favorite uncle."

He grinned, and Leonora saw that he was genuinely excited at the prospect. With determination, she schooled her features to reveal only polite happiness for him. "How delightful."

It would do no good to dwell on what could never be. No matter how much it might hurt her.

"I must have a word with your coachman, Lord Frederick," Aunt Hortense demanded from Freddy's other side, before he could respond to Leonora's lukewarm response. "There is a particular route I must insist upon. My rheumatism insists upon it, you understand."

Grateful for her aunt's managing ways, Leonora allowed Freddy to hand her into the carriage and concentrated on arranging the skirts of her black silk evening gown. She'd had it made up along with several other mourning pieces soon after Jonathan's death. More at the insistence of her modiste than anything else. For she was quite sure she'd have no need for evening dress during her period of mourning. But, of course, Freddy and necessity had changed that.

Once they were situated in the barouche—Aunt Hortense having spoken for several minutes while they waited—Freddy gave the signal for his coachman and they were off.

While Freddy and Aunt Hortense chatted, Leonora

took a moment to study the man seated beside her, hoping to erase the memory of her earlier sadness.

Always one to dress with the utmost care, tonight Freddy was every inch the duke's son. He wore buff breeches and an evening coat of blue superfine. His collar and cuffs glistened white in the evening light, and his cravat was tied neatly in the mathematical—one of his favorites, she'd learned the last time they were engaged. Winking from his cravat was a single stone set in a finely crafted stickpin.

Since he was a younger son in his family, Freddy had often found himself short of ready funds back when they had been together before. He'd told her father that he was quite well off now.

She knew, however, that the pin was a family piece. Once she'd heard him speaking about it to Jonathan who had wanted to purchase it for his own collection. But Freddy had declined. "I always think of my cavalier ancestor when I look at it," he'd told Jonathan with a grin. "He was a bit of a scoundrel, but he was always rigged out in style—or so family legend would have us believe."

She wondered with a smile if he had thought of the cavalier when he donned the pin tonight.

"A penny for them," Freddy said as the carriage slowed a bit. "I should dearly like to know what's going on in that head of yours." His expression was thoughtful, as if he suspected the answer wasn't all pleasant.

"Are you quite sure?" she asked. "For I sometimes am quite grateful that no one could ever see into my mind. Otherwise I'd find myself at constant odds with almost everyone."

"It can't be that bad," he said with a wink. "I'm quite convinced that any number of people think of putting a period to my existence on a daily basis. Certainly my brothers do."

Leonora heard her aunt cough but from mirth or blood thirst, she couldn't say. "I have little doubt that your brothers adore you, Lord Frederick," she said carefully. "And that goes for most people in the *ton*. Indeed, it makes me quite ill at times to consider just how well loved you are. How on earth is anyone else allowed to be fallible when there is such perfection to consider?"

Just then, the carriage rolled to a stop, but it was much too soon for them to have reached Hampstead.

"Ah, this will be my stop," Aunt Hortense said, gathering up her reticule and shawl.

"I don't understand," Leonora said, exchanging a glance with Frederick. "What is this place?"

"It is my friend Agatha's house, my dear," Aunt Hortense said, patting Leonora's arm. "You didn't really suppose I was going to reverse a lifetime of avoiding soirees, did you? Besides, Leonora, I know you're in safe hands with this young rapscallion," she added with a wink at Freddy

"But what about Papa?" Leonora asked with a shake of her head. "He'll be livid!"

"What he doesn't know won't hurt him," her aunt assured her, opening the carriage door and letting the footman hand her down. "No need to worry about coming to fetch me, children. I will simply have one of my friends drive me. I have my own house, after all, and there can be no objection to an old woman begging her young niece to take her home first."

The interior of the carriage was silent for a moment as the coach once more was on its way.

"That was . . . unexpected," Freddy said at last, from the opposite seat.

"That is an understatement," Leonora replied, still somewhat surprised. "But, definitely fortuitous. This will allow us to move freely at the party, as we originally intended."

"There is that," he said thoughtfully. "And I somehow do not think that your aunt would have been quite comfortable with tonight's entertainment. So it's just as well."

"What do you mean?" A prickle of unease ran down Leonora's spine.

"It's just that this soiree was supposed to be for club members and their guests only," Freddy responded. "And I'm not sure they deal in chaperones as a general rule. Aunt Hortense would have stood out. And I have a feeling that would have impeded our progress."

"Why didn't you say anything?" Leonora asked as the carriage slowed.

Frederick shrugged. "I knew your father wanted your aunt to accompany you. And it's in my best interest just now to keep him happy."

"For the sake of our investigation," she said flatly.

"Naturally," he responded, his expression bland. "For the sake of the investigation."

They were saved from further conversation by the footman opening the carriage door.

Frederick's first thought on stepping into the entryway of Sir Gerard and Lady Fincher's Hampstead mansion was "new money."

While his cousin's family was indeed connected to the Lisles by marriage, the Finchers had never been particularly plump in the pocket. Sir Gerard's household, however, must have acquired wealth somehow for the floors gleamed with Italian marble and the walls were hung with fabrics that Frederick knew from furnishing his own small house in Mayfair were quite expensive.

He exchanged a glance with Leonora, whom he could

see from her pointed look at the gilt and crystal chandelier was thinking along similar lines.

"If you will both follow me," the butler said, leading them up the grand staircase to the upper floors.

"I thought you said Sir Gerard's father was a younger son," Leonora said in a low voice as they followed the majordomo up the lushly carpeted stairs.

"I did," Frederick said as they reached the landing, where framed portraits of ancestors bearing no resemblance to the Fincher clan glared out at them. "I'm just as surprised as you are. Last I heard my cousin had already run through his wife's dowry. One can only assume this has been bought on credit."

"Either that, or he has some means of getting funds that we don't know about," Leonora said in a low voice. "It could very well be connected to whatever my brother discovered."

Aware that they were now in hostile territory, he placed a hand on Leonora's lower back to guide her up the narrow stairs, and felt her stiffen then relax. It had been meant as a protective gesture, almost instinctive. It must have been some time since she'd been to a social function with a gentleman, he realized. The thought sent a primitive sort of satisfaction coursing through him. Though he'd at first been careful not to become too attached to her again, he was quickly coming to realize that whatever this was between them was inevitable.

Like a rising tide, it could not be held back.

"Lord Frederick Lisle and Miss Leonora Craven," the butler announced to the room at large.

They were no more than a few moments late—thanks to Aunt Hortense's detour—but it seemed that even so, the party had begun without them. The lavishly furnished drawing room only boasted twenty or so guests, but they somehow managed to make the room feel crowded beyond bearing. That might have been because of the fog of cigar smoke that hung like an impending thundercloud over the room. At the butler's announcement of them, the raucous laughter stopped, and for a moment, the partygoers turned to assess the newcomers.

From his place of pride, on what would in another place be termed a throne, Sir Gerard held court, surrounded by eager young men and ladies whose gowns exposed a shocking amount of naked flesh. "Excellent, my dear cousin! I am so pleased you decided to join us!"

Glancing at Leonora, Freddy saw that she was scanning the room with watchful eyes. She might think that her own artistic set was shocking, but they were probably quite tame when compared to the Lords of Anarchy and their hangers-on. Still, she didn't seem traumatized. Only curious.

"May I present my fiancée, Miss Leonora Craven?" he asked a bit loudly, making sure that the other men in the room, most of whom were eyeing Leonora with open interest, knew that she belonged to him.

Leonora stiffened beside him, but he squeezed her hand. If she let her displeasure show, it might provoke the assembled group to demand a display of dominance from him. Something he was loath to do, but would if it was required to keep her safe from these wolves.

Sir Gerard laughed knowingly at Frederick's declaration. "As usual, cousin, you display exquisite taste," he said, gesturing for them to come stand before him. Like supplicants to the king. To Leonora he said, "I'm delighted to meet you, Miss Craven. My cousin is a lucky man."

Freddy didn't much care for the way Gerard allowed his gaze to rake down Leonora's figure, like a wolf eyeing a tasty morsel. Nor did Leonora, he surmised, feeling her stiffen beside him as his cousin leered at her. It went against every bit of his natural inclination to allow such liberties, but it was a necessity if they were to learn the true nature of Jonathan's death.

Only that knowledge kept him from declaring the gathering to be the farce it was and carrying Leonora bodily from the house.

"A lucky man indeed, Frederick," Sir Gerard said, his gimlet gaze belying the languid tone of his voice. He wished to convey ease and calm, but it was obvious—at least to his cousin—that his every muscle was poised for action. "If she were mine I'd keep her close to my side, as well. One can never be too careful with women, after all."

"The tasty morsel has a name, Sir Gerard," Leonora snapped before Frederick could stop her. "I'm Leonora Craven. I believe you were well acquainted with my brother, Mr. Jonathan Craven, who was a member of your little club, was he not?"

There was nothing to do but wait for Gerard, who had never enjoyed having his authority questioned, to react. But to Frederick's surprise, his cousin threw his head back and laughed.

"This one has spirit, Freddy," he said with a wink. "I will enjoy seeing her lead you a merry chase."

"As for you, my dear," he said, turning to Leonora with a deceptively sorrowful mien, "your brother was indeed a member of our company. I was sorrier than I can say to lose him. As his sister, you are, of course, welcome at any time in my home and in our club. Jonathan was a valued friend and his loss has been felt keenly by all of us."

As if on cue, the assembled members murmured their agreement. Frederick wondered if they really agreed or if it was simply a rote parroting of their leader's statement.

Whatever their motives, however, Leonora seemed to take it at face value. She inclined her head regally. "I thank you, Sir Gerard, for the sentiment. My family has been quite bereft without him."

"I am sorry to hear it," Gerard responded with what seemed to Frederick like sincerity. "But," he continued, addressing the room at large, "life goes on, as we all know. And we are gathered both to honor the late Mr. Jonathan Craven and to welcome a new member in his stead."

Rising, he clapped his hands together, and to both Frederick and Leonora's surprise, the assembled guests divided into two groups: men on one side and women on the other.

Before Frederick could stop them, two ladies came and took Leonora by the arms, leading her to file out of the room with them in a line of two by two.

It took every ounce of self-control he had to stop himself from going after her. While he suspected Leonora would be safer in the ladies' company than she would be here with the men, instinctively he disliked having her out of his sight. Especially in his cousin's home, where anything could happen.

"Lord Frederick Lisle," Gerard intoned in a voice that would have drawn derision from his younger self only a few years ago, "you have been invited to join the most exclusive and exalted Lords of Anarchy. Is it your wish to enter into this sacred order?"

If he weren't flanked on either side by men he suspected would not hesitate to use their massive strength to snap him in two, Freddy would have found the whole situation amusing. As it was, however, he had a role to play. And he did not wish to do anything that might endanger Leonora, wherever his cousin's wife and her cohorts had taken her.

"It is, Sir Gerard," he said, hoping he displayed the proper amount of sincerity for such an occasion. He'd never been inducted into a glorified fraternity before.

"Then by the power vested in me as the founder and leader of the Lords of Anarchy, it is my pleasure to welcome you into our brotherhood, Lord Frederick," Gerard said with a sudden grin. "Enough of this solemnity!" he shouted. "Bring the ladies back in and let us celebrate with some dancing!"

To his surprise, Frederick found himself surrounded by other club members who pounded him on the back in the time-honored tradition of men celebrating with other men.

"What happened?" Leonora asked in a low voice as she stepped up beside him and slipped her arm through his. "I asked the other ladies, but none of them has any idea of what goes on at the induction ceremony."

Grateful to have her once more under his watch, Frederick shrugged. "There wasn't much to it," he said, stepping to the side of the room so that the footmen who'd suddenly flooded into the room could roll up the Aubusson carpets. "If I had blinked I think I'd have missed it."

A line appeared between Leonora's brows, a sure indication that she had more questions. But before she could speak her query aloud, Sir Gerard stepped up beside them. "I hope you will allow me a dance with your lady, cousin," he said with a smile that didn't quite reach his eyes. "I would like to bid her welcome to the family."

"It isn't for me to allow or disallow her from dancing, cousin," Freddy said, exchanging a glance with Leonora. "I think if I were so foolish as to do that I'd see a swift end to our betrothal."

"My dear," she said with a merry laugh, "you make me sound like a veritable tartar. I should think if you were to request it of me, I'd dance with most anyone you recommended to me. Anyone within reason, that is."

"And am I within reason, Miss Craven?" Gerard

asked, a glint of genuine amusement in his eyes. "I'm sure your brother thought so, though he never saw fit to introduce us."

At the mention of Jonathan, a chill seemed to wash over the three of them. As if his ghost had chosen that very moment to make his presence known.

"Don't be ridiculous, Gerard," Frederick said a little more sharply than he meant to—it was proving difficult to stem his natural commanding tendencies around his cousin. Clearly Gerard liked to think of himself as the strongest personality in the room, so for the time being Freddy would have to play at being the follower. It wouldn't be easy, but if he and Leonora were going to learn what really happened to Jonathan, then he'd simply need to exercise a bit of control.

"I mean to say," Freddy continued in a more conciliatory tone, "it's doubtless true that Jonathan intended to introduce you to one another before he died. What reason could he possibly have to shield his sister from one of his most valued friends?"

"None that I can think of," Leonora assured their host, still all smiles, not revealing a hint of what Freddy knew must be rage at Gerard's criticism of her brother. "Unfortunately, Sir Gerard, though I would enjoy it very much, as you can see from my attire, I am still in mourning for Jonathan. And though he would doubtless have insisted I forgo the conventions, I'm afraid my conscience won't allow me to celebrate when I am not finished grieving for him. I know you, as his dear friend, will understand."

Freddy watched as a range of emotions crossed his cousin's face. From surprise to rage, then carefully neutral interest. "My dear Miss Craven, you must forgive me," he said smoothly, placing a hand over his breast—as if the very thought of his own thoughtlessness was too painful to contemplate. "I was so pleased to meet you at last that I simply forgot the protocols of mourning behavior. If you will allow it, however, we may sit out this dance together." He gestured to a cozy corner near the fire where two chairs had been placed, away from where anything there could be overheard.

"I believe that will be quite unobjectionable, Sir Gerard," Leonora said, before turning to Freddy with a bright smile. "I hope you won't mind me abandoning you, my lord."

Trying to convey to her with only a smile and his eyes that he'd be watching out for her, Freddy nodded. "Of course not, my dear. I know you wish to become further acquainted with my cousin. He was, after all, quite close to your brother."

She nodded. "I knew you'd understand," she said. "Now, shall we go chat, Sir Gerard?"

Freddy was amused to see that his cousin would be forced to descend from his throne in order to walk with Leonora to the chairs. Gerard was a bit on the short side, so Freddy guessed he'd chosen the height of the chair to give him a sense of power. But when he stepped down, he proved to be half a head shorter than Leonora.

Neither Gerard nor Leonora remarked upon it, however. "Cousin, I hope you will enjoy yourself while you are here. I promise to take excellent care of your betrothed."

Something in the other man's eyes made Freddy want to pry his hand from Leonora's arm and run away with her. But instead he nodded and watched them cross the room.

"I am so pleased to have a moment to give you my condolences in person, Miss Craven," Gerard said as he led her to the corner he'd chosen for their chat.

She couldn't help but notice that the fireplace was quite ornate, an exquisite carved marble. But when she looked closer she saw that what she'd at first thought were cherubs were in fact satyrs engaged in just the sort of things one might imagine satyrs would get up to.

To her embarrassment, Gerard noted the direction of her gaze and smirked. "You are not the first lady to be drawn to those carvings, my dear," he said silkily. "I feel sure any number of gentlemen would be happy to show you precisely how to reenact the satyrs' frolics in the flesh."

Unsaid was that he himself would be the first in line, but the desire hovered in the air between them. Leonora felt her stomach roil at Gerard's undisguised lust. Especially when his cousin, her betrothed, was only a few feet away. She had known he was bold, but she hadn't quite realized how bold until now.

"I thank you for the compliment," she said coolly, wishing she were a man so that she could call him out—both for insulting her, and for killing her brother. "However, as you well know, I am betrothed. And as you also know, this subject is entirely inappropriate for an unmarried lady and a married gentleman. If you have no care for your cousin, you must at least have some respect for my brother, who counted you among his friends."

Though she hadn't expected Gerard to respond with a quick apology, or embarrassment, she was surprised by his gleeful laughter.

"My dear, Miss Craven," he said, gasping for breath. "You should see your face. I vow you look quite ferocious. Just like my old nanny when I was a boy. I hope my cousin knows just what he's getting himself into."

Not deigning to respond to her host's strange mirth, Leonora waited until he was finished with his fit and said, "I believe you wished to talk to me about my brother?"

Wiping his eyes, Gerard calmed himself, and smiled sheepishly. "That wasn't well done of me, was it? I'm afraid I let your responses get the better of me. Pray, forgive me, Miss Craven." He placed his hand over his breast as he had done earlier. It must be something he did frequently, she thought. "It was devilish of me to behave so. Especially when you are so clearly overset by the loss of your brother. You were twins, were you not?"

Unsure of what he would do next, Leonora nodded slowly. "We were twins. Though we were quite different in any number of ways."

"Indeed," Sir Gerard said, stroking a finger over his chin. "You, the thinker, the poet, and Jonathan, the doer, the driver. Opposite sides of the same coin, it would seem."

"If that is how you wish to see it," she said, wondering what he was getting at.

"I only mean to say, Miss Craven," Gerard said with a smile, "that you were very different from one another. You, for instance, would never betray a friend. Would you?"

A jolt of surprise, then anger shot through her. "Are you implying that my brother would have?" she asked softly, keeping her voice low lest the rest of the room hear them.

Gerard shrugged. "Not in as many words, my dear. Only that your brother was possessed of a moral code that was—how can I put this delicately?—not quite as strong as yours."

"You know nothing about me," she said hotly.

"Do not be angry with me, Miss Craven, I implore you. I only meant that if your brother had been more careful about things. If he hadn't been so determined to win at any cost, he might still be alive today."

So that was it, she fumed. He was accusing Jonny of cheating in the race that took his life. She knew the accusation was absurd, but even so she felt the sting of outrage as it curdled in her gut. "My brother would not race at all if he could not race honorably," she said through her teeth. "Something you would know since he spent most of the past year and a half in your company."

"Oh, I never said he wasn't honorable," Gerard said with a thoughtful stare. "Only that he was willing to do whatever it took to win. And sometimes that meant risking things that weren't his to risk."

"You speak in riddles, Sir Gerard," she said, unable to endure another minute of his cross talk. "Either my brother cheated or he did not. Either he caused his own death or he did not."

"I rather fear, Miss Craven, it's more complicated than that," Gerard said, rising and offering her his hand. Which she refused. "Suit yourself. It was a pleasure speaking to you. I believe you'll make an excellent match for my cousin. I believe he too has a very strong sense of right and wrong. You may be very happy looking down your noses at us mere mortals."

When he was gone, Leonora took a moment to calm her nerves. She could hear the dance end on the floor behind her and was grateful for the diversion. She wasn't quite sure what she'd expected from Sir Gerard, but it hadn't been outright accusations against Jonny. Though he'd never come right out and said what it was he thought Jonny had done.

One thing she knew for a fact was that Gerard was more than aware that Jonathan had learned something about the club leader. Something illegal, and perhaps even immoral.

They were on the right track, she thought with relief.

Now more than ever she was convinced of Gerard's guilt in the matter.

Rising, she went to seek out Freddy.

"He won't do anything to her while you're watching," Lady Fincher said from where she'd slipped up beside him. "At least nothing overtly insulting. He's much more careful than that, my husband. He's a coward at heart, and would rather not die in a duel if he can help it."

Surprised by her candor, Frederick turned to look at his hostess. "I suppose you've seen this sort of thing before?"

"More times than I can say," she said, slipping her arm through his and leading him toward a group of guests. "He has always had a wandering eye, but I do wish he would not hunt in his own preserves. It leads to unpleasantness among the club members. Though at first they seem eager enough to please their leader. Even if it means giving over their wives and sweethearts to him. Not like you, my lord."

"Did I seem so aloof, then?" Freddy asked, accepting a glass of brandy from a footman.

"Let us call it instead," Lady Fincher said, lifting her own glass in a silent toast, "possessiveness. It's nothing to be ashamed of, my lord. Indeed, it's quite admirable in a newly betrothed gentleman."

Before he could comment on her assessment, they reached the other guests. "I'm sure you all know Lord Frederick Lisle," Lady Fincher said by way of introduction.

Lord Hastings, a hard-faced viscount whom Freddy knew a little from their school days, nodded. "My condolences, old fellow. I mean to avoid the parson's mousetrap for as long as I'm able. Though one could do worse than the lovely Miss Craven, despite her ridiculous poetry."

"I quite like her poetry." This was said by a blowsy lady whose cheeks seemed to indicate she'd already had quite a bit of champagne. "It's lovely and decadent. Quite the thing if you're trying to woo the ladies, Lord Hastings," she said with a glance at the man that suggested she'd not be unamused should he try such a thing with her.

"Her brother was quite proud of it," Lady Fincher said with a solemnity that surprised Frederick. He'd not suspected the lady of possessing any great sentimentality. "He spoke of her quite often."

"A shame about his death," Frederick said, hoping the others would join in the conversation. "Were any of you there that day?"

"I was," the other gentleman in the group, Lord Payne, said. "It was a damned shame. Jonny was one of the best whips I've ever seen. Don't know how he could have made such a mistake. Not when his wits were about him, at any rate. He would never have taken that turn like that. Even if there was a—"

He broke off as Lady Fincher touched him on the arm. "I'm sure we don't need to rehash the details, Lord Payne," she said sharply. "Especially as I believe Lord Frederick was a good friend of Mr. Craven's."

To Frederick's surprise the other man paled at the admonition. Interesting, he thought. So Lady Fincher wielded just as much power within the group as her husband did.

The sound of clapping as the dance ended gave Freddy a reason to excuse himself and seek out Leonora. He didn't think his cousin would try anything untoward in a room full of other people, but he did not like leaving her alone with him for longer than he could help.

To his surprise, he found that either she or Gerard had ended their tête-à-tête a little early, and Leonora was deep in conversation with a pretty redhead near the fire-place.

"This is my betrothed, Lord Frederick Lisle," Leonora told the other woman as she took Freddy's arm. "He was good friends with my brother and would never betray a confidence."

An odd way to begin a conversation, Freddy thought as he greeted the matron.

"Freddy, this is Lady Payne," Leonora told him, her eyes bright with excitement. "She was there the day that Jonny was killed." There was much more to the story than that, Frederick knew, but she dare not speak it aloud in this room full of possible suspects.

"I'd better go back to my husband," Lady Payne said with a tight smile. "He begins to wonder if I'm away from his side for too long. And I feel sure he'll want to dance."

When she was gone, Leonora turned to Frederick. "I have much to tell you."

"You've been busy," he said with a smile. "I only spoke to a few people before I came over here and it would seem you've already gathered more intelligence than I did in half the time."

"I saw you speaking with Lady Melisande," Leonora said, leading him to the corner where she'd conversed with Gerard. "And those club members. I feel sure you learned quite a bit."

"In a minute," he said. "I am on tenterhooks to know what my cousin was so eager to tell you."

"He has quite the wandering eye," she said in a low voice. "I don't think there is a lady here whose bosom he hasn't ogled."

"He always did have a taste for the ladies," Frederick responded, grateful for the privacy afforded by the corner. It would not do to have Leonora's disparagement of their host overheard. "But did you learn anything about Jonathan?"

"He was quite sympathetic about Jonny's accident," she replied easily, though there was something in her eyes that made him think she was keeping something about her conversation with his cousin to herself. "But I'm sure he knows something more about what happened. He seemed to blame the accident on my brother doing something untoward in order to win the race. Like cheating or sabotaging the other carriage."

"What?" Freddy demanded with a scowl. "He called Jonathan a cheater?"

Leonora shifted uncomfortably. "Not exactly. It was not something he said explicitly, but I definitely got the idea that he was trying to blacken Jonny's good name to me. Perhaps in an effort to hide his own misconduct. I'm not sure precisely. But it was not a comfortable conversation."

Quickly she told Freddy about Gerard's conduct during their talk. The accusations, the laughter, and how he'd left her so abruptly. She did not tell him about the satyrs. As much as she wished to see Sir Gerard Fincher punished for his bad manners, she did not wish for Freddy to call him out. Because she was not quite sure that Sir Gerard had any honor at all. And would do whatever it took to escape punishment for his misdeed. Even if it meant killing a blood relative.

"I am shocked he spoke so freely, though I somehow do not think that my cousin holds much faith in the intellect of the female sex," Frederick said apologetically. "It has nothing to do with you. He simply doesn't think about women that way."

"Somewhat surprising since his wife is quite cunning," Leonora said, her brows raised. "But perhaps it is just women who are not Melisande whom he thinks of as imbeciles."

Out of the corner of his eye, Frederick noticed that on the dance floor behind them, the couples were not adhering in any way or fashion to the rules that Almack's had set forth regarding the distance between partners in the waltz.

But then, this was hardly the sort of crowd that would value the opinions of the patronesses of Almack's.

"Do you get the feeling, Freddy," Leonora said, her eyes widening as she spied a couple kissing openly amid the other dancers, "that this party isn't quite . . . proper?"

Since another couple were about as close as they could be without the interference of clothing between them, Frederick agreed with her assessment. "I think it's time for us to get a bit of air," he said, deciding that it would do her reputation better to be found with him in an empty chamber than to be seen among these dancers. "Come on."

Taking her by the hand, he led Leonora from the room and toward the hallway.

Seven

*H*er mind awhirl with the memory of the amorous couples on the dance floor, Leonora felt her heart beat faster as she followed Freddy from the drawing room, his hand warm as it clasped hers.

This night had been a maelstrom of surprises. From the foolishness of Sir Gerard Fincher's throne, to the couples all but coupling on the dance floor, she'd seen things this evening that would be difficult to burn from her mind.

Even so, she thought as she felt Freddy slide an arm around her waist as they walked, she was surprisingly sanguine about it. As long as she was with Freddy, she wasn't afraid. And both her conversation with Sir Gerard and her words with Lady Payne had given her much they could use in the plot to prove the former had killed her brother.

Still, the thought of Gerard's coldness when he spoke about Jonny's accident gave her chills. Against her better judgment, she nestled a bit closer to Freddy as he led them farther down the hall.

Finally, he opened a door off the hall and led her inside a room that was dim but for the glow of the firelight. "Here we are," he said, shutting the door behind them.

"My cousin's study. And if he catches us here, we can simply claim that we were looking for somewhere to be alone."

Seeing him move to the desk and begin opening and closing drawers, Leonora stepped over to the sideboard behind it and began her own investigation of its neatly stacked papers.

The first pile she looked through appeared to be bills for Lady Fincher's rather expensive purchases from Madame LaForge, the most celebrated modiste in town. And more shocking, they were all marked paid. It indicated that Sir Gerard was much wealthier than Leonora had supposed. Something that the sumptuousness of the Fincher house also indicated.

"Freddy," she said, in a low voice. "Look at these."

He took the bills from her and sorted through them.

"Where does he get his money? There must be a thousand pounds worth of charges for gowns alone in that stack." It was not unheard of for ladies of the finest families to spend freely at London establishments. So long as there was some expectation of monies to come—whether from an inheritance or some other source, so long as it checked out—most shopkeepers extended credit. Indeed, it was fashionable among some to go as long as possible without paying one's bills. Brummell had been one of those people. Before he had to flee to the Continent when his debts were finally called in.

"I admit, I had no idea my cousin was doing so well for himself," Freddy said finally, handing the notes back to her. "As you said, his father is a younger son, and as far as I know he always lived off the allowance his father gave him. Gerard has never seemed to want for things but I suppose I always assumed he'd inherited something from the other side of his family. If he's paying bills of this size, though, he's got quite a bit of cash on hand."

"He might be involved in any number of schemes," Leonora suggested. "Blackmail, extortion, cheating at cards."

Freddy rubbed the furrow between his brows, thinking. "Something tells me it's got to be connected to the thing in his life he's most passionate about."

"The club," she said with a nod. "It has something to do with the club. Or its members. I noted quite a few members from some of the finest families in the *ton* in that drawing room tonight. All of them with fortunes ripe for the picking."

"It's possible," he said, handing the notes back to her. When he did so, one piece of paper slipped out and sailed to the carpeted floor.

Frowning, he crouched down and picked it up. It was a plain sheet of foolscap, folded in half. Leonora stood beside him and leaned down to watch as he opened the page.

Pay your debts or pay the forfeit.

There was no address. No signature. Nothing whatsoever to indicate it even belonged in the study of Sir Gerard Fincher. But Leonora knew with every bone in her body that it was somehow connected to her brother's death.

"What does it mean?" she asked him, frustrated at finding yet another clue that added up to precisely nothing. At least nothing that could be used as evidence to present to a magistrate.

"I think the real question," Freddy said, standing up again and turning the page over and over, as if some heretofore invisible mark would appear, "is for whom is it intended? It was in a stack of paid bills, so it isn't as if it were being prepared to be sent out. And the fact that it's here at all, among my cousin's received mail, seems to indicate that it was sent to him."

"So someone is threatening *him*?" Leonora asked, dumbfounded. Of all the scenarios she'd imagined involving Sir Gerard Fincher, it was not the one in which he was the victim of a crime.

"Until we find out how it got here, or who it's from," Freddy said with a shrug, "that's the only logical—"

He broke off at the sound of voices in the hallway outside the study.

"Quickly," he said, slipping the note into his coat and taking Leonora in his arms.

Before she knew what was happening his mouth had covered hers.

There was no preamble. There couldn't be. Not when they had to convince anyone who might enter the room that they'd been caught in the midst of something.

But it wasn't the threat of discovery that sent her heart racing. It was the ache of finally being held in Freddy's arms again. The sweetness of taking him into her mouth, the strength of his biceps as she clung helplessly to him and let him kiss her until her toes curled.

This, she thought as she stroked her tongue against his, this is what I've needed.

It was all so familiar. His clean scent: sandalwood and male. His hard body pressed against her soft one.

It had been five years since she'd felt this right. Five years since she'd felt the press of his firm chest against her breasts, the shiver of his hands spread wide over her bottom, the wet heat of his mouth. But here they were, together again as if nothing had changed.

For the life of her, though, she couldn't understand what about that could possibly be wrong. Shutting out the voice of reason that warned her this could be dangerous, she gave herself up to the pure heaven of being held by Freddy again.

Deep in the heart of her, she felt something awaken that had been dormant since she'd lost him.

Teasing him with her tongue, she set her hands free to explore the wide expanse of his shoulders, slipped her fingers through the curls at the nape of his neck. Shivered as his hand stroked up her side and cupped her breast.

As he kissed his way over her jaw and paused to dip his tongue into the hollow of her collarbone, Leonora let out a sigh. And when his thumb stroked over the peak of her nipple she bit back a cry. Her body was on fire. Alive with wanting him.

From some distant corner of her mind she heard voices, and though the haze of sensuality still lingered, she tried to hear what they were saying.

"Sir Gerard has asked me to move the package. I think it's making him nervous what with all the questions. Meet me on Thursday morning and we'll see to it."

"Can't blame 'em for asking, I suppose," said another voice. "I'd do the same thing if it was my brother."

Then the door to Sir Gerard's study opened with a loud click followed by a sharp burst of surprised laughter. "I might have known Freddy Lisle would find a quiet corner," said a low voice as the door closed. "He always had a way with the ladies," she heard his companion snigger before their voices faded away.

With the interruption, the gauzy nostalgia that had cocooned them dissolved, and as if by mutual decree both Leonora and Freddy pulled back slightly. Leonora rested her forehead against the disheveled ruin of his cravat while he rested his chin on the top of her head. Their breathing was a little ragged.

"I think we fooled them," Leonora said, pulling back

further, and slipping out of the warm circle of his arms. Though he did so with obvious reluctance, Frederick let her go.

"Let's hope so," he said, straightening his coat and sliding a hand over the surface of his golden-brown curls. "I recognized their voices—Lord Darleigh and Sir Richard Ewell. Not men I'd trust with the true reason for our being in this room."

At the mention of Lord Darleigh, Leonora frowned. "My brother spoke of Lord Darleigh in his journal," she said with excitement. "I hadn't realized he was a member of the club."

Frederick's head snapped back as if she'd struck him. "What journal?" he demanded. "Why is this the first time I'm hearing of it?"

His ferocity startled her. "Because I forgot about it in all the excitement of the day," she said mildly, despite her fluttering heart. "I found it last night in my brother's rooms. It was hidden in a secret compartment behind his desk."

Quickly, she explained to him about the second break-in and how her brother's bedchamber had been ransacked. And that this time the safe had been taken.

"Leonora, how is this person able to get into your father's house so easily? Are there no locks on the doors?" He ran a frustrated hand through his hair. "I do not like you staying there when it is so clearly not secure."

"I believe I discovered the problem," she assured him, touched by his concern for her. "Jonny often liked to leave his bedchamber window open to get some fresh air. And there is a trellis just outside. A trellis we both took shameless advantage of when we were younger. I feel sure that whoever did this, is climbing into the room and then back out again with no one the wiser."

Freddy swore. "I hope you've locked the window

now," he said in an aggrieved tone. "I greatly dislike the idea of you there where anyone might simply climb into your home and spirit you away when no one is looking."

"It is locked now," Leonora said, fighting the urge to roll her eyes at his exaggerated concern. Really, she was perfectly able to look after herself.

"Good," he said, pulling her to him. "I couldn't bear it if something happened to you. We must endeavor to keep you safe through all of this or I will forbid you from continuing to participate."

She pulled away, her eyes wide. "You wouldn't dare! I'm a grown woman and I am quite capable of—"

"Of course you are," he assured her calmly. "But even you are not indestructible. And your brother has already lost his life in this fiasco. I simply wish to keep you safe, Nora."

His use of her nickname melted her despite the fury his ordering her about had caused. She supposed now wasn't the time for protesting anyway. Until he actually did something, it was still just a threat.

"Back to my brother's journal," she said pointedly.

As if he too were ready to put their cross words behind him, he asked, "What did it say? Did you read it?"

Leonora raised an imperious brow. "Of course I read it. And it had very little to say on the subject of the club. Only a few mentions here and there of Sir Gerard and that reference to Lord Darleigh—it was barely a sentence, really. Jonny said that Lord Darleigh was helping him locate a ledger of some sort."

Frederick's brows drew together. "And did he ever locate it?"

"No, as it happens," she replied with a shrug. "That notation was made on the day before he was killed. So I have no idea whether it was found or not. But perhaps I could ask Lord Darleigh about it later."

But Frederick was already shaking his head. "Better let me do it," he said with a grimace. "I'm afraid Darleigh isn't best known for his manners where ladies are concerned."

Leonora put her hands on her hips. "Are you suggesting I am incapable of handling an ill-mannered gentleman, because I can assure you that I've grown quite accustomed to it in the years you were away?"

"Why the devil would you?" he asked, not bothering to apologize for the profanity. "You're a lady poet, not a Bow Street runner."

Oh, poor misguided man. "Surely you must have read the papers when you were in Paris," she said calmly. "I became something of a thorn in the side of the Tories when I spoke out about the disgraceful way married ladies are treated by the laws of this country. I received quite a bit of unpleasant mail."

"Spoke out *how*"? he asked with deceptive calm.

"Just a few well-placed essays in ladies' magazines," Leonora said, feeling a little defensive. It wasn't her fault that Frederick hadn't bothered to keep up with the papers in his absence from London. Besides, it was none of his affair, really. "And my last book of poems was an epic ballad about famous heroines in history. And may have included a verse praising Judith over her treatment of Holofernes."

Frederick swore. "Didn't you think this was something I should know about before I brought you here? My cousin is many things, but a champion of rights for women is not one of them. His views are such that he might very well have barred us entrance to his home over it!"

"But he didn't," Leonora said, placing a placating hand on his arm. "Indeed, I think my reputation has stood me in good stead here. At least two of the ladies compli-

mented me on my poem that appeared in the *Ladies'
Journal* last month."

He opened his mouth to speak, then closed it. Clearly
he was still agitated, but rather than divulge his thoughts,
Frederick took her arm in his and offered her his arm.

"Where are we going?" she asked.

"To make our good-byes," he replied, leading her back
to the drawing room. "I think our business is done here
for now. And I am suddenly fearful for your safety in this
house. I knew that as Jonathan's sister you were at risk,
but it never occurred to me that you might be a target
because of your writing."

And with that, they left.

As they rode through the streets of Mayfair, the horses'
hooves on the cobblestones making a distinctive clip-
clop, Frederick fumed over what Leonora had revealed
to him.

First of all, there was the fact that she'd kept her discovery of Jonny's journal from him. He'd known from
both his own history with her and Jonny's hair-raising
tales of their childhood that Leonora was as headstrong
as they came. But he'd not expected her to keep information from him right from the start of their new part-
nership. Most troubling at all was the way his heart
had clenched on learning she'd held back the find from
him. It felt like such a betrayal in light of all they'd been
through together. He thought they were working together
as a team, but at the heart of things she simply did not
trust him.

It might be a false betrothal they were engaged in, but
there was a part of him—a much larger part than he'd
realized—that wanted it to be real. He could admit that
now. He wanted to claim her as his own in the most public of ways. Not only out of affection for her, which he

did indeed feel, but also out of some primitive need to mark his territory.

It was nothing he could—or would—ever tell Leonora. If she was indeed the woman who had become known to the press as Miss Bluestocking—he had read the essays while he was in France, he simply hadn't known they were written by Leonora—then she would reject him if she knew how like an animal she made him feel.

It didn't matter that he did his best by every woman he came into contact with. What she'd remember was that he had, in a moment of weakness, wanted all the rights over her a legal marriage would afford him.

A fool's errand if ever there was one.

"You're still angry, I suppose," Leonora said from the opposite seat of the carriage.

The top of the barouche had been lifted and now covered them from the prying eyes of passersby. Thus it was impossible for Frederick to read her expression. Acting on instinct rather than common sense, he took both her hands in his and pulled her over onto the seat beside him.

"Not angry," he said, lifting her into his lap. "Worried about you."

"I've done a good job of taking care of myself in the past five years, Frederick," she responded sharply, though she rested her cheek against his chest. "There's little reason to think that I will suddenly become enfeebled because you've returned home."

"It's not just that and you know it, Leonora," he said, his exasperated voice in contrast to the comforting arms that held her. "Has it even occurred to you that Jonathan's death perhaps had nothing to do with the Lords of Anarchy? That it could have been one of your detractors who killed him?"

Her sharp intake of breath told him that this was a line of inquiry that she'd not considered before now. He regretted frightening her, but even so, the idea of just how little she valued her own neck made him incredibly angry.

"But surely it was Sir Gerard," she protested. "After all, the driving club was the most dangerous thing that my brother was involved with."

"It very well might have been," he responded with feeling. "But that doesn't mean that they are necessarily responsible for his death. My cousin is nothing if not brilliant. He will have already thought through all the pros and cons of the situation. Whether he's acted upon them is another matter altogether. He might be responsible for killing Jonathan, but so too might any crank who feels he owes you an ill turn because of your political views. God knows there are enough of them walking about the streets of London."

She was silent for a moment. Which made him nervous even as he cradled her against him.

"It is true," she finally admitted, "that I have received some threatening letters thanks to my essays, but those were always threats against Miss Bluestocking. Not me, or my actual family. The writers never even knew my direction. They were sent to the offices of the journal, and my editor forwarded them.

"I think what really bothers you about my essays," she continued, "is not that they put me in danger, but that I didn't tell you about them."

She leaned back to get a closer look at his expression. Which he kept carefully neutral lest she see that she'd hit a nerve.

"Don't be absurd," he said with studied calm. "I am concerned for your safety and that's all. What do I care what you were up to while I was away in France?"

"If we are going down that road," she said, toying with

the pin in his cravat. "Then I might begin to wonder how you were spending your time while you were away. Who you were . . . seeing." The pause was a speaking one. And opened up a line of questioning with which he was decidedly uncomfortable.

Sighing, he decided to concede. A bit.

"You may be right that I dislike not being taken into your confidence about your political writings," he admitted. "But that doesn't negate the fact that your writings could very well have put you in danger. And I won't apologize for being worried about your safety. I would hardly be any sort of man if I shrugged my shoulders and went about my business upon learning that my fiancée had received threats because of her political leanings." He slid a finger beneath her chin and tipped her head so that he could see into her eyes. "I never stopped caring for you, Leonora. Not even after you sent me away. It's always been you."

Her lashes lowered. "I wish I could believe that," she said, biting her lip. "I wish—"

The carriage pulled to a stop then, and he bit back a curse because the moment was lost.

She drew back and settled onto the seat beside them as she waited for the footman to open the door.

Taking advantage of the moment, he gave in to temptation and kissed her with every bit of the emotion and desire he'd been unable to give words to.

She was breathless when he pulled back and Freddy smiled wickedly. "Think of that tonight as you lie alone in your cold bed."

"You're a rake and a scoundrel," she said with a rueful shake of her head. "You know this, I hope."

"And this is a surprise to you?" He pushed open the door and leaped to the ground before the footman could lower the steps.

"Of course it's not," she responded as he took advantage of the opportunity to lift her from the carriage. "I know you of old."

"Yes," he said in a low voice, holding her against him for a fraction of a second longer than was entirely proper. "And I know you. Trust me, Leonora. I promise you, I will keep you safe."

But her sad smile told him she wasn't quite there yet. He'd simply have to wait.

Forever if he had to.

"I shall call on you tomorrow afternoon," Freddy said as he walked beside her up the front steps of her father's town house.

"Tomorrow afternoon is my salon, I'm afraid," she said with what looked like sincere disappointment. "You are welcome to attend, of course, but I know how much you disliked attending in the past."

If it was a test, he thought, she couldn't have devised a cleverer one. He had loathed those afternoons when they were betrothed previously. Mostly because it meant watching hopeful young swains read awful poetry in hopes of a kind word from her. But he'd learned a great deal about self-control in the past five years, and a few hours of discomfort would hardly register with him now.

"I will be delighted to attend," he responded, bowing over her hand. "I shall see you tomorrow."

He felt her gaze on him as he descended the steps, but when he turned to look back, she was gone.

Eight

$\mathcal{T}$he Duchess of Pemberton is here to see you, Miss Craven," said Leonora's maid apologetically the next morning. Peggy said everything apologetically. But today her words felt especially doleful. As if a duchess coming to call were something akin to a diagnosis of scurvy.

"Show her into my sitting room," Leonora said, placing the last pin in her hair and rising. "And have cook send up some tea and biscuits."

She didn't anticipate the visit being altogether pleasant, but at least she could have some biscuits to soothe her temper.

It was no secret that the Duke and Duchess of Pemberton hadn't been especially joyful when Freddy told them about their betrothal five years ago. So there was little doubt in Leonora's mind that this was not a pleasant social call.

The Lisle family was very close, and Freddy's parents had high hopes for all their sons. As for Freddy, they hoped for a bride much higher in birth and breeding than a mere gentleman's daughter. But it was Leonora's writing that was the real impediment in their eyes.

It was one thing to write for the sheer pleasure of

it, but Leonora wrote for money. She'd never seen the point of refusing the payment for her publications, especially when she worked hard to make it the best she could. That, among other things, had been a point of contention between Freddy and his parents almost from the first.

There was also the matter of Leonora's outspokenness on political matters. Like many of their generation and class, the duke and duchess thought a lady's place was in the home. And a true lady had no business dabbling in politics, no matter how worthy the cause.

She wished that she could assure the duchess that this latest betrothal was a pretend one—that there was nothing to worry about—but the fewer who knew the truth the better. She'd simply have to tell her pretend future mama-in-law that she intended her precious boy no harm.

When she stepped into her sitting room, however, it was to see not one duchess, but two.

"I hope you won't mind that I accompanied the duchess, Miss Craven," the young dowager Duchess of Ormond, Perdita, now Mrs. Archer Lisle, said, crossing the room to take Leonora's hands in her own. "But I simply could not pass up the opportunity to visit one of my favorite authors."

As Freddy had said, his sister-in-law was very much with child, and she was practically glowing with happiness.

Unconsciously, Leonora's hand stole to her own flat stomach. She would never know that sort of joy, and for a moment the knowledge sucked her breath away.

The Duchess of Pemberton broke through Leonora's heavy thoughts. "Perdita can be quite persuasive, Miss Craven. When I informed her that I was coming to call upon you, I could not persuade her to let me come alone."

Called back to herself, Leonora focused on the duchess.

Frederick's mother was a lovely woman, though some gray had crept into her honey-blond hair—just a few shades lighter than Freddy's. Her blue eyes, so like his, were sharp with intelligence, and Leonora thought not for the first time that it was a shame she'd been unable to persuade the duchess to the cause of women's rights. For it was clear that the lady possessed a keen intellect, and a woman of her grace's poise and station would be highly influential.

"I am delighted to meet you both," Leonora said aloud to her guests, gesturing that they should take seats. "I've asked for refreshments to be sent up. I hope that you'll join me, for I cannot abide a pot of tea without biscuits."

The ladies exchanged polite conversation for a few minutes while they waited for the tea tray. But before long the tea arrived, and Leonora, ready to end her suspense, asked, "To what do I owe the pleasure? Not that I am displeased by the visit, of course. I am delighted."

The two other women exchanged a speaking look. The Duchess of Pemberton finally said, "Miss Craven, my son informs me that you are once again betrothed, a circumstance that leaves me with much trepidation I am sorry to say."

Perdita winced at the duchess's declaration. "What I think her grace is attempting to say, Miss Craven, is that she has some reservations about your betrothal given the circumstances of your previous connection with Frederick. Especially given his exile when you broke things off."

"Exile?" Leonora asked with raised brows. Leaving for France had been Freddy's decision entirely. And Leonora was not about to admit fault in that at least. "I am quite sure that Frederick left England on his own initiative. Yes, perhaps it was as a result of my breaking things off, but that is neither here nor there. It was not my decision to send him away. It was his own. A circumstance I'm sure you cannot hold me liable for, no matter how you might wish to."

"Piffle," the duchess said with a shake of her head. "We all know that Frederick left because he was heartbroken when you jilted him. And I will have your promise, Miss Craven, you do not intend to do such a fool thing again."

Leonora fought to keep her temper. "Your grace, you'll forgive me, but you know nothing about what went on between Frederick and me. And I would hope that you are aware he would be livid if he knew you were here speaking on his behalf."

"Well, someone has to!" the duchess said heatedly. "It nearly killed him. Were you aware of that? He drank himself into a stupor for days, until finally his father and I sent him to France to get him away from his cronies here in London. I sincerely feared for his life, Miss Craven. A circumstance I should think you would appreciate given your recent loss."

Closing her eyes, Leonora took a deep breath. She hadn't known the situation behind Frederick's withdrawal to France. She'd been too enmeshed in her own misery at the time to notice much beyond the routine of daily life. But she was sorry to hear of it.

She'd broken things off with him to protect him. From further attachment to her. For his future. But it would seem she'd almost done more harm than good.

Aloud, she said, "I regret that Frederick suffered like that, your grace. I sincerely do. It was not my intention to destroy him. Far from it. But I must tell you that what happened between us before is between us. And no one else. I can, however, assure you that I will do my utmost to ensure that our betrothal now will bring him no harm."

Though she was less than convinced that was within her power, she would, for both their sakes, try.

Leonora could see that the duchess was struggling with her own emotions. It was clear that she wanted to ask Leonora why she'd done what she'd done. But there was no way she would tell the older woman. Especially not when she'd not even told Freddy.

After a moment of silence, the duchess said, "I will have to be content with that, then, I see. Though I will ask that you give me your word that you will go through with the marriage this time, and will work through any problems that you encounter before your wedding. I rather think that young people are far too apt to dissolve their matches without doing the work that must be done to save the relationship."

It was a promise she could not make.

In part because the betrothal now was a mere fiction, but also because she had no idea how Frederick would respond if he learned the truth about what had forced her to release him five years earlier. It would be so easy to marry him despite her inability to give him children, but that would be unfair to him without telling him the truth. And once he learned that truth it was doubtful he'd go through with the marriage anyway.

What a coil.

For now, she would simply have to prevaricate to the duchess. Bringing Sir Gerard to justice was too important a matter to jeopardize by telling Freddy's mother the true circumstances of their current betrothal.

"I have no wish to part with Lord Frederick," Leonora said truthfully. "And I will do my utmost never to hurt him again." She did not promise to go through with a marriage. And she hoped her words would be enough to satisfy the older woman.

Fortunately, Perdita, who seemed intent upon mending things between the duchess and Leonora, spoke before her mother-in-law could.

"Thank goodness that's settled," she said with obvious relief. "I must admit that I was concerned when the duchess told me she wished to extract a promise from you, Miss Craven, but I might have known you'd handle things so wonderfully. A lady of your obvious sensibilities could not possibly deny a mother's request."

It was far more complicated than either of Leonora's guests could fathom, but she was happy to have the matter settled.

"Now, let us speak of your poetry," Perdita continued, and began asking about various poems that Leonora had published over the years.

Talking to readers had always come easily to Leonora, because she was a reader herself and understood the desire to know more about her favorite pieces. Still, she was not prepared for Perdita's questions about one poem in particular.

"Please, can you tell me," the young matron asked, "what was the inspiration for 'Angel Child'? I was so touched by your obvious understanding of the emotions of the speaker. I don't believe I've ever read a more thoughtful explanation of what it means to lose a child."

If Leonora could have conjured the subject she'd most wish to avoid across the tea table it was that of her poem written soon after her miscarriage. She'd decided to publish it against her better judgment early in her career because she'd sent it along with another set of verse to her editor, who'd convinced her of its quality.

Readers had asked about it before, but never one so great with child. That Perdita was also Freddy's sister-in-law only made the subject more painful.

Determined to hide any hint of discomfort about the subject, she said easily, "Thank you so much, Mrs. Lisle. I am pleased you were so moved by that particular verse. I had a neighbor in the country who suffered such a loss, and I found the idea of losing a child so touching, so poignant, that I couldn't help but imagine the meeting between bereaved mother and angel child."

Suddenly Perdita's eyes filled with tears. "I lost a babe, you see. When I was with my first husband. And I felt the loss of that child so keenly. I took great comfort in your poem, in the notion that my dear one was with me, giving me strength to survive his loss."

She reached out and Leonora found it impossible to refuse the other woman's hand.

"Thank you," Perdita said, squeezing Leonora's hand tightly. "You made my grief so much easier to bear. And I feel sure I speak for any number of other women who have miscarried."

Blinking, Leonora felt the sting of tears in her own eyes. That poem had been the encapsulation of her own grief and heartache at the loss of the child she'd loved despite the perfidy of its absent father. And sitting here, now, with these two ladies not knowing the true circumstances of her own situation, and how it had affected Freddy, she felt as exposed as if she'd run naked down Rotten Row.

"I just recalled that I did not tell cook that we will have an addition to dinner this evening, Perdita," the duchess said, clearing her throat delicately. "I hope you won't mind leaving now. We have trespassed on Miss Craven for far too long this morning."

Perdita pulled her hand away, dabbed at her tears with her handkerchief. "Of course, your grace. I vow, Miss Craven, I apologize for my unruly emotions. I'm afraid this child is turning me into a watering pot. I am usually much more stoic than this."

Despite her own discomfort, Leonora had found her conversation with the young woman cathartic. And knowing that her verse had perhaps given women like herself some comfort in their grief made her own pain more bearable.

"Think nothing of it, Mrs. Lisle," she said with a smile. "A poetess never finds emotion evoked by her words a burden. Indeed, it is the response we crave." Turning serious, she continued, "And I am sorry for your loss. I hope this child gives you great comfort."

"Indeed it does," Perdita said with a smile, laying her hand possessively over her belly. "And I hope to speak of more than that single poem with you this evening."

Puzzled, Leonora frowned. "I'm not sure I understand. Where is it we're to see one another?"

"The additional guest at dinner I spoke of will be you, my dear," the duchess said with a smile that removed twenty years from her face. Leonora suddenly realized how much she'd longed for the approval of Freddy's mother, so great was her relief at the duchess's shift from disapproving to welcoming. "If you are to marry my son, then you must come to dinner at our home tonight. I realize it is short notice, but I do hope you'll consider it. If not for my sake, then for Frederick's."

There was no way she could decline given how sincere the duchess's invitation seemed. And besides, she felt a curious desire to see Freddy among his family, to see how they got along together. Their first betrothal had been so brief she'd not even met his family.

"I thank you, your grace. I should be honored to attend this evening."

"Excellent," the duchess said, pulling on her gloves. "We dine at seven. I will have Frederick come fetch you."

To Leonora's surprise, she leaned forward and kissed her on the cheek. "I look forward to getting to know you better, my dear."

Perdita winked at her as she followed the Duchess of Pemberton from the room.

Utterly flustered by the whole affair, Leonora collapsed onto the settee.

What a debacle, she thought numbly. The more time she spent with Freddy's family, the more painful it would be when their pretend betrothal ran its course. And the last thing she wanted was to cause him or his family more pain.

If only she could contemplate marrying him without the burden of her inability to conceive. In every other way, they were well suited.

Taking a sip of her now cold tea, she looked forlornly at the door her visitors had just exited.

I'm sorry, Freddy.

"You're a bastard," the Earl of Mainwaring said, thrusting his arms into the banyan Frederick had just tossed to him. "You know this, yes?"

"I have it on excellent authority that my parents were married when I was born," Freddy said, unrepentant, crossing his arms over his chest. "What with all the brothers who came before me and all."

He'd arrived at an admittedly early hour in his friend's rooms thanks to his own inability to sleep past daylight. The night before had left him with too many racing thoughts to settle properly into sleep. And besides that, there were things he needed to do this morning. Things that would require the help of Mainwaring.

The earl grunted as he accepted a glass of the foul concoction his valet conjured up for those mornings when his master suffered from overindulging the night before. To Freddy's disgust, Mainwaring swallowed it down in one gulp, shaking his head as he did so.

"I don't know how you stand the stuff," Freddy said with barely restrained revulsion. "Do you even know what's in it?"

"I neither know, nor care," Mainwaring responded, setting the empty glass on a side table, then tying his robe. "All I care about is that it takes away this accursed headache. And of course, learning your reason for waking me at the arse-crack of dawn so that I may murder you for it. A man likes to know the reason why he's killing his friend."

"You can't kill me," Freddy said, dropping into an armchair before the fire as his friend sat down before a tray of tea and toast his valet had left for him. "At least not before I figure out who is responsible for Jonathan's death."

The mention of Jonathan brought them both back down to earth. "What news on that front?" the earl asked as he bit into a piece of toast. "I see from the page Hoskins has helpfully marked for me in the post that you've made your betrothal to Leonora official. Again."

Freddy sat up and unceremoniously plucked the paper from Mainwaring's hand. "Is it in there already? That's fast work. I gave them a bribe to put it in this morning's edition, but one never knows." He scanned the page, and saw that sure enough, there was the announcement that Lord Frederick Lisle and Miss Leonora Craven were planning to marry. It was rather startling to see it in black-and-white and Freddy found that he rather liked seeing it spelled out. He wondered if Leonora had seen it, then cursed himself for being a sentimental idiot.

Turning his attention to the matter at hand, he looked up to see that Mainwaring was watching him.

"What?" he asked, not liking the knowing glint in his friend's eye.

"Nothing," Mainwaring responded, chewing his toast. "It just seems that you're rather pleased with yourself over the announcement."

"Need I remind you, Mainwaring," Freddy said in his

most glacial tones, "that this is a pretend betrothal? I am pleased to see that my bribe worked. That is all."

The other man's brow quirked. "If you say so, old fellow."

"I do."

"I know. I heard you."

"Then there is nothing more to discuss."

Mainwaring looked as if he'd like to discuss the matter further, but after a long look he shook his head as if to clear it.

"Well, then, I suppose you had a reason for rousing me from my bed this early," he said, crossing his arms over his chest. "It doesn't take a mathematical genius to figure that out. So, what is it?"

Quickly Freddy told him about almost everything that had transpired at his cousin's home the night before.

The earl whistled. "I wondered about that induction ceremony. It's rather disappointing to learn it was so unspectacular. I suppose Gerard uses his imagination for something other than the club. Dashed if I know what that could be though."

"My point," Freddy said, "was not to discuss the ceremony, but to make it clear that my cousin is being blackmailed by someone."

"Well, yes," Mainwaring responded with a shrug. "But, as my nanny used to say, 'lie down with dogs, wake up with fleas.' "

"Too right. However, the reason I've roused you from your bed at this ungodly hour is so that you can accompany me to Jackson's. My cousin invited me to pay a visit to Jackson's this morning to spar with one of the other members. It's part of the initiation apparently."

"That should be easy enough." Mainwaring nodded. "You're already there once a week or so. I'm pleased to hear it's another club member you'll spar with. I've got to maintain my gorgeous exterior if I'm going to woo the delicious Mrs. Creighton into my bed. She said she likes my pretty face. And it would be a shame to disappoint her. Especially given how you always ignore my admonition to keep any bruising away from *mon visage*."

Freddy rolled his eyes. "You and your pretty *visage*. Fortunately for you and your face, I have need of you only as a distraction so that I may speak to the other club members in attendance without being caught out by my cousin. Someone among their number knows the truth of what killed Jonathan and I want to hear it."

At the mention of their friend, Mainwaring sighed. "All right. Give me ten minutes to dress and we'll be off.

"However," he said as he rang for his valet, "I must remark that for a driving club, the Lords of Anarchy devote a great deal of time to doing anything but."

Nine

*O*ne hour later—Mainwaring had taken longer to dress than promised, claiming that a gentleman could not make his toilette in haste lest he disappoint his public—they stepped into the bastion of masculine fisti-cuffs, Gentleman Jackson's boxing saloon.

The man himself was watching a pair of young gen-tlemen Freddy recognized as the scions of two of the *ton*'s most influential families. And leaning against the wall, deep in discussion, he recognized the Anarchists Sir Horace Meade and Lord Payne.

Indicating to Mainwaring that he was going to speak to them, he strode across the room, which was already crowded with men wagering or watching the matches al-ready under way.

"It's finished," he heard Payne saying in a low voice as he approached. "And Sir Gerard would like very much for you to keep the matter to yourself. If the authorities find out, it will be a loss for the entire club."

From the expression on Meade's face, Freddy knew that the topic was not a happy one. Unfortunately, the other man noticed Freddy's approach and bit back his reply before it could be overheard.

"Lord Frederick," Sir Horace said pointedly, and sure

enough Lord Payne turned and glared at the approaching man. Clearly their discussion had been of some import.

Interesting.

"I thought you might put in an appearance this morning," Sir Horace continued. "Would you care for a bout?"

Before he could respond, Lord Payne turned and scanned him with a cold eye. "I think you'd better let me fight him, old man," the large man drawled. "I think he's more up to my weight than yours."

It was true that Sir Horace was half a head shorter than the other two men, but Freddy had a feeling that Lord Payne's desire to spar with him had little to do with the suitability of their weights. Even so, Freddy inclined his head. "I'd like nothing better," he said. "In fact, Jackson owes me a favor, so I'll see to it we don't have to wait."

Sir Horace, evidently acceding to Lord Payne's authority, shrugged. "It's all the same to me. I'm not overly fond of fisticuffs anyway. I came because Sir Gerard encouraged it and you'll soon learn, Lord Frederick, that one would do well to do whatever Sir Gerard asks. He expects obedience from club members in all things."

Something about the other man's nasty grin set Freddy's teeth on edge. Sir Gerard might expect obedience, but he was damned if he'd take orders from the man he'd known since he was a schoolboy tearing the wings off flies.

"I'll keep that in mind," he told the other man blandly, neither agreeing nor disagreeing with the advice. Turning to Lord Payne, he gestured that they should proceed to the empty ring, where Gentleman Jackson himself was standing just outside, talking with one of the men whose fights had just finished.

When Jackson's conversation was finished, it was only a matter of a few words' conversation to secure the center ring for Freddy and Lord Payne.

While Payne stayed behind to talk with Jackson, Freddy headed for the dressing room, where other men were dressing and undressing for their own matches.

"I thought you were here to speak with Sir Horace," Mainwaring protested while Freddy removed his cravat. "Payne is not overly fond of rules. Especially the ones that involve fighting fair. I learned that the hard way at school."

Mainwaring, as a mathematical genius, had not had a pleasant time at school before he fell in with Freddy and Trent and Jonathan Craven. Freddy hadn't forgotten, but his focus now was not on Lord Payne's trustworthiness. He already knew it was nonexistent.

"Perhaps," he said, flexing his shoulders, "it's time he fought someone his own size."

"Definitely," the earl responded, "but you must know the man has blood in his eyes. He wants to bash your head in for some reason, and given half a chance he's going to do it."

"Dear Mainwaring," Freddy said with a grin. "I didn't know you cared . . ."

"Don't be an arse," the other man responded with disgust. "I'm serious, Fred. He's not known for pulling his punches. And I do not want to be the one to explain to Leonora that you've gone and gotten yourself killed."

At the mention of Leonora, Freddy sobered. "I'm doing this for her," he said in a low voice. "Payne knows something about what happened to Jonny. As does Sir Horace. Fighting Lord Payne will encourage them to see me as a member of the club. And hopefully will loosen their tongues."

"If you say so," the earl said, looking skeptical. "I suppose I'll just have to trust you."

"My lords," Gentleman Jackson said in a loud voice. "Are you ready for the match to begin?"

"I'm off," Freddy said in a low voice. "Wish me luck."

"You'll need it," Mainwaring muttered as they approached the ring, where a bare-chested Lord Payne stood bouncing on the balls of his feet.

Before Freddy could move into the ring, however, Sir Gerard Fincher stepped up beside him. "I am pleased to see you followed my advice to come this morning, Lord Frederick. I am always happy to welcome new members to the club who are able to follow instructions."

Biting back a retort what would likely get him ejected from the Anarchists, Freddy instead nodded and said, "How could I resist, cousin? I have always enjoyed a fight. And Lord Payne was happy enough to oblige me."

Payne flushed, clearly disliking the notion of obliging anyone about anything. "I was ready for a fight," he said in a clipped tone. "And I knew that as a new member, he needed testing." Unsaid but implied was his suspicion that Freddy would not be passing Professor Payne's pugilistic exam.

"I am grateful for your enthusiasm, Payne," Gerard said to the other man. "But I'm afraid I must ask the two of you to accompany me to my house for an emergency meeting."

Turning to Gentleman Jackson, Gerard added, "I will be sure to compensate you for the time lost while we held this ring, Mr. Jackson."

The big man shrugged, as if it were all the same to him whether they stayed or left. Turning, he walked away to call for someone else to use the now empty ring.

Mainwaring, who had been watching the exchange with a frown, spoke up. "Might I come along as well, Sir Gerard? I'm quite curious about your club, despite being an indifferent driver."

Freddy had to give his friend credit. He was bold. But it was clear from Gerard's expression that he'd rather

invite an asp to sup at his dinner table than have Mainwaring accompany them. He wasn't sure if it was because the other man outranked him or if it was simply a
desire to keep prying eyes away. Whatever the case, his
response was negative. "Unfortunately, Lord Mainwaring," Gerard said coolly, "this will be a meeting for club
members only. I should very much like it if you would
attend the ball my wife and I will be hosting later in the
season, however."

Rather than look offended, Mainwaring shrugged.
"That's disappointing, but not unexpected. Though I suppose club business is club business, and not being a
member . . ."

To Freddy, he said, "I'll see you later, old chap. I hope
you have a very interesting meeting."

Then, before Freddy could protest, he continued, "Oh,
and I'll just drive your curricle to Brooks's for a trice. I've
gotten much better at handling the reins, so have no fear."

"How the devil am I supposed to get to Half Moon
Street?" he called after his friend. Archer was going to
kill him if Mainwaring so much as scratched his curricle, he thought with a sigh. Never mind he hadn't precisely given his permission for his ham-fisted friend to
drive the thing in the first place.

Deciding to catch a ride with one of the other club
members, he hurried into the dressing room and quickly
put his clothes and boots back on.

Just what, he wondered as he tied his cravat, was so
important that Gerard had felt it necessary to call a
meeting of the entire club? Especially when they'd all
been together only the night before.

It was damned strange.

When he stepped back out into the main room of the
saloon, he found his cousin in deep conversation with

Payne, who closed his mouth as soon as Freddy approached.

"Ah, cousin," Gerard said into the pregnant silence. "I will see you and Lord Payne in Half Moon Street in a quarter of an hour."

With that, he bowed and strode toward the door leading out to St. James Street.

"You'd best not tell your friend Mainwaring anything about club business," Lord Payne said as soon as Gerard was out of earshot. "Otherwise Sir Gerard will get it into his head that you're not loyal. And he has a particular disgust for disloyalty. As do I."

Unruffled by the other man's threat, Freddy grunted something that could have been an assent or a suggestion that Payne go jump in the Thames.

Turning his back on the other man, he went in search of a more palatable member of the club to give him a lift to his cousin's house.

He'd spent quite enough time with Lord Payne that morning to last a lifetime.

"What a lovely ode to motherhood, Mrs. Jeffries," Leonora said, grateful that the lady's fifty-stanza-long epic was finally complete. "I especially liked your metaphor comparing the stars to God's daisy chain."

After her meeting with Freddy's mother and sister-in-law that morning, she'd been forced to hurry her preparations for the literary salon. Though she opened her father's drawing room to artists and philosophers of all sorts each week, she usually had some new writing of her own to read. That had proved impossible since Freddy had come back into her life, however.

Fortunately, there were plenty of other attendees who were more than willing to share their own work. When

she'd first started, she'd needed to request things personally before the salon, but now so many vied for the center
of attention at her weekly meetings that there were usually
more than enough pieces for other writers to present.

It was just bad luck that Mrs. Jeffries, whose work was
generally cheerful, would be about the ghost of a small
child returning to warn his mother of her own impending death.

Today, it seemed, she was unable to escape reminders
of her own sorrowful secret.

She'd hoped that Freddy would put in an appearance,
but thus far he'd not shown up. Which was just as well,
because she wanted some time alone with her thoughts
before she saw him again. The meeting with his mother
and Perdita that morning had left her feeling exposed,
and she needed to consider just what the impact of their
charade would have on the people closest to them.

So far, she'd been focused so keenly on proving the
truth about Sir Gerard that it hadn't fully sunk in that
when she and Freddy ended their betrothal this time, it
would affect their friends and families, as well. But the
visit that morning had left her with a heavy heart. And
she was no longer positive that the ends would justify
the means.

Turning her attention back to the salon, she glanced
around the room of attendees. "We have a quarter of an
hour left," she announced to the gathering in a cheerful
voice that belied her mood. "Does anyone else have a
contribution? Perhaps you, Miss Arnot? I believe you
were working on a sonnet sequence when last we spoke."

"It's not quite finished, Miss Craven," said the timid
lady, her customary powder and patch harkening back to
the days of her youth. "But I believe it will be ready next
week."

"Then, if no one else has a contribution, let us have

some refreshment," Leonora said with a smile of relief. Miss Arnot was a nice lady but her poetry tended to be rather tedious and after Mrs. Jeffries's performance she was in no mood for it.

As the tea tray was brought out and glasses of cordial and sherry were handed round, Leonora allowed herself to relax a little as she stood near the front window, surveying the group at large.

She'd started the weekly meetings of writers and intellectuals not long before she and Freddy parted ways the first time. It had proved a godsend in the aftermath, when she'd desperately needed a reason to get out of bed in the morning.

Now the gathering boasted some thirty or so members, though the number was often in flux, with people joining and dropping out from week to week. Month to month. With creative people, there was often a tendency toward following the dictates of the muse, so Leonora wasn't very rigid in her rules for the membership. She considered the changing numbers to be a boon rather than a detriment. After all, the unexpected was often the very thing that made poetry and parties entertaining.

Her reverie was interrupted then by a familiar voice. "I hope you don't mind that we stopped in, Miss Craven," said Corinne, Lady Darleigh, whom she had met at Sir Gerard's home the evening before. "We were so intrigued by the idea of an artistic salon, we couldn't pass up the opportunity to attend."

"Indeed," said the mousy woman at her side. Mrs. Brown, Leonora remembered. She'd met her last night but they'd exchanged nothing beyond greetings.

"I'm pleased you decided to come," Leonora said with the enthusiasm she reserved for new members. "I hope you enjoyed the offerings this afternoon. They vary from meeting to meeting, of course, but are always entertaining."

A blatant lie, but she could hardly cast aspersions on the other writers in her group. It wasn't their fault their verse wasn't quite what she enjoyed.

"Millie," Lady Darleigh said to Mrs. Brown, "why don't you go get a cup of tea while I speak with Miss Craven. Didn't you say that you were famished earlier?"

With a nod, Mrs. Brown moved over to the other side of the room and the tea tray.

Left alone with Lady Darleigh, Leonora raised her brows. "Is there something you wished to speak with me about, Lady Darleigh?" she asked, curious what the other woman could want from her on so brief an acquaintance.

Sometimes near strangers attempted to trade on her popularity by asking her to send their writings to her editor. Or worse, to read their work. For the most part, she eschewed such involvement. Mostly because she knew how fragile a writer's spirit could be. The world was hard enough on a writer's spirit, she reasoned, and she would not be the one to tear down someone else's work. Whether they asked for it or not.

Somehow, though, she knew that Lady Darleigh's request wasn't related to poetry at all.

"I'm afraid I wasn't very subtle," the pretty blonde said with a rueful smile. "Is there somewhere we can be private?"

To Leonora's surprise, the other woman was trembling visibly.

"My dear lady," she said softly, taking Lady Darleigh's hand and leading her to a little parlor the butler used for storing unwanted guests.

Once they were seated on two very uncomfortable Elizabethan chairs, she said, "Please let me know what it is that troubles you. I should hate to think that it's something I've done."

"Not at all," the other woman said with a watery smile.

"I shouldn't have come here if you were the cause of my misery. I am not such a glutton for punishment as that."

"That's a relief, at least," Leonora said truthfully. "Now, you really must tell me what it is you want from me."

Lady Darleigh took a deep breath. "I . . . that is to say, my . . . I mean," she began, and stopped, unable to complete the thought. "I didn't think this would be so difficult," she continued with a frown. "You see, Miss Craven, it's just that I'd like to ask for your assistance. I wish to help my husband sever his membership in the Lords of Anarchy."

Leonora's breath caught in her throat. She'd been expecting some plea or other, but not this.

"My dear Lady Darleigh," she began. "I don't know why you believe I have the sort of influence that will help your husband, but I can assure you I only met Sir Gerard last evening. And I'm not even sure he likes me. Which to my mind makes me the least likely person who could help in this situation."

"Perhaps so," Lady Darleigh responded, "but I know that you and Lord Frederick Lisle are investigating your brother's death. And I very much fear that what happened to him will happen to my own husband."

Leonora's eyes widened.

What fools they'd been to think their true reasons for getting close to the Anarchists would not be discerned at once. Her mind raced, searching for something, anything, to tell the woman seated across from her that would correct her assumption.

Finally, she decided just to pretend ignorance. "I'm sure I don't know what you mean, Lady Darleigh."

The blonde's eyes sharpened. "Please, Miss Craven," she said, her mouth white with anxiety, "do not pretend ignorance. I have guessed your true purpose, but I am confident no one else has. My husband told me he found the two of you in Sir Gerard's study last evening. There were any number of anterooms between the drawing room and his study. You chose that particular room because you were looking for something."

Stunned, Leonora shook her head. Was there no end to the amount of intelligence the other woman had gleaned from one night's acquaintance?

"Your brother was kind to us," Lady Darleigh continued. "He and my husband intended to leave the club together, but Sir Gerard threatened me. So my husband decided to wait. And when he saw what happened to your brother—which was no accident, no matter what Sir Gerard says—he decided to keep his suspicions to himself."

This was just the sort of thing Leonora had hoped to learn during her visit to Sir Gerard's home last night.

"What do you know, Lady Darleigh?" she asked in a low voice, leaning in to keep her voice from being overheard. "What happened to my brother?"

"It is because of that I wish my husband out of that awful group," Lady Darleigh said cautiously. "He has met with several accidents, Miss Craven. All of them either while driving or while in the company of club members. I very much fear that something like what happened to your own brother will also happen to my husband. And I cannot, will not, let that happen!"

Leonora nodded, not daring to speak lest Lady Darleigh stop.

The other woman continued, "He seemed to have some new bruise or bump each time he came home. Lord Darleigh swears it's nothing serious, but I don't like it. They are supposed to just drive to some tavern in Dartford, show off their driving prowess and their expensive coaches, but there is more to the club than that. Things that have nothing to do with driving."

"What?" Leonora couldn't stop herself from asking.

"For one thing," Lady Darleigh said with a frown, "there are the prizefights."

Leonora thought perhaps she'd misheard. "Fights?" she asked. "As in fisticuffs?"

"Precisely," Lady Darleigh said, frowning. "Soon after my husband joined he arrived home one evening with two broken ribs and a black eye. He told me he'd been set upon by thieves on his way home from the club. But the next day Sir Gerard visited our home and told me that I should be proud of my Robert for proving himself to be such a strong fighter."

Shaking her head at the memory, she went on. "It was as if the devil himself had come to call," she said with disgust. "As if I would be pleased to learn my husband was engaged in fisticuffs with those other men. Gentleman Jackson's is bad enough, but this was a private fight. One my husband hadn't seen fit to tell me about."

"Why wouldn't they just use Gentleman Jackson's saloon for their bouts?" Leonora asked, puzzled.

"After I hounded him about it, my husband finally admitted that they fight in private because it is agreed upon by the participants and the audience that there will be no rules of fair conduct."

Leonora gasped. "That's barbaric!" She thought back to a time the year before when her brother had come home with a black eye. At the time he'd excused it as a souvenir from a bout at Jackson's but he'd been a member of the Anarchists at the time.

She hadn't thought it possible to be more disgusted with Sir Gerard Fincher, but clearly she'd been mistaken.

"What do you know about my brother's death, Lady

Darleigh?" she asked quietly. She was torn between need-
ing to know, and wishing to protect herself from what
she knew would be a chilling story. Still, she had to know.
"Please."

With a nod, Lady Darleigh continued. "Two weeks
ago my husband overheard Sir Gerard and another club
member talking, and what they said made it abundantly
clear that your brother died in the most horrific of circumstances."

"How so?" Leonora asked, her fists clenched against
the other woman's words.

"He was set upon, Miss Craven," said Lady Darleigh,
her eyes bright with tears. "They overtook his curricle
on the Dover Road, beat him and tossed his body to the
side of the road. I'm not sure which members did it, but
my husband is sure of what he heard. Sir Gerard was
congratulating them on a job well done. And he also said
that he'd hidden your brother's curricle somewhere
safe."

Leonora felt a cold chill rush down her spine.

She'd been desperate to learn the truth about Jonny's
accident from the moment she'd learned of it. He was a
careful driver, skilled enough to navigate that stretch of
the Dover Road in his sleep. That his driving record remained unblemished, however, was no consolation for
the fact that he'd been murdered by men he thought to be
his comrades.

If Sir Gerard Fincher were so foolish as to appear before her now, she'd find herself hard-pressed not to tell
him exactly what she thought of him and his depraved
club. It wasn't a club for gentlemen. There were any number of members who might better be called brutes.

"Miss Craven." Lady Darleigh's eyes were shadowed with worry. "I do hope I did the right thing in telling you the truth. I simply thought you deserved to know

what really happened. And I wished . . ." She trailed off, bowing her head in shame. "I did so wish to ask for your help. I can tell that you are a lady with true courage. And I know that if you and Lord Frederick would agree to help us, my husband would be able to leave the club for good."

"Do not fret, Lady Darleigh," Leonora assured her, despite her.shaken composure. "I did wish to know. I needed to know what happened to him. And I am more grateful than I can say."

The blonde's eyes widened. "Then you will help us?" she asked, her features bathed in relief. "Oh, you cannot know how grateful I am."

Taking the other woman's hands in her own, Leonora nodded. "I will discuss your concerns about your husband with Lord Frederick. He will need an ally during his time in the club, and if you will tell your husband of our willingness to help, I feel sure that together we can bring Sir Gerard to heel. Preferably with the assistance of the authorities."

"I will tell him," the other lady promised. They both rose and crossed to the door leading to the hall. Leonora was surprised when Lady Darleigh gave her a quick hug.

"I will not forget this," she said, before hurrying to where Mrs. Brown was seated chatting with an elderly cleric with a passion for sonnets.

Not long afterward, the company began to disperse, and when the last guest was finally gone, Leonora collapsed in one of the so recently vacated chairs that were now scattered throughout the room.

She'd thought it would be best to continue with her usual routine so that no one would guess that she and Freddy were actively investigating the Lords of Anarchy. But she hadn't considered that her routine would be invaded by acquaintances from that world.

Her poetry, she'd thought, could prove a welcome distraction from dwelling on her brother's untimely death. But there was no longer any corner of her life that had not been touched by grief.

At least, she thought, sipping a cup of cool tea, it looked as if there were cracks in the foundation of the Lords of Anarchy. Cracks that might prove to be Sir Gerard Fincher's undoing.

Not bad work for a lady poet, she thought, picturing Sir Gerard's expression when he learned she'd been instrumental in exposing his crimes.

The image made her grin.

Not bad work at all.

Ten

When Freddy arrived in Half Moon Street, the butler showed him into the first-floor ballroom and he saw that most of the other club members were already assembled there.

Somehow he'd arrived before Payne, and when his cousin approached him he took the opportunity to ask, "What is so important that it necessitated another meeting so soon after the one last night?"

Gerard looked displeased by the question, but said, "Sometimes things happen that require us to come together as a group much sooner than anticipated. And this was an opportunity for you to solidify your standing within the group that I could not, as your cousin, let pass."

Freddy frowned. What on earth? "I thought I was already a member after the induction ceremony last night. There is more to it than that?"

"There is always room to move up—unless of course, like me, you are the president." Gerard showed his teeth in the pretense of a grin. "And I do wish you to succeed in our group, Freddy. Don't you?"

Everything about the conversation was making Freddy uncomfortable. He wondered idly if it had been this way for Jonathan, as well. Being welcomed in, then having the rug pulled out from under him. It was not the way clubs usually worked, but he was damned sure that his cousin had planned things that way.

But Freddy had to appear to be the eager recruit his cousin thought him. "Of course I wish to gain position within the club, cousin. I would hardly have accepted your invitation if I didn't. What's the point in joining a club where you remain a plebeian for the entirety of your association? I'm simply surprised at how quickly things are progressing."

Which was true enough. He'd never expected Gerard to take him under his wing to ensure his swift climb up the ranks.

Gerard clapped Freddy on the back and grinned. "Of course I want to help you, Freddy. We're family, are we not? And family looks out for one another."

If only Gerard knew, Freddy thought.

"Now," his cousin continued, "tell me about your betrothal to the delectable Miss Craven. How on earth did you manage that?"

Something in Gerard's tone set Freddy's back up. He disliked even hearing her name come out of the other man's mouth. Let alone describing her as delectable. Swallowing his ire, he shrugged, saying, "I should think you of all people would understand the nature of that arrangement. Mama has been on me to marry, and you must admit that Miss Craven is quite beautiful. And the size of her father's fortune is hardly a deterrent. One must keep oneself in good boots, you know. And Papa has become rather tight with the purse strings of late, if you must know."

Fortunately, Freddy's recent windfall had not yet become common knowledge, so he could paint a portrait of himself as pockets to let without fear of his cousin finding out.

"Interesting," Gerard said with what looked like genuine surprise. "I hadn't pegged you for a fortune hunter, but I suppose it makes sense. Especially since your little brother has just wed a duchess. I always thought you were a romantic. I'm impressed, cousin. I believe your years on the Continent have hardened you."

Again Freddy shrugged. "I had to grow up sometime. And I thought that I might toy with her a bit to make up for the way she broke things off with me the last time. You know. A bit of payback."

His cousin grinned and threw an arm over Frederick's shoulder. "I like it," he said with enthusiasm. "You have changed. I must say that I'm impressed. I thought you must be smitten given how closely you attended her every word last night."

"All for show," Freddy said with a cruel smile. "Poor chit."

Gerard laughed at the words. "I vow, I am quite looking forward to seeing how you handle things with Payne. With your new attitude, I suspect you might end up the victor. Though I must admit, my money was on Payne before our little chat."

"So, there are to be fisticuffs this morning despite our abandoning Jackson's," Freddy said thoughtfully. "I must admit you continue to surprise me, Gerard. You're up to every rig."

Gerard preened. "I try," he said with what was supposed to look like a modest shrug but instead seemed smug. "And without the presence of Jackson, we can be . . . freer with our fighting."

Which Freddy translated to mean that the Queensbury rules would not be first and foremost on the minds of the participants.

Just then Payne arrived, and after acknowledging the newcomer, Gerard led Freddy over to where a chair had been placed on one side of a makeshift ring, with a corresponding chair on the other side—presumably for Payne.

Lords Rudyard and Fleming, who seemed to have appointed themselves his pugilistic seconds, stood by while for the second time in as many hours Freddy removed his cravat, coat, and shirt.

Across the room he saw that Payne was also stripping to the waist, and was unsurprised to see that the other man was surrounded by a cluster of club members wishing him luck.

Deciding that he would do better to concentrate on his own readiness for the fight, Freddy twisted his head from one side to the other to loosen the muscles in his neck. He jabbed the air a few times and danced around a bit in his stocking feet.

"He's a mad bastard," Rudyard said in a low voice from his left side. "I've never seen anyone fight with as much fervor. He's going to beat you bloody."

"You don't stand a chance," said Lord Fleming mournfully. "It's a shame because I quite like you. Of course I'd prefer anyone to Payne, but there's no way you're going to best him. I'd say you should concede now, but I think it would end up being just as bad for you. Then Sir Gerard would kick you out of the club, and we all know what happens to men who try to leave the club."

Before he could ask what that last remark meant, Sir Gerard himself stepped into the center of the open circle formed by the other men. "Gentlemen, you know that from time to time we like to indulge in a bit of fisticuffs. The sort which is not allowed by the civilized likes of Gentleman Jackson and his lot. We are men, and as such we fight with the determination of soldiers facing their final battle."

Gerard strode a few feet, warming to his subject.

"Ours is the kind of fighting that has been around since the beginning of time. And as such, I will warn both of today's players—Lord Frederick Lisle and Lord Payne— that there will be no quarter. The fight ends when one of you falls and is incapable of getting up again. You may neither give quarter, nor may you delope."

Freddy hadn't realized just the extent of his cousin's taste for drama until that little speech. Soldiers facing their final battle, indeed. He had a feeling that real soldiers like Trent would find his cousin's bombast particularly loathsome considering how many of his compatriots had died in true war.

Still, it was the sort of thing he'd expect from his cousin, who had always found ways to feed his need for power and control. This wasn't about sport or bravery. It was about creating a situation over which Gerard could rule. And manipulating other men into fighting at his urging.

"I will leave you to it, gentlemen," Gerard said with a loud clap before he stepped back and let Freddy and Payne move to the center of the open circle.

"I'm going to hurt you," Payne said with vicious fury as he swung and missed. "I'm going to bloody that pretty face so much that your mother won't even recognize you."

"I really must insist that you don't do that, old chap," Freddy said, ducking another powerful punch. "I should hate to upset my mama. And I have a feeling she would be quite capable of drawing your cork should she take such a notion into her head."

"Prepare yourself for pain, you cur," Payne growled, this time his fist connecting with Freddy's cheekbone.

It hurt more than Freddy was willing to admit, but he managed to keep his voice light. "A pun! I hadn't thought you capable of even that simple form of wit, Payne. I'm quite impressed."

Having his intelligence denigrated made Payne angry, and he missed seeing Freddy's right fist, which connected solidly with his chin. The other man roared and managed to land a blow on Freddy's jaw.

Damn, that hurt. But the pain sent a jolt of bloodlust through Freddy that made him impervious to the pain. All he cared about was annihilating his opponent and for the next fifteen minutes they danced around one another, first Freddy hitting Payne, then vice versa, neither of them daring to stop lest the other use that pause to gain an advantage.

Finally, his anger getting the best of him, Payne made the mistake of paying more attention to Freddy's right side than his left, and Freddy managed to use his left fist to snap the other man's head back with a force that surprised even him. Stunned, the large man lost his balance and dropped to the hard parquet floor.

Gasping, Freddy shook out his hand, which ached like a bastard, while the two men who had served as Payne's seconds—or whatever one called them—tried and failed to get Payne back up on his feet.

"Gentlemen!" Gerard pronounced loudly to the assembled room. "I declare Lord Frederick Lisle the winner of this bout!"

A cheer rose up from the assembled men and Freddy collapsed into the chair in his corner. For the next hour, he found himself the recipient of congratulations from all the club members in attendance. Even the ones who'd been cheering for Lord Payne at the beginning.

What a difference an hour made.

He was also praised by some other men he was quite sure had not been at the gathering the evening before.

Had his cousin invited outsiders to attend the fight despite his rejection of Mainwaring?

Curious.

"You showed well today, cousin," Gerard said once the crowd had thinned out. "I am pleased at how well you're coming along."

Freddy started to shrug but found his right shoulder was hurting like the devil. "Glad you think so, Gerry," he said with what he hoped sounded like deferential gratitude. He still wasn't sure what the purpose of the fight today had been. To remove Payne from his position of authority in the club? To prove his mettle to the other club members?

"It will be good to have someone I can trust in my inner circle," Gerard continued. "I had to see to it that you proved yourself to the rest of the club, however, before I could bring you in. After all, how strange would it look for me to simply invite an untested man into my confidence?"

So, Freddy reflected, that was the reason for all this. "I am honored that you thought me worthy, Gerry. Truly."

"I can see that you are, old fellow," Gerard said with a nod. "Now, I am sure that you are longing for a bath. And perhaps a beefsteak for that eye. I will not detain you."

He'd been dismissed. And Freddy was indeed eager to remove himself from his cousin's house to lick his wounds. There was no way he'd show the degree of his pain before the other man. Not knowing how capable his cousin was of using that pain against him.

"Thank you, cousin," he said, rising with an involuntary groan. "I definitely think a hot bath is in order."

"I'll see you later, then," Gerard said before leaving Freddy in the front hall.

Blinking at the brightness of sunshine as he stepped out onto the steps, Freddy was surprised to find Mainwaring waiting beside a hackney cab on the street outside. "Do not worry," the other man said with a nod. "I got one of my coachmen to drive your curricle back to your house. And since that was how you got here, I assumed you'd need some way of getting home. Though since you were the winner someone should really have offered to drive you home."

"How did you know I'd won?" Freddy asked, hauling himself up into the vehicle.

"Mostly by the fact that you're able to leave the house under your own power," Mainwaring admitted. "You did win, didn't you? Otherwise I don't see how we can be friends any longer."

"'Course I won," Freddy responded, wincing at the pain in his split lip when he spoke. "I bloody thrashed Payne."

"So it wasn't a simple meeting like your cousin tried to convince me?" the earl asked. "I'm shocked that your dear cousin would lie. Devastated really."

Freddy laughed, but that hurt his ribs so he stopped.

"It was simply a relocation of the fight with Payne from Jackson's to Half Moon Street," he told the earl, resting his head against the seat while the coach jostled through Mayfair toward his town house. "I'd say more but I've got the devil of a headache."

"I'm sure you have, old fellow," said Mainwaring. "I vow, Payne's fists are the size of claymores."

Changing the subject, he went on, "I'm sorry to say that I won't be able to tend your wounds myself. Which is to your benefit. I'm rubbish in the sickroom. Much too restless to sit quietly and knit, or sew, or whatever it is nurses do. I have, however, thought of the perfect person to act in my stead."

But by now Freddy was too exhausted to pay attention to his friend's prattle. All he cared about was getting out of this rattletrap of a carriage and into a quiet room.

"I don't care who tends 'em," he told Mainwaring without opening his eyes. "So long as there's a glass of brandy as big as my head to go with it."

"I feel sure that can be arranged," Mainwaring said.

Eleven

*L*eonora was on her way upstairs to massage her aching temples after her delicate interview with Freddy's mother and sister-in-law, when she heard a knock on the door. Thinking to escape the visitor, she hurried on her way. Until, that is, she heard Freddy's voice in conversation with her father's butler, Greentree.

Reversing course, she made her way back downstairs to find Mr. Greentree standing in the entrance hall giving orders to one of the footmen as Freddy assured the older man that he was as right as rain.

"No need to make a fuss, Greentree," he was saying as Leonora hurried forward. "It's not as bad as it looks, I promise."

When she got within sight of her betrothed, Leonora gasped. "Good God, Freddy!" she exclaimed. "Who did this to you?"

Unable to stop herself, she reached out to touch his face.

"Careful," Freddy said with a wince. "It might not be as bad as it looks, but it hurts like the very dev . . . deuce."

At his switch to the tamer epithet, she rolled her eyes. Now was not the time to be concerned about offending her with his language.

"The other fellow looks much worse," he continued in a cheerful tone that made her want to scream. "I apologize for descending upon you in this state, but Mainwaring threatened to call for the surgeon if I didn't promise to come here at once. He is remarkably squeamish for a gamester. I'd have thought he'd have had his share of beatings given his reputation for winning all the time, but he says not."

"Mr. Greentree," Leonora said, not bothering to respond to Frederick's rambling, "will you please see to it that a pot of tea and a plate of sandwiches are sent to my sitting room? And have cook send up a beefsteak for his eye."

"Very good, miss," the butler said with a brisk nod. "I'll also see if I can get some ice."

Once Greentree was gone, Leonora turned to Freddy. "Are you able to walk?" she asked briskly, moving to drape his arm around her neck.

"Careful," Frederick said on a hiss as she slipped her own arm around his waist. "I think I might have a couple of broken ribs."

Gingerly, she moved to his other side and slowly they made their way up the stairs, Leonora using every bit of slang she'd ever heard her brother use.

"I had no idea you had such a command of cant, my dear," Frederick wheezed as they finally made it to the door of her sitting room. "I'm quite impressed. Though I'm not sure you quite understand the meaning of 'boxing the Jesuit.' Even so, you're quite skillful. I suppose it's because you're a poet and fond of language. I had a tutor—"

"Freddy, this is not the time to compliment me on my swearing abilities," she said as she lowered him to the settee. "After what I've heard today, seeing you in this state is the last possible thing I could have wished for."

"The poetry at your salon was that bad?" he asked as he tried to find a comfortable position. "I'm sorry to have missed it, if only to lend you support, but I was detained at Jackson's, and then my cousin called another meeting of his infantile club. I could hardly refuse given that we are attempting to gain a foothold with the Anarchists. I think that's going rather well, by the way."

Hoping to find some comfort in the ritual of pouring out the tea, Leonora took a seat beside him on the settee. After learning how her brother had died—from a beating not wholly different from what Freddy had endured today—seeing him in this state was unsettling in the extreme.

"So," she said as she handed him his cup, "your cousin's club requires bouts of fisticuffs from its new members, as well? It seems to me they spend time doing everything but the one thing they were created for. Namely driving."

"Just what Mainwaring said," Freddy said with a laugh that turned into a cough. "I begin to think that driving might be the reason they were formed, but that it's for a more sinister reason they continue to get together."

"What do you mean?" she asked, curiosity dampening her anxiety for a moment. "I mean, there must be something, otherwise my brother wouldn't have been so keen to leave, surely. But what have you learned?"

"It's just that Lord Payne—in between attempts to beat me into a fine mash—said as much." He stretched out on the settee, wincing at the motion. "I suspect he hoped I'd die of my wounds, but I didn't grow up with four brothers without learning how to fight dirty."

"You might be surprised to know," Leonora said, watching as he brought his forearm up to shade his eyes from the light, "that I just today learned about these no-rules fights your cousin arranges."

Freddy lowered his arm to look at her. "How?" he demanded. "I thought you had your salon this morning."

"I did," she said, rising to get her medical supplies from a small sideboard. Busying herself with removing the things she'd need, she continued, "Lady Darleigh paid me a visit during the salon."

"And?" Freddy asked, hissing as Leonora cleaned a cut above his eyebrow.

"And she told me about the fighting," Leonora said, narrowing her eyes to see if there was any debris in the cut. "She was horrified when her husband told her about it."

Freddy was silent for a moment. Perhaps he was considering her own response to finding him bloodied and bruised in the entry hall a few moments ago, she thought.

When he didn't speak, she moved on to another cut on his jawline. It was already swelling and would probably get worse before it got better. She hoped Greentree had found some ice for it.

"What else did Lady Darleigh have to say?" Freddy prompted after she'd worked in silence for some minutes. "Did she know anything about Jonathan?"

Sighing, Leonora looked up from where she'd been bandaging his split knuckles. "She did, I'm sorry to say. Or happy?" She shook her head. "I wanted to know. Needed to know, even. But the truth of what happened is so much worse than I'd imagined."

"Tell me," Freddy said, taking her hand in his free one. "Sit, tell me everything."

Wordlessly, she set aside her bandages and carefully sat beside him on the sofa. Gaining strength from his mere proximity. When he put an arm around her, she closed her eyes and told him what she'd learned from Lady Darleigh.

Freddy listened without interruption, only cursing when

she got to the part about how the club members had thrown Jonathan's body to the side of the Dover Road.

"And that's it," Leonora said, accepting the handkerchief he'd pressed into her hand. She hadn't even realized she'd been weeping. "They left him there, then hid his curricle away somewhere so that the authorities would think it had been stolen."

Despite his injuries, Freddy pulled her into his lap and held her while she cried, whispering soothing words against her hair.

When she'd run out of tears, Leonora stayed in his arms, unable to resist the safety she felt there. "Lady Darleigh asked for our help," she said, smoothing the lapel of his coat just to have something to keep her hands occupied. "Her husband wants to leave the club, but is convinced he'll end up like Jonathan if he tries."

"That's not entirely improbable," Freddy said, stroking her back. "It's very likely that was the reason your brother took those documents from Gerard. To blackmail him into letting Jonathan leave unharmed."

Leonora sat up and looked him full in the face. "So, Lady Darleigh was telling the truth."

Reaching up to cup her face, Freddy stroked his thumb over her cheek. "It makes logical sense. He loved driving but, as we have learned, driving is only a fraction of what occupies the club's time. I cannot imagine Jonathan was best pleased with that. He certainly would have objected to no-rules fisticuffs on a regular basis. For one thing, it's dashed near impossible to drive properly when your arm is in a sling and you can't see straight."

Nodding, Leonora settled back down against his chest. "I don't quite know why, but the idea that he was unhappy with the Anarchists eases my mind. I think on some level I was afraid that he'd become one of them. Someone who enjoyed violence, and the kind of lechery we saw at your cousin's house last night."

Freddy kissed the top of her head. "I think it's safe to assume that Jonathan joined for the driving and realized not long after that it wasn't what he'd signed on for. And seeing that no one else was able to escape with their lives, he decided to protect his life by stealing some of my cousin's papers."

"And lost his life anyway." Leonora was glad to know the truth, but the fact was that her brother was still gone.

"I told Mainwaring to take me home," Freddy said into the quiet. "But he insisted on bringing me here. Said he'd arranged things with you—which is a bald-faced lie."

"Did you not want to see me?" she asked, surprised at how hurt she was by the idea of him going home alone in his current state.

"I always want to see you," he said, kissing her. "But I didn't want to upset you. I know I'm not looking my handsome best at the moment."

"As if I care for such things," she said, kissing him back. "I only want you safe. If I'm upset about anything it's that you're now involved in your cousin's detestable club. I wish more than anything that we'd never embarked on this investigation."

"You worry too much," he said, stroking a lock of hair from her forehead. "I know how to handle Gerard. And I don't intend to let him harm either of us."

But they both knew that it might not come down to their intentions.

"I'm glad Mainwaring brought you here," she said with a smile. "Though I don't know why you didn't just have Greentree send you home in one of the carriages. He would have been happy to do so."

He looked sheepish. "I wanted to see you," he admitted. "It was stupid of me since you were bound to be unsettled by the sight of all these bruises, but I couldn't help myself."

She sighed, and with gentle care for his injuries, wrapped her arms around him. "You are the most foolish man I've ever met. And the bravest. Not many men would allow themselves to be beaten senseless for any reason. Much less to learn the truth about what happened to a friend weeks ago. What good could it possibly do at this point?"

"It could do a great deal," he responded, kissing the end of her nose. "Especially if it could ease the mind of the friend's sister. Who happens to be unutterably beautiful."

"I'd hardly call myself that," she responded with a laugh. "But if you are giving out compliments, I shall take them. If you are willing to take mine in return."

"I suppose one could do worse than accept being called foolish and brave," he said with a laugh.

"Speaking of foolish and brave," she continued, "in addition to the salon, I had a visit this morning beforehand from your mama and your sister-in-law."

Now it was his turn to curse fluently.

"Oh, it's not as bad as all that," she said with a shrug. "I quite liked them."

Though she'd been unsettled by Perdita's condition, she couldn't help but like the redhead. Remembering their conversation, though, reminded her of their talk about miscarriage. And she was suddenly very aware that she was behaving with Freddy as if there were no reason in the world they couldn't be together.

Carefully, she extricated herself from his arms. Which he seemed not to notice so incensed was he by his relatives' impromptu visit.

"Was ever a man so beset by meddling relations as I am?" he asked, thrusting his uninjured hand into his messy curls. "Perdita I can forgive because she's enceinte, and could possibly just wish to welcome you to the family. Mama, on the other hand, knows better than to come here before telling me. She's a busybody, and always has been."

"I would hardly call your mother calling upon your betrothed the behavior of a busybody," Leonora protested. "Indeed, I rather liked them. Your mother was rather fierce at first, but once we spoke a bit she thawed. And Perdita was quite charming. I can quite see why your brother fell in love with her."

"I suppose they're all right," Frederick responded with a frown. "But it does grow tiresome to have my mother intruding into my affairs. I should have been able to present you to her myself. Not have her present herself. Especially since our last betrothal ended before you could even meet."

At the time, not meeting his family had seemed like a blessing, Leonora remembered. Though their social circles overlapped a bit, there was enough variety in their acquaintance that she could safely move around town without fear of running into the Lisles. Or if she did, not having been introduced, they didn't need to speak.

Now, though, she feared that things were moving dangerously fast. So fast that they might soon find themselves going from a faux betrothal to a very real marriage.

And that would be an impossible situation for both of them.

Steeling herself, she moved to the chair opposite, saying briskly, "I think you're forgetting, Lord Frederick, that we are only pretending to be engaged. For the sake of our investigation."

At her words, Freddy lifted his head and narrowed his

eyes. Apparently seeing that she had not misspoken, he shook his head in disgust. "I might have known you'd turn cold at the first indication that what's between us is real, Nora. Whenever things get the least bit complicated you run away."

Leonora stiffened. "That's not fair," she said, unable to keep the hurt from her voice. "I told you from the beginning that this was not a true betrothal. That hardly means I am incapable of handling complex situations. Indeed, I should think a pretend match is a great deal more complicated than a real one. At least with a real engagement, one is able to be oneself."

"Funny you should say that," Freddy said mirthlessly. "Because I am never more myself than when I'm with you. Clearly, you are not burdened by the same degree of comfort in my company."

It wasn't true. Only moments ago in his arms she'd felt more relaxed than she had in years. But for both their sakes, she couldn't tell him that.

"I think it's time you go home," she said tersely. "Your valet will be able to wrap your ribs, I think. And if necessary you can call a physician."

He stalked stiffly to the door of her sitting room. When he reached the door he turned. "I suppose I should be grateful you tended my wounds at all. It showed a disregard for convention that would be upsetting to a lady involved in a *false* betrothal."

She listened as he descended the staircase with as much speed as a man with his injuries could.

Too late, she remembered the invitation his mother had conveyed that morning.

Closing her eyes, she wondered when this infernal day would end.

Twelve

Despite their disagreement earlier, when he'd gotten home to find a summons from his mother for dinner that evening, he sent a note round to Leonora informing her he'd pick her up at six.

His valet had indeed wrapped his ribs, which could very well be broken, but might be said optimistically to be only bruised. Freddy wasn't sure if he cared about the difference. Either one hurt like the devil.

Rigged out in evening dress, with his unruly curls tamed to something like a fashionable style, he felt close to human again. The liniment his valet had given him for his bruises had helped, too.

The ride from the Craven house to the Pemberton town house had been blessedly short. Which meant he and Leonora had exchanged only inane pleasantries instead of insults and recriminations. Which was good, he supposed, but he wished somehow they could get back to the closeness they'd shared that afternoon before she remembered his mother's visit.

Now, he stood on the threshold of his mother's drawing room and glared. "What are you doing here?" Freddy demanded of the room at large. He'd expected to see Archer, since apparently he and Perdita had returned from the country, but his mother's summons had said nothing about the rest of his brothers attending this evening.

If Leonora had been frightened by his mother's un-scheduled visit that morning, then being swarmed by the entire Lisle brood without warning would send her into a conniption fit.

"Is that any way to treat your dearest siblings, Fred-dykins?" asked Lord Benedick Lisle wickedly, his clerical collar shining white against his dark coat. "We wanted to meet this paragon who has agreed to leg-shackle herself to you for the rest of her days."

Freddy glanced at Leonora to see what her reaction was to the crowded room. To his relief she seemed to be taking the surprise family reunion with aplomb.

Turning to Benedick, he frowned. "You're a vicar, for pity's sake," he protested, his arm tightening around Le-onora's waist. Damned fellow was too handsome by half. It was a wonder he'd not been killed by the husband of some lovesick parishioner. "I would expect this sort of remark from Cam, because he's a heathen scientist, but you? I thought it was against the church code or some such to embarrass one's siblings in front of their fian-cées."

"You'd be surprised about what is and isn't against the church code, old fellow," retorted Benedick as he stepped forward and bowed over Leonora's hand. Only Freddy noticed that his eyes lingered on her bosom as he did so.

Vicar or no, he was going to bloody his brother's nose as soon as his knuckles healed.

"I hope you've been warned about this one, my dear," Benedick said to Leonora with a grin. "I'm afraid he might be the least civilized among us. Though I do sup-pose he's right about Cam, who lives in primitive sur-roundings and collects rocks, being a heathen. Really, I'm the best of the lot, as you have doubtless noticed."

"They are specimens," Cam interjected, edging out his elder brother so that he could kiss the back of Leonora's hand. Like Benedick before him, his eyes brushed slowly over her bosom.

Mentally, Freddy added Cam to his list of future victims.

"Lord Cameron Lisle at your service, Miss Craven," his brother said, the gold highlights in his light brown hair glinting in the firelight as he held Nora's hand a bit longer than entirely appropriate. "I hope you will give me the chance to prove to you that not all of us are—"

"I apologize for these barbarians, Miss Craven," interjected another brother, elbowing Cam out of the way. "I'm Lord Archer Lisle, my dear. The handsome one."

"The newly married one," Freddy said with a growl as his youngest brother bowed over Nora's hand. So far, he'd been the only one of the Lisle brothers to keep his eyes to himself.

He supposed he could thank Perdita for that small wonder.

Even so, he wasn't going to put up with any funny business. "Don't think you're going to turn her head with your diplomat's tongue, Archie. I don't care how handsome you are."

Leonora sniggered beside him but Freddy couldn't stop himself. "Nor you, Cameron. No lady wants to talk about rocks all day. She'd die of boredom in the first quarter hour."

"Speaking of rocks," Benedick said as Freddy led Leonora to a chair by the fire. "Who's been throwing them at your face?"

Freddy was saved from replying by the arrival of yet another Lisle.

"Boys," the Duchess of Pemberton, matriarch of the House of Lisle, said as she stepped into the room and surveyed it until her eyes lit upon Leonora. "All of you are being boorish. Stop it at once. You know how to treat a lady better than that."

In unison, as if they were all still in the schoolroom, the brothers said, "Yes, Mama."

"You must tell me later how you manage that," Leonora quipped, looking round the room in wonder. "It is a rather impressive skill to have in one's quiver."

Freddy just bet she'd like to be able to quiet him as easily as that, he thought grimly, remembering their argument earlier.

"They are a rowdy lot, but my own," his mother was saying as she handed Leonora a glass of sherry. "And here is my husband to show you where they got their charm."

Turning, Freddy saw that his father had indeed entered the room. A still handsome man in his fifties, the duke's brown hair was shot through with silver now, but no one would mistake his age for feebleness. The Duke of Pemberton had been a man of power for some years, and would be for several more to come.

"It's my pleasure, Miss Craven," he said as he crossed to take Leonora's hand in his. Fortunately, his back was to Freddy, so the bosom test was not possible. Which was all well and good, because if he caught his father looking at her bosom, he'd just have to blind himself with one of Cam's rocks.

"I've long wished to meet the lady who has the power to tame Frederick," the duke said to Leonora. "He's the most troublesome one, you know."

"I'm still here," Frederick said sulkily from his post against the mantelpiece. To Leonora he said, "Pay no attention to these people, my dear Miss Craven. They have a fondness for exaggeration and half-truths."

Before Leonora could respond, Archer spoke up.

"Did you hear something, Cam?" he asked with a puzzled frown, cupping his ear. "It's like a bee buzzing."

"Now that you mention it," Cam said, cupping his ear, too. "Yes, I may have heard a wasp."

"You are hilarious," Freddy said in a flat tone. "Really, you must be loads of fun at children's parties."

"My dears," said Perdita, coming to his rescue. "You mustn't tease your brother. Or his fiancée. You're being very rude to mob her like this on her first visit to Pemberton House."

"Hardly mobbed, Mrs. Lisle," Leonora said with a laugh. "Though I can see now where Lord Frederick gets his quick wit. It's rather overwhelming to be in the room with five of him."

"I quite understand, Miss Craven," Perdita said with a smile. "They can be intimidating, can't they?"

Freddy had yet to see the day that Miss Leonora Craven proclaimed herself to be intimidated. He knew quite well that it wasn't today.

"I hope you don't mind, my dears," his mother said in that way she had of apologizing without actually apologizing. "I've invited a few of the extended family, as well. It's not every day that one of my sons becomes betrothed and I wanted them to celebrate with us."

Damnation, Freddy thought. Leave it to his mother to make the misery of this evening complete.

With a sense of inevitability, he saw that Sir Gerard Fincher and Lady Melisande Fincher had entered the room.

Before Nora could do anything but look up and gape, Freddy was at her side. He couldn't say anything aloud, but he hoped at least his presence would offer her some comfort.

"Leonora has already been introduced to Gerard and his lady, Mama," he said cheerfully, resting his hand on Nora's shoulder.

The duchess looked puzzled at the change in his tone, but she didn't remark upon it. "How delightful," she said. "Then you will not mind that I've put you beside Gerard at supper, my dear Miss Craven."

Freddy clenched his teeth. But before he could object, his cousin spoke up.

"What a pleasure, Duchess," Gerard said as he and Melisande stepped farther into the room. "I've not yet had a chance to speak to Miss Craven about her poetry. I must say that I find the creative process such a fascinating subject. I wonder sometimes whether such talent runs in families. After all, I believe her brother was quite the fantasist, as well."

At the mention of Jonathan, Freddy felt Leonora stiffen. What the devil was his cousin about, taunting her like that?

"I have read a bit of Jonathan's prose, Gerard," he said with asperity. "And I found it to be quite grounded in reality. Indeed, I feel sure he left some of it in his family's safekeeping."

As he'd hoped it would, Freddy's arrow found its mark.

His eyes narrow, Gerard said, "How interesting, cousin. I should like to come by Craven House one of the days to look it over. As I said, Jonathan Craven was quite imaginative. Why, you'd be shocked to hear the stories he came up with."

Perhaps sensing the dark undertone in the exchange, the duchess chose that moment to announce dinner.

"Will you be all right?" Freddy asked Leonora softly as the others rose. "I can speak to my mother if you don't wish to sit beside him."

But his Nora was made of sterner stuff. "I will be

fine," she said firmly. "I will not let that man think he's frightened me with his veiled threats."

And since Gerard approached with his arm out, Freddy had to bite his tongue and watch them walk away.

"I hope you will tell me more about the workings of your driving club, Sir Gerard," Leonora said as she tasted the first course of her dinner—a delicious turtle soup. "My brother was never very forthcoming about it, and I do so wish to know how he spent his time over the last few months of his life."

But if she thought it would be as easy as that, she was mistaken. "My dear Miss Craven," Sir Gerard drawled, "I cannot possibly share any details about the club with you. It's for gentlemen only, you understand. And there are some things that our club holds to be sacrosanct. Though of course I regret the need to disappoint you."

"I'm sure you do, Sir Gerard," she responded, a mask of indifference hiding her annoyance at his condescending tone. "I suppose there are some things that will forever remain a mystery to us poor ladies. What with our feeble minds and oversensitive emotions."

Thirteen

Y ou are mocking me now," said Sir Gerard, his lips tightening almost imperceptibly. "But I can assure you that we have our reasons for keeping our secrets. If word were to get out, I am quite sure that any number of persons might be harmed. It's not all fun and games for the Lords of Anarchy, you must understand."

"On the contrary, Sir Gerard," she said with what she hoped seemed like sincerity. "I do quite understand the need to segregate some activities by sex. We could hardly last very long as a civilization if gentlemen were to suddenly take over the running of the household or—heaven forbid—the rearing of children. No, sir, I am quite content with the knowledge that there are some things I should be protected from, but it is my tender woman's heart that wishes to know these things about your club. For instance, what actually happened when my brother's curricle had an accident. He was such a skilled and experienced driver, you see, and I should hate to think that he lost his life because of something that might have been prevented."

Sir Gerard looked at her from beneath hooded eyes for a moment. Finally he sighed, and placed his hand over hers. "Then let me assure you, Miss Craven," he said in a condescending tone that made her want to stab his hand with her fork, "your brother was very much enjoying himself when he died. He loved competition, your brother, and it was one of my greatest joys to watch him at the ribbons. And he was racing when he died. I assure you he will be missed by our entire membership."

Leonora bit back a wave of sadness. Gerard was right about one thing. Her brother had loved racing. More than almost anything. It was just a shame his last race had been with the man sitting next to her.

"You are very kind, Sir Gerard," she said with a sad smile. "I don't suppose you or a club member have his curricle, do you? I mean the one he drove. That day." She paused, waiting for some response. But Gerard was not so easy to manipulate.

"But I'm sure you were told already, Miss Craven," he said with a frown, "that Jonathan's curricle was stolen by whoever caused his accident. That is what the local magistrate decided at any rate. I was sure your father would have related this information to you. But I daresay he was trying to spare you from further pain."

Then, perhaps thinking to forestall more questions, Gerard patted her hand. "I really do understand your need for answers, but I think it would be best for all of us if you were to simply go on with your life. It's what your brother would have wanted. I'm sure of it."

Leonora fought to keep her temper under control. The nerve of that man to tell her what her own brother would have wished to happen after his death. Especially given the blackguard's involvement in that death.

He truly was without conscience in the matter, she fumed.

Well, she was finished playing mouse to his cat.

Looking up from her shaking hands, she saw that Freddy was gazing at her from across the table. He raised his brows as if to ask if she were well.

Silently she gave a short nod. Freddy nodded back, then turned his gaze on Gerard beside her. Who was blithely eating his dessert without any awareness of the death stare his cousin was giving him.

Leonora was startled from her observation of Freddy by the voice of his brother.

"I must tell you, Miss Craven," said Lord Benedick from her other side, "that I am very fond of your latest essay in the *Ladies' Gazette*. The one about the rights of married women."

Thankful for the distraction, Leonora settled in for a lively discussion of political philosophy. And if she glanced at Freddy far more than was entirely healthy for her, then it was her own fault for failing to protect herself against his charms.

She very much feared that despite her better judgment she was falling in love with him.

From his seat across the table, Freddy watched with barely concealed anger as his cousin spoke to Nora. He could tell from the condescending look on Gerard's face that he was pontificating about something to her. Or threatening her as he'd done earlier.

All he'd wanted to do when Gerard spoke about Jonathan's imagination was plow his already bruised fist into his cousin's face. But despite his savage anger, he knew that they needed to bide their time to ensure Gerard was caught out in a way that would get him a punishment more lasting than a broken nose.

"If you keep looking at her like that, you're going to scare the poor girl off again, Fred," said Archer from beside him. "I don't think I've seen you look this jealous since you were at Eton."

At least his brother mistook his rage against Gerard for jealousy over Nora, he thought glumly. He almost wished to ask for help in this matter from his brothers, but that would be far more trouble than it would be worth.

Sitting up, he flashed a fake smile at Archer.

"That's better," his younger brother said approvingly. "What's got you staring daggers at Gerard? I know he's not our favorite relative, but he hardly warrants the evil eye you've been giving him since he arrived."

Drinking liberally from his wine goblet, Freddy reconsidered whether to tell his brother about Gerard. Given that Archer had dealt with a threat to his own lady just a few months before, he might be just the man to talk to. And unlike Benedick and Cam, he could be trusted to keep the story to himself.

"Let's just say," he said finally, "that our least favorite cousin has been up to something nefarious. Something that ended with the demise of Leonora's brother."

His brother's brows drew together. "Jonny Craven. I knew he'd died of course. A carriage accident, wasn't it?"

"Indeed," Freddy said, glaring at his curried lobster. "Though it may not have been as accidental as all that. And, given that it was during a race with Gerard at the time, there's no way our cousin isn't involved somehow. He might not have landed the killing blow, but he damned well ordered it."

"Really?" Archer hissed in a low voice. "I knew Gerard's driving club was up to no good, of course. Anything he's involved with has a tendency to be a bit dodgy. But . . ." He glanced around at the table to make sure they weren't being watched. "Murder?"

"That's right," said Frederick, grateful to his brother

for understanding the gist of things so quickly. "Separately Leonora and I came to the conclusion he was involved somehow, then decided to work together to look into it."

"I'm surprised you're allowing her to look into it at all," Archer said with a frown. "I know I tried my damnedest to keep Perdita from looking into the matter of her blackmailer."

When Freddy didn't answer, Archer looked at him more closely. "Aha," he said. "You didn't want her working on it."

"Of course not," his brother said with a scowl. "She shouldn't be involved in this business at all. I certainly want her as far away from Gerard and his bloody Lords of Anarchy as possible."

"And Mama invited him to dine with us, and seated Leonora next to him," Archer said with a shake of his head. "I'll give the mater this," he said. "She's got a particular talent for finding exactly the thing we don't want and doing it."

"Doesn't she?" Frederick said, laying his fork and knife down as the footman took his dinner plate. "At least I don't think Gerard has become so bold that he'd try something at the dinner table with a passel of Lisles watching him."

"No," Archer said thoughtfully. He glanced across the table, where Leonora was laughing at something Benedick said. "He wouldn't do that. He values Papa's status too much. It would be foolish for him to offend the most powerful relative he possesses."

"I just wish there were a way to get him away from Leonora permanently." Freddy knew that if anyone were going to understand his point of view on this, it would be Archer. "He's already had her brother killed. I'm afraid that if she asks too many questions he'll take it into his head to harm her, too. Especially given the veiled threats he made when he arrived this evening. Clearly he was taunting her about her brother to see if she'd take the bait."

"It is troublesome," Archer said. "When I was in a similar situation, I took Perdita away, but I have a feeling that Leonora would have your guts for garters if you tried something like that. Perdita almost did that to me, come to think of it."

For a moment Freddy was distracted by the glow of happiness that virtually shone out of his brother's face. "You are so disgustingly pleased with yourself, aren't you?" he asked. "I would never have guessed it would be you who settled down first. Though you were always wanting to mark off your own space from the rest of us. So it stands to reason you'd do the same with your lady."

"And you aren't marking your own territory?" Archer asked with a raised brow. "It is perhaps indelicate of me to say it, but you all but pissed in a circle around her when you entered the drawing room earlier. I think we've got the message. Loud and clear."

"So what if I did?" Freddy said without remorse. "I know what our brothers are like. You might be spoken for, but Cam and Ben certainly aren't. It nearly broke me the first time she jilted me. I'm not going to stand aside and let her leave me again."

"So, it's a true betrothal, then?" Archer asked thoughtfully.

"Damn right it is," Freddy said, without a pang of conscience for the lie. He might trust Archer with the story about Gerard, but the news that Freddy was involved in a faux betrothal would simply be too juicy a tale to keep to himself.

Still, it bothered him that his brother had even asked if the betrothal was real. "Why, what have you heard?"

"Nothing," Archer responded with a shrug. "It's just that I get the feeling something isn't quite settled between you. Otherwise you wouldn't feel it so necessary to mark her as yours."

Leave it to his little brother to ken the situation correctly from the first. But he was hardly going to admit to it aloud. "Don't be daft. Of course everything is settled between us. I have no intention of letting her go this time around. And she's simply going to need to come to terms with that."

"I'm not quite sure that's how it works, Freddykins."

"That's what you think, Archie."

Fourteen

γou know how much I've wanted to become a member of a driving club," said Lady Hermione Upperton as she and Leonora wandered the aisles of Castle's Bookshop.

For the first time in weeks Leonora had fallen right to sleep upon seeking her bed the night before. Of course that might be because she'd had a day that would exhaust a cheetah. From the visit from Freddy's mama and sister-in-law, to the revelations from Lady Darleigh, and finally ending with the fraught dinner party at the Pembertons', it had been the day from Hades.

She'd not only needed sleep, she was unable to keep her eyes open from the moment her head hit the pillow.

The first rest she'd had in weeks, however, didn't make her eager to rise from her bed when her maid awoke her not long after dawn with the news that Lady Hermione Upperton had called and needed to speak to her about an important matter.

Her friend was always up before the dawn, and had difficulty imagining that anyone would wish to sleep past the sunrise.

"Of course I know of your longing to join a club, Hermione," Leonora said, pulling down a volume of

Shakespeare's sonnets that their Ophelia might like. Ostensibly, it was to find her a birthday gift that this shopping trip had been embarked upon. "It's all you've spoken about for years."

"Yes," Hermione agreed. "And of course I would never dream of trying to join the Lords of Anarchy, though they are the only club that uses curricles instead of larger carriages."

"That's a relief," Leonora said, glancing at her friend. Despite the other woman's protestation, Leonora knew how tempting the thought of a club that drove racing carriages would be for her friend. "I am quite positive now that the Lords of Anarchy are not all they seem."

"There's just something I don't trust about Sir Gerard," Hermione agreed. "Especially given what happened with your brother. And from what I've heard the club doesn't spend a great deal of time driving."

"That is quite true," Leonora said, flipping through a book of sonnets. "Anything but, really."

"I had thought that perhaps the Whipsters would have me," Hermione said diffidently, leaning her back against the shelf beside Leonora. "They said that a lady would be better suited to take up some more feminine pastime. Like needlepoint. Or . . . you will be amused at this . . . writing poetry."

That did spark a reaction from Leonora. "They didn't!" She stomped her booted foot. "It infuriates me that poetry gets lumped into those so-called feminine occupations. Why cannot they simply think of it like anything else? Like playing whist? Or I don't know . . . painting? Both men and ladies paint but you don't see anyone telling Gainsborough to leave the daubing to the ladies. Why then must people like that say that poetry or needlepoint or any occupation is particularly suited for females."

"Well, they do say that watercolors are especially suited to ladies, Nora," Hermione said defensively. "And what of needlepoint? I don't think I've ever known a man who sews."

"That is because a man who sews is given his very own specific title—he's a tailor." It was an old hobby-horse for them both. One that never failed to leave each of them feeling angry and out of sorts.

"Why must people insist upon separating occupations and pastimes into those for men and those for women?" Hermione was perhaps even more upset about the situation than Leonora since from an early age she'd wanted nothing more than to spend her every waking moment with horses and in carriages.

Leonora at least had loved the written word, which, granted, was not entirely thought to be a proper occupation for a lady, but was at least known for having female practitioners of it. So far as Leonora knew, there were no truly famous lady drivers.

"Why cannot we simply do what we wish? It's too frustrating!" Hermione closed the atlas she was examining with a snap. "The Whipsters didn't even put my name up for a vote. The main chap just scribbled out a note to me telling me how foolish it was even to apply to them."

Knowing it would take some time to boost Hermione's spirits after such a setback, Leonora linked arms with her and they purchased the book of sonnets for Ophelia—though she did question the wisdom of buying any of Shakespeare's works for a girl named Ophelia, her friend was genuinely fond of the bard—and they stepped out into the spring air and let the waiting footmen hand them into Hermione's landau.

She'd been driving on her own for ages—ever since the Upperton coachman at their country estate had taught her to handle the reins of the gig. Now, of course, she was better than most men, and Leonora had no hesitation to be driven about by her friend. "I wish I had your spirit, Hermione," she said as they neared the edge of Hyde Park. "You are so sure of yourself in the carriage. And I have no doubt that you would not stand to let Sir Gerard Fincher lie to your face as he did to me last evening. When I think of it—how he smiled as he did it, like a particularly odious snake—I cannot help but think that I am a poor sort of opponent for someone like him."

Flicking the ear of the leader, Hermione skillfully drove them through the gates of the park. "But you spoke to him, Nora. That's more than most ladies would have the gumption to do. And I'll bet he was smiling to cover up how frightened your questions were making him. You must recall that men are quite good at pretending to emotions they don't actually feel."

Unbidden, Leonora's thoughts turned to Freddy's open protectiveness of her the night before. Had he been pretending to a possessiveness he didn't feel? she wondered. After all, she'd pushed him away quite effectively earlier that afternoon in her sitting room. The idea that he had been pretending last evening for the sake of his family made her fists clench.

He hadn't even tried to kiss her before walking her to the door of her house. She'd thought it was because he was still angry at her earlier rebuff, but perhaps it was simply that there was no audience to see them.

She knew she had to protect him from falling in love with her, for his own sake. Especially if he wanted the same sort of marriage, with children, that his brother Archer was enjoying.

But some corner of her heart wept at the thought of severing herself from him forever. She was almost sure now that there would never be another man she would love as much as Freddy.

Love.

The word echoed in her mind. She had fallen in love with Freddy.

How utterly foolish of her.

Hermione cursed under her breath, and Leonora shook off her thoughts.

They had reached the promenade by now, and to her dismay, the first carriage they encountered was an open barouche driven by Sir Gerard.

Lifting his hat, Frederick's cousin, whose wife, Melisande, was seated beside him, spoke first. "Miss Craven, it seems that you are everywhere I look these days." Turning his gaze to Hermione, he said, "You've a pretty hand with the whip, Lady Hermione. I am quite impressed."

"I am rather like the proverbial bad penny, aren't I?" Leonora said with raised brows.

Noting that Lady Melisande had not greeted them, she turned to Hermione. "Have you been introduced to Sir Gerard's wife, Lady Melisande?"

Gesturing to the other woman, Leonora said, "Lady Hermione Upperton, meet Lady Melisande Fincher."

Sir Gerard's wife looked imperious, but polite. "I am pleased to meet you, Lady Hermione. I've heard quite a lot about your driving skills. I believe Miss Craven's brother was quite impressed with you."

"He was indeed, Lady Melisande," said Leonora, wondering what Jonathan had said about her friend. She'd once suspected the two had shared a mutual *tendre* but that had been before he became so wrapped up in the Lords of Anarchy. She'd hoped that he would settle down and thought perhaps he might consider doing so with her friend once his infatuation with the club passed, but that hadn't happened. "As are we all."

"I regret that the rules do not allow for the club to

invite a noted whip like yourself into the club, Lady Hermione," said Sir Gerard, though Leonora doubted very much that he felt any real chagrin over the technicality.

"We can always use another steady hand with the whip," he continued apologetically. "And I would have considered a recommendation from Jonathan Craven to be quite as good as one from myself. He was as skilled a driver as I've ever known."

"That's just as well, Sir Gerard," Hermione said before Leonora could speak up. "I think Jonathan's untimely death has put me off the idea of joining a club like yours. One with so much competition, I mean."

She smiled, but it didn't reach her eyes, Leonora noted.

"I rather think being a member of your club might be dangerous to a driver's health." Hermione's gaze was as cold as ice. And Leonora realized that her friend felt more strongly about what had happened to Jonathan than she'd realized.

A flash of something cold and implacable flashed in Gerard's eyes before he schooled his features into something closer to pleasant. "I think you might be right when it comes to a certain sort of driver, Lady Hermione. There is no room at all in the club for drivers who take risks unnecessarily. I regret to say that Miss Craven's brother was one of them."

Before either Leonora or Hermione could respond to Gerard's taunt, the driver of the carriage behind them indicated that he wished to pass, so Hermione steered them back into the line of traffic, and for the next forty minutes they waved and chatted with various members of the haute *ton*.

All the while, the memory of Sir Gerard's words lodged in Leonora's mind like a thorn stuck in the pad of a thumb.

It was the hour to see and be seen, and Leonora tried to focus on the attention her friend received. Both for her driving, and if Leonora weren't mistaken, for her pretty face as well.

The way Hermione had defended Jonathan to Sir Gerard just now made her think that the *tendre* she'd suspected had indeed been a reality. But thus far, Hermione had never revealed anything but sadness for the death of a friend.

Perhaps Hermione would find happiness with someone else. Someone who might share her love of driving as Jonny had.

Yet another life that had been touched by the evil that was Sir Gerard Fincher.

They had reached the gate on the other side of the park now, and as Hermione expertly used the ribbons, Leonora watched with interest. They'd just passed into the street beyond the gate, where a crowd had gathered to watch the swells on their promenade through the park, when Hermione slowed the carriage to avoid the bystanders.

Just then, a white bundle flew through the air, just to the right of the leaders. The horses spooked and reared, and then when the loud pop of an explosion sounded they bolted altogether.

"Hold on!" shouted Hermione as Leonora clung for dear life to the sides of the carriage.

"A package?" Mainwaring's brow furrowed as he put his substantial brainbox to work on the problem. Freddy had always appreciated that his friend's mind worked in mysterious ways. His skill at cards was only the half of it. While the rest of the world labored over their account books—well, while Freddy's man did, at any rate—Mainwaring had already calculated the whole in his head and was on to the next task. "It must have been some kind of code. I can hardly think the members of the Lords of Anarchy are doing something as menial as moving boxes about. Unless Sir Gerard is making them do so as some kind of punishment, which I wouldn't put past him."

The two men had met at Brooks's to discuss the matter of Sir Gerard and the various mysteries of his club.

Fortunately Freddy's ribs no longer felt as if they were being stabbed with a hot knife on a regular basis. And applying ice again as soon as he'd gotten home last evening from taking Leonora home had reduced the swelling in his jaw and his shoulder.

He'd not kissed her as he wanted to. He might be a rascal, but she'd been quite clear that afternoon when she said she wanted their betrothal to remain a false one. He'd shown himself to be possessive of her at his parents' house, but that had been in keeping with the ruse. And he'd have found it impossible not to warn his brothers off when they were all watching her like a starving dog watches a bone.

"Are you even listening to me?" Mainwaring asked, leaning back to get a better look at his friend.

Freddy rolled his eyes. "Of course I'm listening. I simply have a great deal on my mind at the moment. I'm perfectly capable of holding more than one thought in my head at a time."

"I'm glad to hear it," said the earl with a grin. "Because you're going to need that ability if you're to outwit your cousin."

Freddy thrust a hand through his hair in frustration. "I know that, damn it all. He's just so slippery. Every time I think we've figured out a way to get the truth out of him, he twists out of the trap."

"Not unlike most criminals," Mainwaring said, crossing his arms over his chest. "You're going to have to get him to lower his guard somehow. Or trap him into revealing himself without realizing it."

The earl rubbed his chin thoughtfully. "I don't suppose you'd consider using his obvious wish to harm Leonora against him, would you? He might not be able to resist if you dangle her before him."

"Leonora is not some minnow we can use to lure a larger fish, Mainwaring," Freddy growled. "I am unhappy with the degree of risk she's exposed herself to already. I most certainly won't put her in a position where my cousin might be able to grab her before I have a chance to act."

He glared at Mainwaring, daring him to argue.

"Just an idea, old fellow," his friend said with a staying hand. "I simply thought it might be a way to break past Sir Gerard's defenses. But if Miss Craven is to be kept away from him then we'll think of something else."

"Perhaps we should talk to her," Freddy said, rubbing a weary hand over his face. "She is stubborn as a mule, but she's dashed clever." Truth be told, she was a better strategist than he was. He'd grown accustomed to having his way paved for him thanks to his charm and good looks, while as a lady, she had been forced to work out sometimes complicated paths to get what she wanted. It was a skill he found impressive when he wasn't the obstacle she was trying to get around.

"Lead on," Mainwaring said, drinking the remainder of his brandy and rising from the table. "I'm curious to see what she'll come up with."

Retrieving their greatcoats the two men left the club and headed for the Craven town house.

Unfortunately when they arrived, it was to discover that Miss Craven had gone out driving with her friend Lady Hermione Upperton.

"Upperton?" asked Mainwaring with a frown. "She's not the one who's tried and failed to get into all of the driving clubs in London, I hope. Your lady would be keeping some very unsuitable company if so."

Freddy sighed. Of course Mainwaring, the worst driver in London, would find fault with a lady who drove better than the sum total of every driving club in London.

"Yes, it's that Lady Hermione," he said with a roll of his eyes. "Let's go see if we can find them. It's time for grand promenade anyway. At least that will mean they won't be moving very fast."

Back in Freddy's curricle he steered them in the direction of Hyde Park.

"How can you countenance Miss Craven riding in the carriage with a lady driver?" Mainwaring asked as they sped through Mayfair.

"They've been friends for years, Mainwaring," Freddy said with a shrug. "I can hardly forbid Leonora to have contact with one of her dearest friends. What if she tried the same with me and forbade me to keep company with you?"

"That would be different," Mainwaring replied readily. "You are the man in the relationship and your word is final."

"Spoken like a man who has never been engaged," said Freddy wryly. He feared that his friend had much to learn about relationships with women who were not mistresses. Especially one like Leonora who had opinions and wasn't afraid to speak them aloud.

"I've had relationships with ladies, if that's what you mean," Mainwaring retorted. "And besides that, I thought your betrothal was all a hum anyway. You are naturally concerned about her because she's a lady under your protection. But it's hardly the same thing as a love match.

"And," the earl added, as if he'd just discovered the point that would win him the game. "It's your reputation on the line if she aligns herself with someone like Lady Hermione without your permission."

"First of all, it might be a false betrothal now," Freddy responded with frustration, "but I intend for it to become real by the time this investigation into Jonathan's death is concluded. She might not wish that to happen just yet, but I plan to do my best to persuade her.

"Secondly," he said before Mainwaring could respond, "if I wished to forbid Leonora from seeing her friends I would do it. There is no question of who is the leader in this match. But I simply don't find Lady Hermione's friendship with Leonora to be as threatening as you seem to."

Mainwaring shrugged. "It's up to you, I suppose. But women like Lady Hermione Upperton are dangerous to all men. They go about demanding to be included in activities that are not within the realm of a lady's knowledge and they upset the natural balance of things. Let them join driving clubs and soon they'll be demanding membership at White's and will start wearing trousers. It's absurd. Ladies are not meant to go about behaving like us."

It wasn't far off what most men felt about ladies who stepped outside their proper sphere, Freddy thought wryly. Unfortunately, Mainwaring's acquaintance with actual ladies had been limited, he was quite certain. At least, those who were not afraid to speak their own minds like Leonora and her friends.

"I know you think you're speaking sense, my friend," Freddy told the other with a shake of his head. "But your words are going to get you into a great deal of trouble with one of these dangerous women, as you call them. Mark my words."

They'd just turned onto Park Lane, which was thick

with a line of carriages driving out of the park, when they both saw something go sailing through the air about three hundred yards ahead.

As they looked on, the bundle began to jerk and pop, and already surprised by the unexpected projectile, the horses nearest the explosion began to rear up. Then, as they watched, they bolted.

At first, Freddy was merely intent on getting to the runaway carriage for chivalric reasons. It was the right thing to do. It was what a gentleman would do.

That was before, however, he realized that the passenger in the carriage was Leonora.

Cursing, he maneuvered them around the crowd and set the curricle racing after the speeding landau.

"It's Leonora and Lady Hermione," he shouted as they sped down Park Lane.

Fortunately, the traces had broken only a half mile from where the landau had started out, so the horses continued their frightened escape but left the carriage itself behind.

Freddy pulled his own pair to a stop, and as soon as they slowed, he leaped from the curricle and ran as fast as his injuries would allow to the listing landau.

"Nora!" he shouted as he neared the wreck.

He rounded the carriage to find Leonora sitting with her head in her hands, which were shaking.

"Nora," he said softly, not wanting to startle her. "Darling, are you hurt? Are you injured?"

When she looked up, their eyes met and Freddy climbed up onto the seat beside her, which had been vacated by Hermione, who was nowhere to be seen.

Pulling her into his arms, he breathed a sigh of relief into her hair. "My God, you gave me a fright. What happened? We saw the object sail toward the carriage, and heard the pop, but didn't get a good enough look to identify it."

"I don't know," she said against his shoulder. He was gratified to know that she was taking some comfort in his nearness. "There was some kind of explosion and the horses bolted. You know as much as I do."

At that moment, Mainwaring stepped forward, a bundle of what looked like paper in his hands. "I think this was the culprit," he said shortly. "It looks as if it was made by someone with a knowledge of flammables."

"What is it?" Leonora asked, not moving from the circle of Frederick's arms. "Was someone deliberately trying to frighten us?"

"I'd rather say that they were trying to frighten the horses," Lady Hermione said breathlessly, as she walked up beside Mainwaring. Her hair had slipped from its pins and Freddy noted that she had a black smudge on her cheek. "And I very much doubt it was an accident."

"What do you mean?" Freddy asked with deceptive calm.

"It's a Chinese firecracker," Hermione said grimly. "Someone threw this at my horses in order to make them bolt. They are sometimes skittish, but nothing I cannot control. In this case, however, they were provoked purposely. And are now God knows where, frightened out of their minds."

A shaft of rage ran through Freddy. Leonora might have been killed, he fumed as he pulled her tighter.

"Let me go," she said softly in protest. "We're in the middle of the park, for goodness' sake."

Reluctantly he realized that she was right and let her go. And they'd drawn a bit of a crowd, he noticed as he scanned the area around them.

"You did rather well managing the horses," Mainwaring said to Lady Hermione, with grudging respect, breaking into the awkward silence.

"I would thank you," Lady Hermione replied with a scowl, "but you seem to be so surprised by my ability to control the carriage as to be insulting. Have you never seen a lady drive a coach and four, then?"

Members of the crowd jeered, causing Mainwaring to flush. Freddy was quite certain his friend had not expected to receive a set-down in return for his compliment.

"No, frankly," the earl responded heatedly. "I don't think it's appropriate behavior for a lady. But you do it quite well. I believe you saved not only Miss Craven's life but those of these bystanders."

Lady Hermione made a strangled sound and Leonora chose that moment to speak in a low voice. "Please, Hermione, not here. Let us leave before more gawkers come."

At the strain in her friend's voice Hermione nodded.

"Would you mind terribly seeing Lady Hermione home, Mainwaring?" Freddy asked his friend, who was still gaping at that lady as if she had two heads. "I will see Miss Craven home in my curricle."

He saw the moment understanding dawned in the earl's eyes. And he would have laughed if he weren't so consumed with rage over the attack on Leonora.

Glancing at Lady Hermione, Mainwaring sighed. "I would be happy to escort you home, my lady."

Hermione looked as if she would protest, but perhaps she realized that making a ruckus would only upset her friend. "I am grateful for your assistance," she said formally. "But first, I should like to search for my horses."

Closing his eyes as if he'd been given a fatal diagnosis, Mainwaring nodded. "Of course. Perhaps we will find they aren't too far away."

"Oh, I sincerely doubt it," Hermione said as she turned to stalk down Park Lane in the direction she'd last seen her team. "They're quite fast, you know."

With one last baleful glance in Freddy's direction, Mainwaring trudged after her.

Fifteen

I do not normally drink strong spirits," Leonora said as she lifted her glass. "But I think being nearly killed in a runaway carriage is emergency enough to warrant it."

"Agreed," Lady Hermione said as she drank hers in one gulp. Her eyes watering from the burning liquid, she continued in a hoarse voice. "Now, are we going to do something about Sir Gerard Fincher?"

Hermione and Mainwaring had found the missing horses sooner than Hermione had predicted. And after paying a couple of boys in the neighborhood to walk them back to the Upperton mews, she had insisted Mainwaring bring her not to her own house, but to Leonora's. She'd send a pair of grooms to fetch the carriage later.

Leonora and Freddy had only been there for a few minutes before Greentree announced that Lady Hermione and the earl of Mainwaring had called.

"I'm very much afraid that firecracker was Sir Gerard's doing," Leonora said with a frown. "Clearly he is tired of discussing my brother's death and wishes to swat me like a fly."

The fact that she and Hermione had seen the man only a few minutes before the incident made her even more certain he was to blame.

"If that is the case," Freddy said implacably, "then there is nothing for it but you must stop participating in our investigation. I suppose I'd been relying on my cousin's sense of honor to keep him from physically harming you, but I can see now that was a delusion on my part."

Mainwaring nodded. "I agree. This is much too dangerous now for a lady to be involved. I will assist Frederick and we will report our findings to you, Miss Craven. You have my word."

But Leonora wasn't to be swept aside so easily. "Of course I won't just stop my role in the investigation," she said sharply. "Or have you forgotten what I learned from Lady Darleigh?" Quickly she outlined what the other woman had told her at her salon. "If I hadn't gone to the club's soiree that evening at Sir Gerard's home, Lady Darleigh might not have attended my salon and told me what she knew about Jonathan's murder."

"Be that as it may, Leonora," Freddy said with a scowl, "things have changed. My cousin has shown that he has no respect for the fact that you are a lady under my protection. In fact, once I can prove he was the one who attacked you this afternoon, I intend to call him out."

Leonora's heart constricted. "You most certainly will not!" she said, her voice brittle with horror. "I will not allow you to risk your life for me. We are not even truly betrothed."

"It's not a question of allowing me, or of real or false betrothals," Freddy said, his voice rising. "Even if we are not actually engaged, Gerard believes we are and I'm damned if I'll let him thumb his nose at me like that and get away with it."

"Oh, so this isn't about safety at all, then," Leonora said heatedly. "It's about masculine pride. I might have known."

"There is more to it than that," Frederick said, his jaw

set. "You know me better than to think that's all there is
to it."

"Well, I am not able to look into your thoughts and
divine them on my own, Frederick," she said with a huff.

"I believe there might be another explanation for what
happened," Hermione interrupted. "You know how many
of the London clubs I've approached for membership,
Leonora."

Leonora saw what her friend meant at once. "You think
perhaps it was an attempt to dissuade you from your pur-
suit of a membership?"

Hermione shrugged slightly. "I have become rather
notorious for my quest to join a driving club. Perhaps the
explosion was an attempt on someone's part to put me in
my place."

"It's a possibility," Mainwaring said to Frederick.
"God knows there are some members of all male clubs
who would commit murder rather than admit a lady into
their ranks."

"Like you?" Hermione asked sweetly.

The earl bristled. "While it is true that I am not a pro-
ponent of inviting ladies into all of my clubs, I am not
yet so lost to morality that I would consider murder to
stop it from happening. I should hope you could see that
I am an honorable man, Lady Hermione, even if my behavior is not always in accordance with your wishes."

"She could be right," Leonora said to Freddy beneath
the noise of the other couple's bickering. "I can imagine
any number of men who would attempt to dissuade Hermione by frightening her."

Freddy massaged his temples, as if warding off an
ache there. "Why does this keep getting more complex
rather than less? Every time I think we've unraveled a bit
of the snarl, the matter becomes knotted again."

Before Leonora could reply, Mainwaring interjected,

"Perhaps Lady Hermione and I should be going now. You clearly have much to discuss, and we are contributing nothing to the talk besides more complications." Turning to that lady, he offered her his arm, which she reluctantly accepted.

"Are you agreeable with that, Leonora?" Hermione asked pointedly before allowing the earl to lead her away. "If not I'll stay."

Leonora rose and hugged her friend. "I apologize for our rudeness," she told them both. "I fear my nerves are rattled after our incident."

"Not at all, Miss Craven," said Mainwaring with a smile. "Good afternoon."

When they were gone, Leonora and Frederick stood staring at one another for a moment. Then wordlessly he opened his arms and she walked into them.

They stood there like that for several moments before he said, "I apologize for ripping up at you. If you only knew what it did to me to see you clinging to the side of that careening carriage. I never, ever, want to witness anything like that again." He leaned forward and kissed her, his kiss gentle. As if he were afraid he might break her.

Leonora closed her eyes, grateful beyond measure for the safety of his arms. Wordlessly, Freddy slipped his hand in hers and led her to the sofa and pulled her onto his lap.

For a few minutes, they sat just holding one another. The memory of her fear in Hermione's carriage hovered in the periphery of Leonora's mind, threatening to consume her.

Desperate to blot out the memory, she lifted her head and kissed Freddy with all the fear and desperation she'd felt when she realized she might never see him again.

As if realizing what she needed, he slid his arms around her and opened his mouth under hers, taking the kiss deeper with every caress.

Leonora groaned against his mouth as Freddy cupped her breast and stroked his thumb over the bud of her nipple. Restlessness coursing through her, Leonora slid her own hands around his head, holding his mouth to hers while she caressed the curls at the back of his neck.

Almost without realizing it, she'd loosened his cravat, revealing a vee of naked chest that demanded she put her lips there. She kissed her way down his jaw and over his chin until she reached the newly revealed spot and stroked her tongue over it.

"God, Nora," Freddy hissed as his fingers worked the buttons on the back of her gown. "You're going to be the death of me."

Sliding her hand into the gaping neck of his shirt, she slid it down over his heart. "I think not, sir," she said in a low voice that didn't sound like her own. "Your heart is beating much too fast for that."

"We'll just have to make it beat a little faster, won't we?" he said with a grin as he pulled first one then the other of her sleeves down, revealing her bare shoulders, but also trapping her arms at her sides. "There now," he said with a grin, "I can do what I want with you."

Leonora would not have imagined she'd find such love play erotic, but perhaps because she trusted Freddy, she found the game more exciting than alarming. Selfishly, she wanted only to feel. And he was allowing her to do just that.

He placed his mouth on the hollow at her collarbone and teased his tongue over it, drawing a mewl of desire from her. Then, he kissed down her chest and with one hand pulled the bodice of her gown down, exposing her breasts. The anticipation of his mouth on her was almost better than the real thing.

Almost.

But not quite.

She writhed as he took her nipple in his mouth and stroked his tongue over the sensitive tip. Then, with aching tenderness he suckled her, the pull sending a thread of desire from her peak to the heart of her. The ache between her legs was almost like pain, and with her arms pinned, she could do nothing but shift restlessly against him.

"Easy," Freddy said, moving his attention to her other breast, then to her relief, sliding his hand down over her gown and raising both it and the petticoats beneath. She was nearly trembling by the time his hand touched her inner thigh. Then, with aching slowness, he moved his hand up and stroked a finger over her aching quim.

The pleasure was so intense, she nearly wept. And when he sucked her breast and stroked his finger into her, one, then the other, in a steady rhythm, Leonora had no choice but to give herself up to it. Again and again, he sucked her, stroked into her. And she moved in a desperate rhythm against him until, finally, something broke within her and she felt herself break apart into a million tiny shards of light and fly up into the universe.

She came back to herself some time later, collapsed against Freddy's chest. A lassitude unlike anything she'd ever known weighed down her limbs until she felt like she'd never stand again.

"Are you all right?" he asked, leaning his head back to look at her as he tucked a loose strand of hair behind her ear. "I rather think that might have been your first time to experience *le petit mort*."

Though she'd lain with the father of her child, she'd not known when she was with him that it was possible to feel this way. She'd just assumed that it was the way of things. Men enjoyed lovemaking, but women didn't.

What had just happened was more than she'd ever thought possible. Perhaps Freddy was just more skilled at such things than her first lover had been. He was certainly a better man.

"That was my first time," she admitted, lowering her lashes. "I have put . . . that is to say, I've touched . . . myself, before. But that's a bit different, isn't it?"

Her voice was low and she felt absurdly embarrassed for all that he'd just had his hand up her skirt a moment before.

When she looked up, she saw that his eyes had darkened to an almost navy blue. "I would like to see that sometime," he said in a hoarse voice.

"Oh," she gasped, suddenly aware of the hardness of him pressed against her thigh. Blushing, she continued, "What about your . . . ?" She gestured in the general direction of his rampant body.

He smiled crookedly and pulled her hand up to his mouth and kissed it. "Not your problem," he said with a laugh. "We'll deal with that another time."

It was far more than she'd expected, and Leonora was reminded for the second time that afternoon just how different Freddy was from Anthony. She knew with certainty that Freddy would never make demands on her that made her uncomfortable. Nor would he put his own needs before her own, as Anthony had.

Tears gathering in her eyes, she kissed him. They lay there together for a bit, a comfortable silence between them.

"Tell me what happened," he said suddenly, his expression turning serious.

For a moment she thought he was talking about Anthony, and she racked her brain to figure out how he'd found out her secret. Then she realized he was talking about the incident earlier in Hermione's carriage.

"It was terrifying," she admitted, shameful relief washing over her at the realization her secret was safe.

"But Hermione handled it admirably," she went on, focusing on the topic at hand. "I was so proud of her."

"Remind me to send her a new whip or gloves or something," he said, linking their hands together. "She proved herself an outstanding driver today, though I don't know that any thanks I give her can be enough."

"You aren't really going to challenge your cousin, are you?" Leonora asked in a soft voice. She wanted desperately to repeat her admonition that he not do so, but their betrothal—for all that it had brought them closer together—was still a faux one. What had just happened between them notwithstanding. And she had no right to demand it of him. All she could do was ask. "I truly would not wish for anything to happen to you."

"Neither would I," he replied firmly. "But my cousin seems to be under the impression that he is allowed to place other people in danger at his own will. That is unacceptable."

"Could you not, perhaps, have a discussion with him?" she asked, hating how tentative she sounded. "I mean, warn him off without engaging in fisticuffs or a duel or anything?"

"I could," he replied. "And I'll probably do that first."

"But?" she asked, not liking the direction this was going in.

"But," he replied, "that would hardly teach my cousin the lesson he so richly deserves. In fact, I think he deserves to feel my sword against his throat for what he did to you this afternoon."

"If it was him," she said softly. "We don't know that yet."

"True enough," he said with a nod. "Which is why I won't challenge him just yet. No matter how much I might wish to."

She pulled back from him and looked into his eyes.

And was thrilled to see that he was sincere. "You don't know how relieved I am to hear you say that. I don't think I could bear it if something happened to you because of me."

"Let's get something straight," he said, his expression serious. "Any fight between my cousin and me would be between my cousin and me. Not you. He is responsible for his own actions. So, if I were to fight him, it would not be your fault. Do you understand?"

"I suppose. Though I still hope you'll not duel with him all the same."

"I can't make any promises," he responded. "But what I can promise is that I will not do so without warning you first."

"Will you also agree to let me continue to work to find some way to bring him to justice for Jonny's sake?" she asked carefully.

It was clear that he'd been expecting this. "I won't banish you," he agreed. "But you must promise to do what I ask when I think your life is in danger. I've known my cousin since we were children and I understand on an intuitive level just what he's willing to do in order to get his way. And unfortunately, there isn't much he won't try."

Relieved, she nodded. "I will not needlessly endanger myself. Especially not when your cousin is involved."

"I suppose that's all I can ask for," he said with a sigh.

Then, turning the subject, he said, "I want you to know that I intend to marry you, Leonora."

Her heart constricted. Unable to look away from him, she saw in his eyes that he was serious. It would always come back to this, she feared.

And the danger was that she was losing the strength to resist him.

"Freddy," she said, pressing a staying hand against his chest. "I'm not sure I can—"

But he stopped her with a kiss. "Don't answer now," he said. "I can see I'll need time to persuade you."

It was more than that. So much more than simply allowing herself to be persuaded.

But it had been an eventful day and she was willing to linger in the sweet in-between space where they were now.

"All right," she said, finally. "We can wait until things settle down a bit."

The clock down the hall struck the five o'clock hour. Realizing how much time had passed since Hermione and Mainwaring had left, Leonora scrambled off Freddy's lap and straightened her gown.

She must have been mad to get so carried away with him right here where anyone in the house might have stumbled in upon them.

"Quick," she hissed, "tie your cravat before Greentree comes looking for me!"

An amused glint in his eye, Freddy tied his neckcloth in a loose knot and wordlessly turned her so that he could refasten her gown.

When they were once again decently clothed, they sank back onto the sofa.

They were still sitting too close together for propriety, discussing Frederick's plans for Mainwaring and the Duke of Trent to look into some of the other club members, when a cough sounded from the doorway.

"I beg your pardon, Miss Craven," said George, the first footman. "This invitation just arrived and Mr. Greentree said I was to bring it to you at once."

She gave Freddy a speaking glance then took the invitation from the young man.

"Thank you, George," she said with a smile. "That will be all."

When he was gone, Leonora took the heavily embossed page from him and opened it. She'd expected an unremarkable request for her presence at some fete or other—the season was in full swing, after all—but to her surprise, when she opened the folded page, a glance at the bottom told her it was from Sir Gerard and Lady Melisande.

"Look," she said to Freddy, who had gotten up when the footman entered and now studied the fire as if it held all the secrets of the universe within its flames. "Your cousin and his wife have invited me to a house party at their estate on the south coast. And it says that they've extended an invitation to you, as well."

That got his attention. "Estate? I was unaware that there was such a thing as a Fincher estate. Clearly there are more than just the funds he uses to furnish his house and clothe his wife in my cousin's bank account."

Leonora showed him the letter. "It's called South Haven," she continued. "Could it have been something that Melisande brought to the marriage? One of her father's unentailed properties perhaps?" Gerard's wife was called Lady Melisande because her father had been the Earl of Belhaven and her dowry had been quite large. It wasn't impossible it had included an estate, as well. "Or maybe Sir Gerard purchased it with her marriage portion."

Freddy looked up from the invitation. "I don't know," he said thoughtfully. "My mother will know more about the settlements than I do. I was out of the country when they married. And even then, it's not the sort of thing I'd have paid much attention to. Gerard has never been my favorite topic of conversation."

"And here I thought there was such an abundance of family feeling between you," Leonora said with an arch look. "If that is the case, then perhaps we should decline this generous invitation."

"Not a chance, Nora," he said, leaning down to kiss her. "Pack your bags and prepare yourself for a journey to the coast."

"Just as easy as that?" she asked, a bit startled by his haste. "Don't you need to make preparations or something?"

"We won't leave until the day after tomorrow," he said with a shrug. "And by then I'll have had time to make all the arrangements necessary. I hope you won't be one of those tiresome ladies who lingers over her every choice of bauble."

"Hardly." Leonora laughed.

"So," she continued, sobering. "Does this invitation mean your cousin wishes to remove us from our friends and family so that he can do away with us?"

Freddy shook his head. "It's more likely he's going to attempt to persuade us that he's not the monster he's painted. And I believe I heard a couple of the other men talking about this party at the fight the other day. Now their discussion makes more sense."

"All right then," she said with a nod. "I'll ready myself for a journey."

She only hoped it would get them closer to prying a confession out of Sir Gerard.

For she feared if she spent much more time with Freddy, she'd lose what little willpower she had left.

Sixteen

The drive to Basildon was a relatively short one from London, only a day and a half in Freddy's coach and four, which he had borrowed once again from Archer.

Leonora and her aunt Hortense, who was acting as chaperone, rode inside while the ladies' maids and Freddy's valet followed in another coach with their bags. In keeping with his role as a member of the Anarchists, Freddy led the procession in his curricle.

The weather was, thankfully, good, and they stopped only to change the horses despite Aunt Hortense's complaints, which Leonora was forced to endure inside the carriage. Freddy suggested trying to persuade the older lady to ride with the servants, but Leonora had shrugged off the offer. Her aunt's complaints, though they did seem to annoy Leonora, did not seem to be enough to induce her to ride alone.

Freddy wondered fleetingly if that was because she feared he would choose to come inside the vehicle instead.

She needn't have worried, however. It had been a long time since he'd been able to drive any measurable distance, and it would have taken a great deal of inducement to force him inside on such a fine day.

They turned into the rambling drive of South Haven late in the evening a couple of days later, when the sun was just on the brink of dipping into the horizon. With a keen eye, Freddy watched as he drove past his cousin's lands. They looked to be well-tended acres of farmland and once again he was surprised at his cousin's seemingly boundless supply of bounty.

When finally the poplar-lined drive ended and a half-circle drive before a grand Roman portico took its place, he saw that they were one of many guests arriving that evening.

"Cousin!" shouted Sir Gerard from the top step as he waved in Frederick's direction. "Well met! How pleased I am you've come."

Saluting the other man with his whip, Freddy leaped easily to the ground, and hurried to open the door to the carriage so that he might help Leonora and her aunt down.

"You must get me away from her," Leonora said in a low hiss. "She talked the entire journey. I never knew one woman could possibly find something to discuss about every subject in Mr. Webster's encyclopedia. She read aloud from it."

"I vow, Lord Frederick," Aunt Hortense declared as she stepped down from the carriage, "I believe you did not slow for a moment all the way from London. Were you aware that you were carrying an elderly passenger with aching bones and sensitive nerves?"

Despite her complaints, the older lady climbed nimbly up the front steps of South Haven and fell upon her maid who had hurried from the servants' carriage, which had stopped not far behind them. "Ah, Johnson, I should like a bath and a glass of sherry at once. Sir Gerard, Lady Melisande, I hope you will not mind my insistence upon resting these old bones, but when one reaches a certain age great respect must be paid to them or else they intrude at the most inconvenient moments."

And having blown into the house like a cyclone, she tugged Johnson along behind her and disappeared up the stairs.

"A formidable lady, your aunt," Lady Melisande said to Leonora as she and Freddy stepped into the entranceway.

"Indeed she is, Lady Melisande," Leonora said with a wince. "I do apologize for her boldness. It was not my intention to—"

"Do not think of it, Miss Craven," Gerard interrupted smoothly. "We have aunts of our own, do we not, Frederick?" He winked at his cousin as if to share the joke. "I should be shocked if your elderly relative had emerged from a carriage trip without a word of complaint."

"Welcome to our home, Miss Craven," Lady Melisande said with a smile that was not reflected in her eyes. "We are so pleased to have you here."

"Indeed we are, Miss Craven," Gerard said with a knowing smile. "Speaking of carriages, I heard about your accident in the park earlier this week. I am so pleased that neither you nor Lady Hermione was seriously hurt."

Freddy tensed at his cousin's mention of the firecracker incident. He'd decided upon receiving the invitation to his cousin's country house that he would put off confronting Gerard about the incident. Especially in light of the possibility that it might have been intended for Lady Hermione and Leonora was just an innocent bystander. But he found himself wanting to bring up the topic now. Preferably with his fists.

Leonora, however, must have guessed the direction of his thoughts because he felt a pinch on his arm. "It was rather frightening, Sir Gerard," she said now in a hearty tone. "But my friend and I escaped unscathed so all is well. I cannot imagine who would be so foolish as to set off a Chinese firecracker in the park like that. A very fool-ish person, it must have been. But there was no harm done. And fortunately my friend Lady Hermione is a skillful whip, so I was in good hands. Thank you for asking."

She might very well have escaped without injury from the incident, Freddy thought grimly, but that did not mean that he was finished with the matter. In addition to finding some way to prove what happened to Jonathan, he also intended to find out if Gerard or one of his cro-nies had set out to scare Leonora and Lady Hermione.

"It was a great deal more serious than you are mak-ing it out to be, my dear," he said to Leonora pointedly. "You might have been killed. A point I will make when I find the culprit, I can assure you."

"How ferocious you sound, Lord Frederick," said Lady Melisande with a titter. "I would have thought a bluestock-ing like Miss Craven would not abide such behavior from her betrothed. I was given to believe that followers of Miss Wollstonecraft did not find such protection necessary or desirable."

Watching as their bags were carried inside by their maid and valet, Leonora held tight to Freddy's arm. "Miss Wollstonecraft does not suggest dispensing with gentlemen altogether, Lady Melisande," she corrected gently. "She merely asks whether it would not be possi-ble for them to be a bit more accepting when ladies at-tempt to partake of those activities that are generally ascribed to men."

"Is that correct, Miss Craven?" Sir Gerard asked with a derisive laugh. "I thought it was getting rid of men al-together that Miss Wollstonecraft advocates. It seems to me that's what every lady I know who has partaken of that lady's writings has come away from her saying. I hope you do not intend to harm my cousin while you're both under my roof."

"What are you suggesting, cousin?" Freddy's voice was harsh, and Gerard must have noticed it because he laughed.

"Listen to me," Gerard said with unaccustomed sheepishness that made Freddy suspicious. "I sound like the writer of a gothic novel. Of course you do not mean to harm my cousin. I don't know how such an idea came to me."

"You must be exhausted from your journey," Lady Melisande said after an awkward pause. "Let me show you to your rooms."

"I think you'll be quite pleased with them." Sir Gerard sounded as if he were holding back mirth for some reason. "They overlook the park, which leads eventually to the cliff and the Channel."

Freddy was suspicious, but played along and expressed pleasure at the notion while Leonora told a story about the first time she saw the sea. When they reached the narrow hallway their rooms led off from, he realized what his cousin's mirth was about.

He'd given them adjoining rooms.

"You're here, Miss Craven," Lady Melisande said, flinging open the first door to reveal a prettily decorated room in rose tones. "And Lord Frederick, if you'll follow my husband, you're the next room down."

"Is my aunt's room on this hall, as well?" Freddy heard Leonora ask before she disappeared into her room.

"She is in the other wing," Gerard said, elbowing Freddy in his still sore ribs.

He hissed and Gerard made a face. "Don't tell me you're still smarting from that little episode the other day. I thought your man was supposed to be a dab hand at easing bruises and bumps."

Since his valet was a former prizefighter, it was the

truth, but Chester wasn't a miracle worker. Freddy didn't know of any tincture or cream that could erase a bruised rib. Aloud he said, "He does well enough, but I reinjured it."

Gerard paused and then winked. Freddy really wished that his cousin would remove that particular action from his physical vocabulary. It was quite offputting.

"I'll bet I can guess how," he said with no attempt to hide his insinuation.

A week in this man's company was going to leave him with either a thirst for blood or sore knuckles again from planting his cousin a facer. Either way, the outcome would not be good. Reminding himself that he and Leonora were here for reasons more important than his vendetta against his cousin, he reined in his temper.

Chuckling, he said, "I'll bet you can guess. Still, it doesn't make them hurt any less. So the less you poke at me the better, if you don't mind, old chap."

Gerard laughed rather more than the situation warranted. "Say no more, coz. I'll refrain from touching you, though I can't speak for the other guests. There are some ladies I asked Melisande to add to the guest list who would be quite willing to rub soothing ointment where it hurts."

Wondering how many women his cousin expected him to be bedding at a time, Freddy laughed along, vowing to warn Leonora not to think the worst if she saw him in a compromising position with another guest. He had a feeling that his cousin would think it endlessly amusing to set him up for all manner of embarrassing situations in an effort to sabotage his betrothal to Jonathan's sister. Anything to keep them from further investigating his death.

"My thanks for showing me to my room, Gerry," he said aloud now, wanting to talk with Leonora before they were dragged into the party activities. "I think I'll wash off the travel dirt before dinner."

Accepting his dismissal with surprising good grace, Gerard left him with a reminder that dinner was at eight so he'd better not let his "rest" last beyond that.

After a quick wash and a change of clothes, during which Freddy noted the location of the door joining his own dressing room to Leonora's, he stepped back out into the hallway and knocked on the door to her bedchamber, like the civilized person he was.

"I cannot believe they gave us adjoining rooms!" Leonora hissed when they were safe in the back garden where they wouldn't be overheard. "I know I'm a poet with a rather liberal reputation," she went on, "but am I considered so bold that I would really embark upon an affair with my betrothed while we're at a house party?"

She'd thought it surprising that their rooms were side by side, while her chaperone was in a whole other wing, but when Leonora had discovered the doors that joined their rooms, she'd been aghast. "It's shocking, Frederick. Quite shocking."

But he didn't seem nearly as overset by the situation as she was. Which was, in her experience, typical.

"I hate to be the one to disabuse you of the notion that house parties are always entirely proper, Leonora," he said with raised brows, "but house parties are not always entirely proper."

"I know some are improper," Leonora protested with a moue of distaste. "But I never thought that I would be invited to such a one. I'm an unmarried lady, for goodness' sake. I brought a chaperone!"

"Yes, an elderly aunt who does not have the most sterling reputation for propriety herself. Or are you forgetting that she left you to attend my cousin's soiree alone with me?"

"That was different," Leonora said dismissively. Aunt Hortense was perhaps not the highest stickler, but she wasn't entirely lost to all notions of proper behavior. She simply detested soirees. It was understandable that she would avoid them—even those where she was expected to chaperone—at all costs. Still, she did wonder just how scrupulous her aunt would be during their stay at South Haven. She had retired to her rooms immediately upon arriving. That didn't mean anything.

Did it?

"My aunt's chaperonage or lack thereof notwithstanding, I suppose I didn't have a choice." She sobered, thinking of their true reason for being there. "I came to learn more about what happened to my brother. To see if there is some way to glean information from the rest of the club members. So, if my reputation is ruined in the process, I will gladly endure it so that I can tell my father who it was that killed his only son."

At the mention of Jonathan, Freddy's expression grew serious. "I won't let them ruin your reputation," he said with a frown. "If anyone speaks a word about any impropriety between us, I'll just make him regret it."

"And what if that doesn't help?" she asked, her mind thinking about the connecting doors upstairs. "What if we are compromised?"

"Leonora," he said, his gaze unwavering. "I said I'd marry you and I will. We are betrothed to be married, and though it began as a sham, it's quite real to me. If something happens that makes it necessary for us to marry sooner rather than later, I will certainly do it."

At his declaration she tried to pull away, but Freddy refused to let her go. She wasn't prepared to argue about the truth or falseness of their betrothal just now. Talking that out would mean telling him the truth about her inability to conceive. Something she had to keep from him lest he decide to marry her out of some misguided desire to see her taken care of, to marry her anyway.

"Listen to me," Freddy said, his voice low, his eyes intent on hers. "I won't let you martyr yourself on your brother's grave. We will work to find out who killed him. Because that's what Jonathan would have wanted. He'd want his killer brought to justice. But he would not want his only sister to sacrifice her name and reputation in an effort to do so."

When she would have spoken, he stopped her with a finger to her lips. "I know you feel on some level that you are obligated to find out who did him in. And I understand that. But let me do what I can to protect you. He was one of my dearest friends and I was unable to save him. Let me, if possible, save you in his stead."

"It's not the same thing," she protested, jerking away from him. And this time, he let her go. She walked a short distance to the edge of the garden, which overlooked a stand of trees. "You have done quite enough for us both," she said, shaking her head, as if trying to free her mind from some invisible tether. "I cannot trap you into marriage in addition to leading you into danger."

"You're too damned noble for your own good," he said in exasperation. "Perhaps you have forgot it's my cousin we are trying to prove is a killer. And that twice now he's threatened you, and perhaps even attempted to kill you by throwing an explosive at you."

He swore and ran a restless hand over the back of his neck. "Let me protect you, Leonora. I'm a grown man. I don't need you to fight my battles for me. Or worse, shield me from myself lest I do something you see as recklessly noble."

She stared at him for a moment. He was right about protecting him. He just didn't know what it was she was actually shielding him from.

"And if at the end of this madness we decide that it would be best if we went our separate ways?" she asked, half hoping, half dreading what his answer would be.

But she should have known that he'd evade the question.

"If we get to the end of this party without some evidence to prove my cousin killed your brother," he said firmly, "then I promise that I will not force you to marry me."

There was much that was left unsaid in his declaration. He didn't promise not to use persuasion to win her over—only force. And he had already proven himself too honorable for that. And what if they found evidence against Gerard, but it wasn't enough to bring him before the magistrate?

She rather thought his promise was merely a sop to calm her before she brought the suspicions of the house down around their ears.

And, to her shame, he wasn't wrong to offer it.

"Very well," she said with a nod, hoping she conveyed more poise than she felt. "I think now we should go in search of the rest of the party."

She began to walk back the way they'd come, but Freddy stopped her. "I think you should know," he said, "that I believe the reason we've been given adjoining rooms is not necessarily because this party is particularly unseemly—though it certainly does appear that way. I believe the true reason, however, is that my cousin wishes to ascertain just how real our pretend betrothal is."

As his words sank in, Leonora felt a wave of anger sweep through her. "So, it's a test? I thought it was uncommon for betrothed couples to . . ." She waved her hand in the air to fill in the verbal blank. "Is it not?"

"Having only been betrothed to one lady in my life," he said with a raised brow, "I cannot speak to that. I do know that my cousin knows my reputation as . . ."—he coughed and Leonora saw that his ears were turning red—"a rake, and has determined that I am the sort of man who would insist upon anticipating my marriage vows."

It made a certain kind of sense, she thought. Freddy did have a reputation for consorting with ladies. She'd heard enough rumors about his time on the Continent to last a lifetime. Though he swore he'd been faithful to her. But hadn't she herself experienced his skill as a lover only yesterday in her father's drawing room?

There was some truth to the rumors about his skill.

"So, your cousin believes that if our betrothal is real we will use the adjoining door and if it isn't we won't?" she asked, trying to convey a worldliness she did not feel.

"In short, yes." He spent an inordinate amount of time examining his fingernails as he waited for her response. Leonora was silent.

"How will they know?" she finally asked.

"Know what?"

"Whether we use the door or not."

He frowned. "I suspect they've worked out some way of checking to see if the door has been opened. Or maybe they'll attempt to bribe our servants. Or perhaps it will be their own housemaids they ask. Does it matter?"

Tilting her head to the side, she looked at him for a moment. Had she realized how complicated this would become when she embarked on this quest with him? Maybe she had. What she knew for certain was that her brother's death had changed both of their lives irrevocably. And there was no turning back.

Slipping her arm through his, she led him back through the garden toward the French doors they'd exited from.

"Are you not angry?" he asked diffidently when they reached the house. "I thought you'd be offended beyond measure."

"I can't say that I'm shocked. It is your cousin, after all. He's no angel." She glanced around to make sure that no one was watching, then kissed him full on the lips. "But if your cousin needs to know how real our betrothal is, then we will simply have to prove it to him."

"I don't want to hurt you, Leonora," Frederick said fiercely, holding on to her when she would have pulled away.

"It's my decision," she replied. "My choice."

His blue eyes gazed into hers for a moment, then he sighed and let her step away.

"Ah, Lord Frederick and Miss Craven."

She wasn't sure how long Sir Gerard had been standing there, but Leonora hoped it had been long enough to see their kiss. She wanted desperately to prove this man had killed her brother. Not only for her brother's sake, but for her own, as well.

"I hope you'll join the rest of my guests for drinks before dinner," he said with that knowing look that so infuriated her. "Let me show you to the drawing room."

Aware that the game was truly begun now, Leonora held tight to Freddy's arm, and they followed him.

Seventeen

The first person Freddy saw when they entered his cousin's drawing room was, unfortunately, Lord Payne.

"Quite an eye you've got there, my lord," he said with a sneer, his own face showing the marks that Freddy had left on him during their match. "Thought you'd be laid up in your bed with a beefsteak, if you must know."

Unsurprised by the other man's bluster, Freddy did not give him the pleasure of rising to his bait. "Not at all, Lord Payne. I find that the best thing after a satisfying win is to get out and about as much as possible." Truth be told, *he* was rather surprised at Payne's presence here. He'd been unconscious the last time Freddy had seen him.

"I know from experience that my cousin is a seasoned fighter, Payne," said Sir Gerard as he handed glasses of brandy round to the gentlemen. "He nearly killed a man on our estate when we were growing up, didn't you, Fred?"

He might have known Gerard would bring that up. He had most definitely not almost killed the other boy. He'd been defending one of the local girls from the farm lad's advances, and had landed a lucky shot that knocked the boy out cold.

"There was never any question the boy might die," he said with studied indifference, knowing that responding to the taunt would only make Gerard happy. "Do not paint my exploits larger than they actually are."

It came out a bit more censorious than he wished, but Freddy was pleased to see a flare of anger behind his cousin's eyes before he concealed it.

"Not at all, cousin," Gerard said coolly. "I was just complimenting your skills. That is all."

Then he turned his attention to Leonora with a smarmy grin that set Freddy's skin crawling. "Miss Craven, I must say it's a delight to have you in our home. Isn't it, Melisande?" He slid an arm around his wife's waist and Freddy got the distinct impression that she would rather have been molested by an adder. Even so, she smiled politely. "Yes, indeed. Welcome to South Haven, Miss Craven. I hope you've found everything in your rooms to your liking?"

Freddy watched their hostess for some sign that she was fishing for their reaction to the adjoining rooms, but could discern nothing from her.

Before he could respond, however, Leonora spoke up. "My room is quite lovely, Lady Fincher. I am quite pleased that it opens onto the gardens below. I do appreciate a lovely view."

Unable to resist, he said, "Mine does as well, Miss Craven." Then to his cousin's wife, he said, "I must thank you for giving us rooms on the same hall, Lady Fincher. How thoughtful of you to guess that after my dear fiancée's accident in Hyde Park I would wish to keep a careful watch over her."

Lady Darleigh, who, along with her husband, had come closer when they heard the first stirrings of conversation, interjected. "What incident is that, Lord Frederick? I don't believe I've heard anything about an accident in the park. Surely it wasn't during the fashionable hour or it would have been talked about incessantly."

"I was riding with my friend Lady Hermione, my lady," Leonora said cautiously, "and someone threw an incendiary device at our carriage."

"A . . ." Lady Darleigh looked helpless. "A what? I'm sorry, I must sound terribly ignorant next to a learned lady like yourself, but what is an incendiary device?"

"A bomb," her husband said sharply. "Like Guy Fawkes and that business."

A collective gasp went up among the other guests, who'd been listening in.

"Who would do such a thing?" Lady Payne asked with a hand to her throat. "You both might have been killed."

"Ladies oughtn't to be driving coaches," one of the other men—Lord Colburn—said with a frown. "That's a good reason why. What lady can keep hold of the reins in a situation like that? She shouldn't be expected to. Upperton should know better than to let that daughter of his run wild. Driving carriages like a man. What's it to be next? Wearing trousers?"

"It would certainly be less confining than skirts, you must admit, Lord Colburn," Leonora said, and Freddy was relieved that it generated a few laughs from the rest of the guests. Continuing, she said, "I am quite proud of my friend, my lord. And she is an excellent driver. Indeed, I think if she were allowed to join a club such as yours, she would put many of you to shame."

That did not please her audience nearly as much as her earlier words.

"Was not her name associated with your brother's last season, Miss Craven?" asked Colburn, a dark tone in his voice. "Perhaps she was teaching him bad habits. Bad habits that maybe got him killed?"

There was a collective gasp from the other guests.

Even his fellow club members thought Colburn a boor, Freddy thought.

"Lord Colburn," Gerard cut in sharply. "I must remind you that Miss Craven is a guest and is to be treated with the utmost respect. Her brother has only recently died. Have some manners."

Colburn looked angry, but mumbled an apology. That was followed closely by Lady Fincher's announcement that dinner was served.

As he led Leonora into dinner—Freddy was relieved to note that his cousin did not have a high regard for the rules of precedence at his table—he overheard one of the other men admonishing Colburn for his behavior. "Better watch out, Colly. That chit is betrothed to Sir Gerard's cousin. And he looks after what's his."

But to his surprise, Colburn didn't seem to take the other man seriously at all. "Gerry's got no love for that versifying ape-leader. Didn't you see how he looked at her when she walked in on Freddy Lisle's arm? Like he wanted to strangle her in the bath. I ain't worried about Gerry on that score. He's got a temper, don't get me wrong. But it ain't gonna be over her."

Freddy wanted to turn to see who the other man was, but all he could do was slow down a bit in the hopes that the two men would pass them. Unfortunately he and Leonora reached the table before the others passed them.

Before she sat down, Leonora glanced over at Lord Colburn ruefully. "I might have handled that better," she admitted in a low voice that only Frederick could hear. "I cannot stand it when men dismiss Hermione out of hand because of her sex. I hope I haven't destroyed a possible alliance there."

"I doubt it," Freddy said, thinking about the other conversation he'd overheard. "That fellow is known for being disagreeable. I sincerely doubt he would have unbent enough to give you any help. Even were you to pair it with a bag of diamonds."

Taking her seat, Leonora nodded. "That's good to know. I shall try to avoid him if at all possible,"

"I'm afraid that won't be quite as easy as you think," Freddy said apologetically as he took his seat beside her. "He's one of my cousin's most valued men. After Payne, of course."

"Whatever are the two of you discussing in such a heated manner?" Lady Melisande asked at Leonora's other side. "I begin to understand why the two of you are betrothed. You spend every possible second together, don't you?"

Then the conversation turned to weddings and there was no more time for private discussion.

"I very much enjoy your poetry, Miss Craven," said the rather plain lady who had been introduced as Lady Rutledge as she and Leonora walked from the dining room to the drawing room after dinner.

Leonora had been rather surprised to learn that Sir Gerard and Lady Melisande followed the custom of having the ladies leave the gentlemen to their port, given that their adherence to other social niceties—having betrothed couples not sleep in adjoining rooms, for instance—was not all that strict.

Even so, she was somewhat relieved to be spending the next quarter hour without feeling like the most scantily dressed lady in the room. There was nothing in the least objectionable about her gown—it was a simply cut lavender, in keeping with her mourning for Jonathan, and was no more revealing than any of the other gowns in the room. Indeed, there were a few ladies whom Leonora suspected must be desperately in need of a shawl given the nakedness of their bosoms and shoulders.

Lady Rutledge, on the other hand, had chosen to err on the side of caution. The neckline of her watered silk was almost so far up her neck as to be counted as a cravat, and her sleeves were long, despite the fact that spring was in the air.

"Thank you so much, Lady Rutledge," she said with genuine gratitude. Even if the other woman was offering her meaningless compliments to pass the time, it was better than the suggestive chatter Leonora could hear between a few of the other ladies. And infinitely more pleasant than enduring yet another cold interrogation from Lady Melisande.

"I spend a great deal of time reading to my mother-in-law, the dowager Marchioness of Rutledge," Lady Rutledge continued, her hand nervously picking at her skirt. "She has declared your writing is easily as good as Mr. Wordsworth's. Or, and this is as fine a compliment as she can give, even that of Keats."

The comparisons to other poets—male ones especially—was something Leonora still hadn't quite gotten used to. It was odd to imagine that her work, which felt so unique to her own thoughts and feelings while she was in the midst of writing it, was anything like any other poet's. But that was the nature of reading and being read. The human mind was constantly looking for ways to make connections between disparate things. Poets, poems, novels, even people.

"Is your mother-in-law an invalid, Lady Rutledge?" Leonora asked, curious. She wondered if it were the dowager who had chosen the younger marchioness's attire. "What an admirable thing for you to spend time reading to her."

The other lady blushed. "She is, Miss Craven. She suffered an apoplexy last year and my Thomas was nearly beside himself over it. He insisted upon moving her from the dower house into the estate where he could personally oversee her care."

That was unusual for a gentleman, Leonora knew. But sometimes sons were like that with their mothers. "I feel sure that you had some role in her removal, as well," she told the other woman. "Though it sounds as if both you and your husband are fond of her."

"We are," said Lady Rutledge with a shy smile. "I lost my own mother when I was a girl, so Tommy's mother has taken me under her wing."

Wistfully, Leonora thought of her own mother who had died when she was still but a girl. Unbidden, her thoughts went to the Duchess of Pemberton and her easy ways. If this betrothal between Frederick and her were real, would the duchess do the same with her as the marchioness had done with Lady Rutledge? It was a tempting idea, though a dangerous one, Leonora knew. The less she relied upon Frederick and the ways in which making their betrothal real would affect her, the better.

"How nice," she replied to the other woman, glancing once again at where Lady Rutledge's sleeves reached her wrists.

"I see you have noticed my odd attire," the other lady said ruefully. When Leonora would have demurred, she laughed. "Do not worry. I am not offended. If I were a stranger seeing myself for the first time, I'd be curious, too."

Taking a seat on the settee near the fire, she indicated that she would like Leonora to join her. Unable to resist her curiosity, Leonora did just that.

"I cannot deny that I did wonder," she said carefully. "I thought perhaps you were simply cold natured?"

"That would certainly be easier," the marchioness said with a smile. "But, alas, it's nothing so simple. You see, I was in a fire when I was but a girl. It's how I lost my parents, if you must know. And my skin is quite ugly because of it."

"Oh dear!" Leonora gasped. What a terrible thing to happen to someone so young. That she managed to get about in society at all was impressive, then. "I am terribly sorry to hear it. You must be quite strong."

"Hardly," Lady Rutledge said with a laugh. "But my Tommy is a very social man, and I cannot bear to make him spend all of his evenings indoors with me. Especially when I am suffering with one of my headaches. He is also mad about driving, so when he was invited to join the Lords of Anarchy, I insisted that he accept. He enjoyed the camaraderie of the other members, and I rub along well enough with the other wives." She lowered her voice, and continued, "Though there are a few of the ladies I would just as soon not interact with."

It was impossible not to like such an unaffected, plain-speaking lady. And Leonora found herself warming to the other woman. She would appreciate having Lady Rutledge as a friend, if, that is, she were able to keep up with any such relationships once she and Frederick found Jonathan's killer.

"I cannot blame you," she replied in a low voice that matched that of Lady Rutledge. "I believe in any group there will always be a few members you'd rather avoid if given the choice. I haven't met many in this one, but they are certainly there."

"I hope you don't mind my asking, Miss Craven," the other woman said with a timid smile, "but are you perhaps here because you wish to learn more about your brother?"

It was said in a normal enough voice, but Leonora found herself glancing around at the other women in the room—who, fortunately, seemed not to have heard her companion's question.

"If I said yes, would you take that information to Lady Melisande?" Leonora asked candidly. "Because if you do, I will deny it."

"My dear, what a delightful story," Lady Rutledge said in a loud voice. Then in a lower one, she continued, "I have no wish to unmask you to Lady Melisande, Sir Gerard, or any other club member. I was quite fond of your brother on the few occasions I met him. And I would be very willing to assist you in discovering whatever you'd like to know."

Automatically, Leonora's gaze went to Lady Darleigh, who was engrossed in conversation with Lady Melisande on the other side of the drawing room. She wondered if Lady Melisande had any notion of just how many of her so-called friends were willing to help Leonora. She rather doubted it.

"I thank you, my lady," she said to the other woman in a low voice. "I am in need of any help I can get. You know, perhaps, that my brother's death was not what it seemed. At least that is the conclusion my betrothed and I have come to."

"It is logical," Lady Rutledge replied with a shrug. "My husband is convinced of it, as well."

"What?" Leonora felt her heart beating faster. If another club member was suspicious about Jonathan's accident, then perhaps he knew something about it that would help them. "You must tell me everything."

But Lady Rutledge shook her head. "I've got nothing to tell, my dear. I am sorry to have gotten your hopes up. It's just that Tommy and I have discussed the way your brother's accident happened. And we both thought it strange that it should occur so soon after his quarrel with Sir Gerard."

"You are not alone in that," Leonora said quietly. Lady Rutledge took Leonora's hand and squeezed it. "Jonathan

Craven is one of the kindest gentlemen I've ever known. His loss was a blow to all of us who counted him as a friend."

"Thank you, my lady," Leonora said with a warm smile. She was grateful that she'd decided to break off their conversation then, because the gentlemen chose that moment to file into the drawing room.

"There's my Tommy," said Lady Rutledge as a handsome dark-haired man strode into the room on Frederick's heels.

"He's quite handsome," Leonora said with a smile for the way the man's face lit up on spotting his wife. Whatever had happened to Lady Rutledge in childhood, it was obvious that her marriage was a love match. She wondered for a moment what it must be like to be the object of such affection. From the way the other woman was beaming, it must feel quite nice.

"My dear," Frederick said, bowing over her hand, "I see you've made a friend."

"Indeed," said Leonora, introducing Lady Rutledge. "I was on the verge of offering her the secret recipe for my headache relieving tisane. We can make it up ourselves, Lady Rutledge, if the kitchen gardens have what we'll need."

"I am quite sure they do, Miss Craven," the other lady replied with a smile. "Lady Melisande is known in this circle as a bit of a healer when it comes to herbs. She maintains an extensive herb garden for just such occasions."

"Does she?" Frederick asked, his gaze sharpening. "I did not know that about my cousin's wife. But of course it makes a great deal of sense. He must get all sorts of injuries as a result of driving and whatnot."

"I should say so," Tommy, the Marquess of Rutledge, said with a guffaw. "Sir Gerard is quite the whip, but when you drive as fast as he does on roads that are not quite up to snuff, there will be accidents, don't you know?"

Just then, their host ventured into the center of the room and clapped his hands to get their attention.

"Ladies and gentlemen!" he called, turning in a full circle so that he could catch the eye of every guest. "It is time for a bit of fun, now that supper and the after-dinner drinks are ended."

Eighteen

I'm not sure I expected Sir Gerard's 'bit of fun' to turn
out to be hide-and-seek," Leonora said as she clung to
Freddy's hand on their way up the stairs. He knew his
cousin's tastes ran to the childish, but he rather suspected
that tonight's game was conceived solely for the purposes
of allowing some of the guests to spend an hour or so in
seclusion with the person of their choosing. Be it their
own spouse or someone else's.

It was most decidedly not an appropriate game for a
young unmarried lady like Leonora. But since Aunt
Hortense had spent the entirety of their visit so far in her
so-called sickbed, there was no one to call it to their
host's attention.

"You would be surprised at what my cousin finds
amusing," he said aloud to Leonora as they left the drawing room in an exodus with the other couples while Lord
Payne—the unlucky fellow to be the counter—stayed behind and loudly began to count. "This is a man who still
enjoys snap dragon at Christmas, you know."

"I love a good game of hide-and-seek," Lord Darleigh
said with a grin as he pulled his wife into an empty sitting room, then shut the door firmly behind them.

"I suppose this puts a damper on the idea of questioning club members," Leonora said wryly, her voice low as they continued on toward the upper floors. "It's just as well, as I believe they are beginning to be suspicious of us. Perhaps tomorrow we will have better luck, during the archery tournament."

Freddy laughed softly, causing the candle he was using to light their way to dance. "I think it might be best not to question people while they are aiming a dangerous weapon, my dear."

"Ha-ha," Leonora said sarcastically. "If so, then why are we here at all? Your cousin clearly has no intention of telling us anything. He wishes you to be a part of his silly little club and will spend the rest of his days evading questions about what really happened to my brother. I may as well have my maid pack my bags and take my leave tomorrow."

Turning, he saw that she was looking more defeated than he'd seen in a long while. They'd reached one of the upper floors, but one he suspected was used for housing guests who weren't all that welcome. Testing one of the doors, a quick look inside revealed that it was a small bedchamber overlooking the barn. Pulling Leonora behind him, he entered the room and shut the door.

"What is this place? As hiding places go, I suppose it's all right. Your cousin is unlikely to come this far in search of us."

"I have a feeling that there will be no searching, Leonora," he said, kneeling to light the fire that had been laid in the hearth. "It's the way these parties go. Every opportunity is given for couples to be alone, all under the guise of respectable party games."

Leonora turned from where she'd been running her hand over the counterpane. "What? Why bother pretending if the games are all supposed to devolve into an orgy of sorts?"

"It's hardly an orgy," Freddy said, brushing his hands on his breeches before standing to look at her. In the fire-light he could see the hollows of her cheeks and her eyes looked enormous. "That would involve much more pub-lic displays and there is no way in hell I would ever con-sider taking you to one of those. This, on the other hand, is only on the fringes of respectability and won't damage your reputation too much. Else the other guests would risk their own reputations for a moment. And for their own reasons they'd rather not."

She tilted her head to the side, revealing the soft skin between her neck and shoulders. Freddy felt himself harden as he considered the possibilities of their being closeted in this little room.

"Have you ever been to an orgy?" she asked softly, walking slowly toward him. "I must admit, the idea of being in the same room with other couples while they are . . . touching each other holds a certain excitement."

She was close enough now for him to touch, and softly, he slid his hands up her sides until he grasped her by the waist. Then he stepped closer and her arms went round his waist. "It can be exciting." He exhaled as he leaned his head down and kissed her oh so softly. "To watch," he said, as he took her lower lip between his teeth and tugged a little. "Do you want to watch, Leonora?" he whispered as he leaned in closer and kissed her fully. When she of-fered a little gasp, he slid his tongue between her lips and stroked against her softness.

"Maybe," she whispered, pulling back only enough to give herself a breath before opening her mouth more fully and letting him stroke inside again. Once, twice, he played against her tongue with his own, almost drunk with the heat, the sweetness of her. Her hands against his chest opened and closed restlessly as his own stroked up her sides and over the swell of her breasts. It took only the work of a moment to slip the sleeve down over her shoulder, exposing the soft curve of her breast.

The light was low, but it was enough. "Gorgeous," he whispered, sliding the back of his knuckles over the pebbled peak while his mouth grew more desperate against hers.

As if by agreement, they moved backward toward the bed, and soon they were reclining, Leonora's demands becoming more restless as she pressed herself against his fully clothed body. "Easy, sweeting," he soothed even as his hands stroked over her naked breasts, his fingers drawing the taut skin to points that must have been as painful as they were pleasurable.

"Freddy," she murmured as he kissed down her neck and made his way to where his fingers were teasing her. Finally, he took her in his mouth and suckled. An action that soon had both of them breathless.

"Want to feel you, too," Leonora said restlessly as she arched into him. "Take your shirt off."

Even as he pulled against her breast, Freddy felt her hands at his neck, unwinding his cravat. When that was off, he paused to shrug out of his jacket and waistcoat. Finally he was pulling the lawn of his shirt from where it was tucked into his breeches and pulling it off over his head.

Her hands were there immediately, sliding over the contours of his chest and waist, and when Leonora pulled him down against her so that her breasts were naked against his chest, he hissed.

"Lovely." She sighed against his mouth even as he slipped an arm down to grasp the hem of her skirt in his hand and bring it up, exposing her stockinged legs.

For a moment he held back and just looked his fill at

her, stretched out on the bed like a feast for the taking. "Beautiful." He leaned forward to kiss her navel.

He had thought she might be shy, but when he felt her fingers clutching his shoulders, he realized his mistake. She might be untutored in this, but she was definitely not shy.

To his surprise, her lip quivered as if she were about to cry. "I mean it," he said more harshly. "You're beautiful." He took her hand and placed it over the front of his breeches. "Do you feel how much I want you? This isn't for show, Leonora. It's real. I want you, and this is the proof of it."

Her eyes widened as her hand palmed over his erection and he wanted to howl. But soon enough, she was stroking over him with a sureness that belied her unfamiliarity with the practice. With a curse, he pulled back and began to undo the buttons at his waist.

"Take off your gown," he said, his voice harsh with unquenched lust. "I need to see you. All of you."

She hesitated, but only for a moment before she grasped the bottom of it and pulled the silk over her head, leaving her there in her shift and stays.

While she removed those, he dispensed with his boots and breeches, and soon he was climbing up beside her on the bed, where she'd pulled back the counterpane.

In the firelight, her dark hair was spread out on the pillows in a cloud of softness and he would not forget the memory of her thus for the whole of his life.

"Beautiful," he whispered against her lips, the feel of her naked skin against his more glorious than anything he'd ever known.

His hands on either side of her waist, he parted her legs with a knee and kissed his way down her body, pausing every few inches to lavish her skin with attention.

When finally he reached his destination, she seemed to realize just what he intended and gasped. "You cannot mean to kiss me there . . ." But ignoring her protest, he did just that.

Leonora caught her breath as his tongue swept over the heart of her, sending a maelstrom of sensation through her as he proceeded to worship her with his mouth.

She'd seen etchings that depicted the man with his mouth on that part of a woman's body before. Once when she'd stumbled upon the restricted area of her favorite bookshop she'd seen drawings even more scandalous than that. But nothing could have prepared her for the utter devastation of his tongue touching her there.

Of their own accord her hands found the soft silk of his hair, holding him to her as he thrust first one, then two fingers inside her, moving in counterpoint to the stroke of his tongue on the bud of her pleasure.

When the climax came, it was more powerful than anything she'd dreamed of in her most lurid imaginings. Her body moved of its own accord against him in a rhythm she wasn't even aware she knew.

She was still coming back to herself when she felt him move up to position himself at her entrance. "This might hurt a bit," he said, kissing her swiftly before he thrust into her. "I'm sorry."

It did hurt, but she bit back her cry in the knowledge that this was Frederick joining his body with hers. She reveled in the sensation of his weight pressing into her when he moved, and bending her knees, she gasped at how the change in position eased the pain into something like pleasure. "Better?" he whispered against her ear, as he stroked into her again. This time, the motion had her moving her hips to follow him as he pulled away.

"Better," she gasped as she reveled in the way he filled her, her body clenching with the rhythm they set together. "Oh, yes, better."

"Ah, God, Nora," he groaned, his pace quickening as she felt herself hurtle over the edge into bliss.

Nineteen

Sometime in the wee hours, Leonora and Freddy dressed hastily and slipped back into her rooms.

They made love again, but when Leonora awoke some hours later, it was to find herself alone and feeling sore in places she'd not quite known she even possessed.

Stretching languidly, she remembered every caress, every word. The memories left her flushed with feminine satisfaction.

Lovemaking had been everything she'd hoped it would be. Because that's what it was between her and Freddy. Lovemaking.

What she'd done with Anthony, when she was still such a child, had been confusing. Though she'd wanted to please him, now that she'd been with Freddy, who focused entirely on her pleasure, it was obvious Anthony had not truly cared for her.

Only what he could get from her.

She'd been dreaming of running away with him, and he'd used her. Like a bath towel, or a shovel.

It hadn't occurred to her before Freddy that it was possible to feel so close to another human being.

When Freddy touched her, looked at her, she knew that he was trying to make things as good as possible for her. With every glance, every caress, he made her feel as if they were the only two people left on earth. And making love to her was his only concern.

Not once had he chided her for crying out, or shrunk back when she tried to touch him.

Anthony Townsend had been utterly wrong.

About everything.

She wasn't wrong or unnatural for enjoying what Freddy did to her. If anything it had been Anthony who was unnatural. He certainly hadn't behaved as if he cared about her.

She knew now that her dreams of them living happily ever after had been just that, dreams. She'd imagined him into a charming prince who would whisk her away and care for her and their child.

But in reality, he'd just been a flawed man, who got her with child then abandoned her.

It was impossible to imagine Freddy behaving the same way in such circumstances.

"Miss Craven, ma'am," Peggy said, knocking on the door of the dressing room. "I beg pardon, but your aunt is asking after you."

Since it was long past the time when she should be getting dressed, Leonora threw back the covers and asked Peggy to ring for a bath.

An hour later, feeling much improved, and dressed in one of her favorite morning gowns, a deep violet muslin that emphasized her bosom, she made her way to the wing of the house where Aunt Hortense had taken up residence. When she knocked on the bedchamber door, it was opened by one of the housemaids, who ushered her into the large rooms that her aunt had been placed in.

"What took you so long?" Aunt Hortense asked, her gray hair tucked into a pretty lace cap that Leonora knew the older lady favored because she thought it brought out her eyes. "I rang for you two hours ago. I thought you'd been kidnapped or perhaps had been spirited away by our hosts."

Leonora forbore from pointing out that it was no thanks to her chaperone who'd spent all of her time since their arrival the day before secluded in her bedchamber.

"I had to bathe and dress, aunt," she said, seating herself on the edge of her aunt's bed. "Are you feeling better?"

"Hardly," her aunt said with a hand to her brow. "The drive was such that I am unsure I will be able to return to London if your young man insists upon driving us. I have sent for my own carriage to fetch me in four days' time. Of course I will remain here for the duration of the house party to act as chaperone for you. But I am afraid I won't be able to leave my bed."

It was a familiar refrain, one that Leonora had heard again and again over the years. Her aunt maintained that her health was fragile and as such she was required to spend as much time as possible in her bed, resting her nerves. Leonora and the rest of her aunt's acquaintances knew that the old woman's nerves were as strong as iron and that she took to her bed as much because she disliked interacting with others as anything else. Still, her readiness to chaperone Leonora on those occasions when she was needed, made her a favorite. Especially because Hortense either possessed no curiosity, or indeed had none, about what Leonora got up to while her aunt was ensconced in her bedchamber reading and eating bonbons.

"You must do what you can for your poor nerves, aunt," Leonora said, patting her elderly relative's hand. "I know how they plague you. And I apologize for the discomfort of the journey here. Of course you must not endure that again."

"It is perhaps unseemly for me not to insist that you

accompany me," Hortense said with a mournful shake of her head. "But I will have room only for myself and my maid. As you are already betrothed to Lord Frederick, I believe it will be unobjectionable for you to ride unchaperoned with him back to London."

"Oh, of course," Leonora answered, maintaining a straight face while inside she danced a jig. "Is there anything I can bring you to make you feel more the thing?"

But her aunt had all she needed to see to her comfort and soon dismissed her niece with an admonition to behave herself.

If she only knew, Leonora thought with a grin as she shut the door behind her.

"Miss Craven, the very person I was looking for," Lady Melisande said as she met Leonora on the landing. "Would you be interested in a walk to the folly this afternoon? I would have asked you at breakfast but you were not there. And the others would like to set out in a short while."

Leonora felt her cheeks burn as her hostess waited with raised brows that seemed to imply knowledge of just why Leonora had missed breakfast. Still, the folly sounded interesting and she would like to speak to the other guests to see what they recalled about her brother. "I would like that, Lady Melisande," she said with a coolness she hoped belied her burning cheeks. "Do you know if Lord Frederick has agreed to go?"

"I thought you must have spoken with him already," her hostess said with a touch of asperity. "However, I do believe he has agreed to walk with us. I will instruct the others to wait for you downstairs. You might wish to put on something a bit warmer, for there is a bit of a chill in the air today."

With that admonishment, the other woman hurried down the hall, likely to don her own change of clothes,

Leonora thought wryly as she looked at her hostess's re-
treating back and the short-sleeved round gown Lady
Melisande wore.

She wasn't sure what it was about Sir Gerard's wife
that set her back up, but she certainly did have the
power to annoy. Perhaps it was the way she looked at
one as if you had just trod on her toes, or tipped over a
glass of claret onto a white carpet. Though she supposed
that she was democratic about that look, for Leonora had
seen the same expression on Lady Melisandre's face
when she was speaking to virtually every other member
of their party.

Deciding to change her gown despite her pique at her
hostess's suggestion, she hurried to her bedchamber.

The next morning, despite having slept very little, Freddy
went down to breakfast with a spring in his step.

Last night with Leonora had been beyond his wildest
imaginings of what they would be like together. He'd
known the bond between them was intense, but it wasn't
until he'd held her in his arms—looked into her eyes
while he joined his body with hers—that he'd realized
just how intense.

What he felt for her was unlike anything he'd felt before. A mix of tenderness, affection, passion, and a burning desire to protect her from anyone who might wish
her harm. And while they were together, he'd known in
his soul she felt the same way about him.

He'd promised not to press her, and he wouldn't. But
now he was more eager than ever to settle the business
of Jonathan's death. Not only to see justice done, but so
that he and Nora could start their married life together.

"Good morning, cousin," Sir Gerard said with a lascivious grin as Freddy entered the breakfast room. "You
look as if you slept very well, indeed."

Wishing he'd found someone else lingering over their eggs, Freddy said, "I did, thank you."

He left it at that.

At the sideboard he filled a plate with eggs and bacon. When he turned, despite his wish, his cousin was still there.

"So," Gerard said, toying with the rim of his coffee cup. "Did you enjoy my little game of hide-and-seek last night?"

Freddy was damned if he'd tell Gerard anything about what happened between Leonora and him last night. He could practically hear the questions lurking in his cousin's fetid brain.

"I'm not much for games," he said tersely. Chew on that, old man.

"Oh come now, Freddy," Gerard said with a pout. "Don't be such a stick-in-the-mud. I'm sure there are one or two little anecdotes from your evening you can share."

He bit back a demand for his cousin to leave him the hell alone. If Gerard had planned the game last night so that he could collect stories the following morning, then he would have to live without Freddy's.

Deciding to turn the tables, he took a forkful of eggs halfway to his mouth, then paused.

"I was wondering, Gerry," he said as if it had only just occurred to him. "Where did Jonathan Craven stay the night before the race?"

At his cousin's narrowed eyes, Freddy knew he'd made a hit.

"It's just," he continued, "that I had always assumed the race was from London to Dartford. But someone pointed out to me that they saw the coaches headed in the opposite direction. Did you invite Jonathan and Lord Payne to stay at South Haven since the race was so nearby?

It was truly satisfying to see his cousin gnashing his teeth after the hell he'd put Freddy and Leonora through over the past week. And, if Jonathan had stayed in this house the night before the race, then there was a good chance his things were still lurking about here.

All it would take to find them? One correct answer from his cousin.

"Where are Jonathan Craven's belongings?" he said, laying his fork across his plate to indicate he was finished. "For I do not recall my fiancée ever mentioning a note or letter telling her his things had been found. It's such a shame when people ignore ladies. Especially those in mourning."

"I am growing weary of your looking down your nose at me, Freddy," his cousin said with ice in his eyes. "You are just a man, like any other. You cannot walk on water. And you are not above enjoying the pleasures of the flesh upon occasion."

"I think that's beside the point, Gerry." Freddy spat out the word, as if his cousin's name tasted foul. "I asked you a simple question. Do you, or do you not, know the whereabouts of Jonathan Craven's belongings? The ones he brought with him the evening before your race."

Indifferent to his cousin's glare, Freddy crossed his arms and waited. He'd always been better at keeping his patience than Gerry. It had been one of the things that set them apart, even as children.

Finally, his patience paid off.

"I believe they are boxed up, and were placed somewhere in the attics," Gerard said coldly. "You and your ladylove are welcome to go look for them at your leisure. Now, if you would excuse me, I must go make sure preparations are under way for our trip later this morning."

"One more thing before you go," Freddy called out to him. When he turned as if to ask what the devil he wanted now, Freddy asked, "Why did you not send them home? I would have thought a grieving sister and an elderly father who's lost his only son would wish to have them."

Gerard's lips pursed. "If you must know, it's because the club wanted to keep them. They are just a few fripperies and whatnot. I don't think you'll solve any great mystery with them."

"We'll just wait and see, won't we?" Freddy asked with a smile that didn't reach his eyes.

"I suppose so."

With that, the other man stalked out of the room, anger reverberating in his every step.

Freddy only wished he could be sure Jonathan's things would be of any value. Mostly because his cousin had too readily given him permission to search through them.

Oh, he'd grumbled about it, but that was to be expected when one requested anything from Sir Gerard Fincher, from a shilling to a guinea. He was reluctant to part with things. Even the ones that bore little real or sentimental value to him.

Hoping this time was different, Freddy hurried upstairs to find Leonora.

Upstairs in her bedchamber, Leonora was just pulling a wool gown over her head when a knock sounded on her door.

"Leonora, are you there?"

Her heart sang at the sound of his voice. Leonora grinned in spite of herself.

Meeting her maid's amused gaze, she shoved the girl away as she reached back to button her own gown and called out for him to come in.

"Don't you have a maid for that?" he asked, puzzled as she held up her gown with one hand. "Here let me help you."

Turning obediently, she let him fasten her.

"I have more experience with the undoing of these," he said wryly as he made his way up her back. "Are you changing because you are going on the walk to the folly?"

"Yes, Lady Melisande just asked me," she said, shivering as he kissed the nape of her neck. Turning, she brushed her hands down over her gown, just to give them something to do. "She said you were going, as well."

"I am," he said, reaching out to take her upper arms in his hands. Leaning down, he kissed her. "There, that's better. I don't know why we should feel awkward in one another's presence after what happened last evening, but it happens sometimes, I suppose."

"Perhaps because you left before I woke up," she said, reaching up to fluff his cravat where it had folded in on itself. "I thought we'd go down to breakfast together."

"That would hardly have been discreet, Leonora," he said, his brows furrowed. "It's all well and good that we are betrothed, but I won't have the others at this party carrying tales back to London when the week is over."

"So that's why you left," she said with a sigh. "I thought since Sir Gerard and Lady Melisande gave us adjoining rooms we were going to make them think that we're lovers already. Not that it would be a lie now."

"No, of course not," he agreed, "but it's one thing for them to suspect but quite another to know. And besides that, I wanted to speak to my cousin."

"Did you think of something regarding Jonathan?" Leonora asked, feeling a pang of guilt at how far her mind had wandered from the search for her brother's killer since their arrival.

"Perhaps," Freddy said, kissing the end of her nose. "It occurred to me this morning that your brother might have spent the night here in this house before the race in which he was killed. And I wondered if my cousin had sent his things back to your father."

It was something that had never occurred to her, and she was suddenly glad that Frederick was investigating this situation with her. "What did he say?"

"Jonathan did stay here that night," Frederick said, the frown lines around his mouth pronounced as he spoke.

"And his things?" Leonora asked, trying not to think about what her brother's last moments had been like. Here, in the home of a man who had planned his demise.

Far from the father and sister who loved him.

"They are here," Frederick said with a sigh. "Or they were. Gerard said that he'd had them boxed up and put in the attics, but the footman he sent to retrieve them couldn't find them. I thought perhaps you and I could look for them later."

She wanted to go look for them that very minute, but Leonora knew that if either of them didn't show up downstairs at the appointed time for the trip to the folly, Sir Gerard and Lady Melisande would remark upon it.

As if reading her thoughts, Frederick touched her cheek and said, "We'll go as soon as we can after dinner tonight, I promise you."

Nodding, she went in search of her hat and pelisse and they made their way downstairs to the drawing room.

If the good cheer she'd felt after last night's festivities had dissipated in the wake of recalling their true reason for journeying here, that was all right. Perhaps she'd needed to recall that their engagement was just an illusion created for the sake of the hunt.

Twenty

I couldn't help but notice that you and your young man disappeared last night during the game," Lady Darleigh said to Leonora as they walked behind the others along the winding path leading through the landscaped gardens of South Haven.

Leonora had thought she would escape the walk without any reference to the evening before. After all, the game had clearly been chosen because it offered the opportunity for couples to find a quiet corner in which to euphemistically spend time together. Lady Darleigh, it would seem, either hadn't known, or was simply too curious to stop herself.

"We got trapped in a closet on the upper floors," Leonora lied with ease born of years spent deflecting the snide remarks of society gossips. "By the time we managed to get the door open, everyone else was gone and we decided to go to bed."

"I meant nothing by it," Lady Darleigh said with a dark blush. "I only meant that you missed the to-do when Lady Melisande shouted at Sir Gerard. It was quite a scene, I can assure you."

Despite her dislike of gossip in general, Leonora found her curiosity piqued. "What happened?" she asked, careful not to walk too quickly lest they move into earshot of the others.

"Sir Gerard went to look for a hiding place with Mrs. Chater," Lady Darleigh said in a low voice. "I hadn't realized he had any interest in her. She's such a mousy little thing."

Astonished, Leonora could not disagree.

"I think perhaps they'd come to some sort of understanding about things, because when Lady Melisande found him with Mrs. Chater in the study, she accused him of going against their agreement. It was quite a loud altercation. I'm rather surprised you didn't hear them shouting. I know the rest of us all came running as soon as she shrieked."

Leonora didn't bother offering up an excuse for why she and Freddy—supposedly trapped in a closet—hadn't been able to hear the contretemps. "I must say, I'm rather shocked that her reaction was so strong," she admitted. "I find Lady Melisande to be rather cold, don't you?"

"Yes," Lady Darleigh said quickly. "That is why I was so surprised at her strong response. I supposed she was indifferent to her husband at best. But apparently, she cares about his affair with Mrs. Chater. Either that or she's angry because he went back on his word. Whatever that promise might have been about."

"Perhaps he said he would not see Mrs. Chater during this particular party," Leonora said, pulling her pelisse more tightly around her. It was chilly out today, just as Lady Melisande had said it was. And she was grateful she'd changed into the wool for she'd have spent the entire walk miserable otherwise.

"Perhaps," Lady Darleigh agreed. "But there seemed to be more to it than that. It felt like the ending of something. I don't know, though. One never really knows what goes on within the privacy of a marriage."

Speaking of marriages, Leonora thought. "I wonder about that issue you mentioned to me before—your fears concerning what Sir Gerard might do to your husband if he leaves," she said to the other woman. "Has that changed at all, or are you still worried?"

Lady Darleigh paused a moment before responding. "I did think that it was getting better," she admitted, brushing at a lock of hair that had worked its way out of her chignon. "But that was before we made this trip."

Before Leonora could reply, Lady Darleigh continued, "You know that as the crow flies, Sir Gerard's estate isn't far from the stretch of road where your brother was found."

Leonora gasped at the other woman's words. It hadn't occurred to her the place where her brother had been murdered was in the vicinity.

But if the racers had departed from South Haven, then it made sense. "I didn't know," she said, her voice calmer than she felt. "If you'll forgive, me, I thought the Anarchists were meant to travel from London to Dartford when they drove as a club."

Lady Darleigh shook her head. "London to Dartford is only for the monthly processions involving the whole club. These smaller races, which are only open to those of Sir Gerard's choosing, take the route from Basildon to Dartford."

Yet another circle within a circle for Gerard, Leonora thought, biting her lip. It was becoming difficult to tell the difference between the club for regular members and those aspects of the club Sir Gerard showed only to a special few.

"I'm afraid I didn't tell you the whole truth when we spoke about that day before." Lady Darleigh tucked a strand of her windblown hair behind her ear. "I was afraid, you see. That you would refuse to help us if you knew the truth of the matter."

She might have known it was only a partial truth, Leonora thought with frustration. It seemed that no one involved with the club—not even the wives—was capable of telling the honest truth. Still she could hardly rip up at the other woman when she was prepared to speak now.

"I hadn't realized," Leonora said in what she hoped was a neutral tone. "I hope you'll tell me now."

"I was here," Lady Darleigh admitted. "The day of the race. A few of the club members—including your brother—Sir Gerard and Lady Melisande and my husband and me all stayed here at South Haven the night before the race."

Not unlike the house party now, Leonora thought with a frown. With the exception that her brother wasn't here. But perhaps Freddy's presence made up for that in Sir Gerard's eyes?

"I thought my husband was going to be the one to race against Lord Payne that day," Lady Darleigh continued, "but Darleigh spoke with your brother that morning, and suddenly it was Jonathan who was competing against Sir Gerard. I can't deny that I felt a certain measure of relief at the knowledge."

Thinking of her brother and his propensity for rescuing those in need, Leonora had no difficulty believing that he had convinced Lord Darleigh to trade places. Jonny was one of the best drivers in England, and so too was Gerard. It would have been a much fairer competition than the earlier matchup would have been, since Darleigh, while competent, was no match for Payne.

"I know my brother changed places with your husband because he and Payne were more evenly matched," she said aloud, "but why then did Lord Payne trade places with Sir Gerard?"

"No one knows for sure," Lady Darleigh said in a low voice, "but Lady Payne confided to me that she learned from her husband that Sir Gerard had wished to race your brother for some time, but your brother always refused. In this case, because he was driving in my husband's stead, he could not cry off."

A chill raced down Leonora's spine. It was almost as if Gerard had seen his opportunity to get Jonathan alone on a deserted stretch of the road, and went in for the kill. Closing her eyes against the image of her brother dead on the roadside, she took a deep breath.

Lady Darleigh was watching her closely, worry in her eyes. "I cannot tell you how sorry I am for what's happened."

"I cannot blame you," Leonora said, placing a hand on the other lady's shoulder as they continued to walk several yards behind the rest of the party. "You cannot have known what the outcome would be."

"Certainly not," Lady Darleigh said sadly. "And when I learned what happened, I was guilt-ridden. I hope you know, Miss Craven, that my husband had no idea that the race would have an outcome like that. Your brother took his place purely by chance. If we'd known . . ."

"It's all right," Leonora assured the other woman. "You can hardly be blamed for not foretelling the future. But I wonder if you noticed anything untoward that day? Or perhaps your husband did?"

"It seemed unremarkable enough," Lady Darleigh said, trudging along the path beside Leonora. "We were waiting at the Black Dog in Dartford for them to finish. I didn't know anything was wrong until Sir Gerard came riding up in a cloud of dust calling for a physician."

"He was alone?" Leonora asked, frowning. For some reason, it seemed odd that the baronet would not stay with her brother, though she supposed it was necessary that someone go in search of a surgeon.

"Yes," Lady Darleigh said, shaking her head. "He was

as calm as you please. He said there had been a terrible accident. If it had been me, I'd have been trembling from head to toe, but Sir Gerard kept a cool head."

Perhaps too cool, Leonora thought grimly.

"I didn't know at that point that your brother had taken my husband's place, or that Sir Gerard was riding for Lord Payne," Lady Darleigh explained, shuddering at the memory. "My first thought on seeing Sir Gerard shouting for a physician was that my Robert had been killed. I was beside myself with worry, but finally Lady Melisande managed to get through to me that it had been Jonathan driving and not Robert. I'm so sorry to admit such a thing to you. But if you knew how much I rely upon my husband."

"Please don't apologize," Leonora assured her. She could imagine herself in the same position and knew she'd have been frantic with worry. It wasn't Lady Darleigh's fault that her husband had switched places without her knowing it. "I don't blame you one bit."

"Thank you, Miss Craven," the other woman said with genuine appreciation. "The thing is, my poor husband was devastated at what happened to Mr. Craven. I don't think he knew what was going to happen, either. And I know he was terribly upset about it. That's what made me wonder if he knew that your brother's accident was intended for him."

Something occurred to Leonora. "Lady Darleigh, if your husband wasn't with you, and he wasn't driving the race against Sir Gerard, then where was he that day?"

The other woman started, as if the question had never crossed her mind.

"I . . . I'm not entirely sure," she said with a frown. "He wasn't with me and Lady Melisande at the Black Dog. I suppose I thought he'd just driven back to South Haven when he learned he wasn't going to race."

Hmm. It was a puzzle. Because Leonora wasn't entirely sure that Lord Darleigh was innocent in the matter. A man would do a great deal to protect his own life and that of his wife. A great deal that he might otherwise find unconscionable.

Aloud, however she reassured Lady Darleigh. "I wish you wouldn't trouble yourself so," she said. "Your husband is safe and that's all there is to it. I know my brother would say as much."

"But that's just it," Lady Darleigh said in an undertone. "My husband examined his own carriage later that day before we drove back to London, and he found something that made him think that perhaps despite your brother taking his place, he was still someone's target."

"What do you mean?"

"My husband's groom found that one of his traces had been cut," Lady Darleigh said in little more than a whisper. "They discovered it before we departed for London, thank goodness, else we'd have risked our own necks. But he did wonder if it had been done as some sort of payback. For trading places with Jonathan."

Leonora was quiet. What a tangled mess this affair was.

"Robert never goes anywhere without examining every bit of his leather and checking the vehicle for soundness, as well," Lady Darleigh said in a low voice. "And I rather think he blames Lord Payne for what happened. He believes Lord Payne thinks him a coward for agreeing to switch with your brother in the first place."

Since Lord Payne's whereabouts during the race had been, like Darleigh's, unknown, it was not impossible that the two men had been together.

Working on behalf of Sir Gerard? There was no way of knowing without speaking to the men herself.

By this time they'd caught up with the others, who

were nearing the crest of the hill where a pretty Grecian folly had been built by South Haven's previous owners. The façade looked to be stone, but upon closer inspection, it was revealed to be painted wood. The floor of the enclosure proved to be real marble, however, and as she climbed the steps and walked between the Doric columns, Leonora felt as if she were walking into an adult version of a children's playhouse.

"You looked to be deep in conversation with Lady Darleigh," Frederick said as he stepped up beside her, taking her arm in his.

"Later," she said in a low voice as they ventured into the small edifice and then out the other side into the pretty garden that lay between the folly and the wood. "I wonder that your cousin has kept this place up. It doesn't seem like the sort of thing a sportsman would find interesting."

"I suspect," Freddy said with a wry smile, "my cousin feels that a gentleman of property is required to have a folly on his estate. He once said as much when we were boys, playing in the folly at my father's country estate. Gerard has some very stringent ideas of what it takes to be a gentleman, and most of them have little to do with conduct and everything to do with possessions."

"Like the shelves of books in his library that remain uncut and never read," Leonora said with a moue of distaste. "It goes against my own code to let books go untouched. Especially when they were obviously chosen for the color of binding rather than the content within them."

"Exactly," Freddy said, taking her elbow as she took a seat on a stone bench. "It is about appearances. And perhaps on some level proving a point to those he sees as looking down on him."

"He's certainly not destitute," Leonora said. "He is the nephew of a duke and appears to have as much money as he could wish—no matter how he might have acquired it."

"It might interest you to know that this folly looks a great deal like the one at Lisle House." Freddy dropped down beside her, picking up a blade of grass and splitting it in two.

But Leonora was not distracted by the grass.

"How is it possible that his folly is so like your father's?" she demanded.

"An unusual coincidence?" He shrugged. "I was rather less polite when I saw it from the road yesterday."

"Why didn't you tell me?" she asked, remembering he'd seemed fine when they arrived at South Haven's entrance.

"I didn't really want to talk about it," he said. "Gerard has been jealous of my father from the time he and his mother first came to live in Lisle House. I think he was bitter because my father was a duke, but his father wasn't."

Leonora's eyes widened. It hadn't occurred to her that Sir Gerard and Lady Melisande were trying to compete with anyone in particular. "Just like this one?" she asked, looking back at the folly.

"This is perhaps grander," he said ruefully. "My grandfather built the one at Lisle House. My father has always hated it, though as children we had great fun there. I suppose Gerard recalls only that the Duke of Lisle possessed a folly so he decided that he should have one, too."

"Curious," she said, rising to look closer at a statue of a stone cherub. "His mother is your father's sister, then?"

Freddy nodded. "I suppose he's felt the sting of being a mere baronet when he himself is the grandson of a duke. It's not something I've ever refined upon. I certainly don't envy my eldest brother his position as the heir. I'd find my life constricted in any number of ways that I don't now need to worry about."

"Like being forced to marry a wealthy titled lady?" she asked, suddenly realizing that if he were the eldest he'd never have given her a second glance. Or if he had, they'd be discussing an arrangement far less respectable than the one they had.

"Like that," he said, kissing her head. "But mostly being at the beck and call of any number of poor relations or petitioners who see you as the means to an end. My father has spent most of his adult life responding to various queries from aunts, uncles, nieces, nephews, tenants, villagers, and the like. I'm a selfish fellow. I like being able to come and go as I please, without having to see to the needs of a dozen other people before my own."

His meaning was clear.

He didn't wish to be tied down.

She almost laughed it was so ludicrous. Had she really been protecting *him* from a childless marriage? From the way he spoke now, he disliked the idea of anyone under his protection.

She might have been relieved at his obvious reluctance for children, if only she didn't desperately want them. Yesterday when things had been going so well between them, she'd even allowed herself to imagine that they could find some poor child without parents to adopt as their own.

But clearly that was just a fantasy.

She disentangled herself from him suddenly and walked briskly toward the little pond at the center of the folly's garden. Busying herself with removing a tangle of vines from the plaque there, she heard him approach without turning to greet him.

"I didn't mean you, Leonora," he said quietly from behind her. "I was talking about the myriad of people who place demands on the ducal estate. I would rather not feel that kind of responsibility. That's all I meant."

But Leonora wasn't listening.

She'd managed to remove most of the vines from the plaque.

The pond was dedicated to the memory of a child, whose birth and death dates were only fifty or so years in the past. And possessed of a depressingly small number of years between them.

The child had died long ago, but all Leonora could see was her own babe. Fully formed and so achingly sweet. A little girl, who'd not even lived long enough to draw her first breath.

Her eyes stung from the effort of holding back tears.

When she didn't answer him, Freddy stepped up beside her so that he could read the little memorial. "Just a wee one," he said softly, placing his hand over hers where it rested on the death date. "Darling, I didn't mean to hurt your feelings. I really was speaking of all those other people."

But she was beyond that now. It seemed that every time she began to visualize a way out of her prison of loneliness, some reminder that she was not quite worthy appeared.

Whether it was Freddy's dislike of managing a ducal household or the memorial to a child who'd died before Leonora was even born, the message was the same.

No family for you.

"I'm not angry," she said, regaining her composure. "I was simply bothered by this small child's memorial. Such a short life he had. It is sad. That's all."

He made a noise that sounded skeptical, but to her relief, he didn't press her. "I imagine my cousin didn't even know this plaque was here," he said, helping her remove the rest of the vines from the stone. "It is rather like Gerard to buy something then not pay the least bit of attention to it. It's the owning he likes, not the caring for."

"He's not unlike most men in that," she said wryly. She stood and brushed her hands off on her skirts, and heard Lady Melisande calling her guests to where the army of footmen and maids who'd followed discreetly behind them as they trekked to the folly had set up a table laden with a feast far too sumptuous to be called a picnic.

"Shall we?" Frederick asked, his expression seeming to ask more than that.

Her heart constricting in her chest, Leonora put her hand in his and allowed him to lead her to the table.

Twenty-one

*A*fter the picnic lunch, which Freddy had found a trifle extravagant even for his cousin, the partygoers trekked back to the manor house. Leonora, whom he admitted with a touch of masculine pride hadn't gotten a great deal of sleep the night before, retired for an afternoon nap, while Freddy wandered down to the library in search of one of his cousin's uncut three-volume novels.

When he stepped into the room, however, he found that Gerard was there, albeit not immersed in a book. He was in a discussion with Lord Payne, which stopped abruptly as soon as Freddy opened the door.

"Don't mind me," he said, beginning to back out again.

But his cousin held up a hand. "One moment, Lord Frederick, if you please. I was just about to go in search of you, so this visit is fortuitous."

Curious despite himself, Freddy stepped in and shut the door behind him, sensing that whatever it was that Gerard wished to discuss was not something that should be open to public scrutiny.

"How can I be of help?" he asked, taking the seat beside Lord Payne, who had stretched out his trunklike legs before him. "I must warn you that I cannot let you drive my team as promised because my leader strained a fetlock on the journey here."

Gerard, who'd been watching him with what Freddy could only describe as a speculative expression, touched his forefingers together. "I do not wish to drive, cousin," he said. "Besides I'm the leader of the foremost driving club in England, I've no doubt driven better horseflesh."

Freddy decided it wasn't the best time to inform his cousin that he himself didn't have a spare carriage and he considered himself to be a fine specimen. But then he wasn't the leader of the Lords of Anarchy. He supposed that sort of responsibility would weigh upon one.

"Then you must tell me," he said with a shrug. "I'll be happy to oblige if I am able."

And if it's legal.

"You have no notion of how happy that makes me," Gerard said with a chuckle that sounded just the slightest bit sinister. Or perhaps that was just Freddy embellishing for his own amusement. His mind did that sometimes.

"We need you to do something as a club member," Lord Payne said with a grin that revealed he'd partaken of the spinach pie that had been served at lunch. Rather than inform the other man, Freddy let it pass, considering that he still bore the bruises from their last encounter. "Something that you will perhaps find unpleasant."

Since Freddy had found very little about being a member of the Lords of Anarchy to be anything remotely resembling pleasant, he was not surprised to hear it. "I will simply have to hear what it is and then make my decision."

Gerard laughed again, this time harder. "Frederick, I vow, I find your conversation to be most amusing. Indeed, I don't remember you being such a pleasant companion when we were lads."

Perhaps that was because Gerard had spent much of

their boyhood running after Freddy and his brothers, begging them to let him play with them, he thought ruefully. He wondered idly if their treatment of him as a boy had had some impact on the man he'd become. Then again, it was impossible to know that sort of thing. After all, he'd spent a fair enough time begging his brothers to let him in on their games and he'd turned out all right.

"I beg you will tell me what it is you ask," he said, tiring of the suspense. "I am not a great fan of secrets, I must tell you."

"Very well," Lord Payne said, showing that bit of spinach again. "We have a task that must be done. And since you are the newest member of the club, it falls to you."

"Ah." Freddy sighed. So it was to be some unpleasant chore. Perhaps riding back to town to ask some unsuspecting fellow to pay his dues. Though come to think of it there had been no mention of dues. "Well, I feel sure it will be something I can do. Though I must warn you that I will not leave Miss Craven here alone. I take that part of my duties to her quite seriously and I would not like leaving her here in a house where she is unfamiliar with most of the other guests."

"Your concern does you credit, cousin," Sir Gerard said, doing that thing with his fingers again. "But I assure you that this task is one that will take but an afternoon. And you can do it here at South Haven."

"Excellent," Freddy said, relaxing a bit. He hadn't liked the idea of telling Leonora that they would have to leave before solving the mystery of her brother's death. "So, what is it, then?"

"You proved yourself to be quite accomplished when it comes to bare-knuckle fisticuffs," Lord Payne said, grinning. Really, Freddy was going to have to tell the man about the spinach or it would turn everyone's stomach. "We would like you to use those skills on Lord Darleigh."

Freddy frowned as the other man's words sank in. "You want me to fight Lord Darleigh? As much as I'd like to oblige, gentlemen, I must respectfully decline. Or haven't you looked at my face today?" The bruise on his eye had turned bright purple.

"It's not a request, Lord Frederick," Lord Payne said. Or growled, rather. "It is an order. And you needn't worry about Darleigh messing up that pretty face of yours. For he'll be tied up while you have a go at him."

But this statement did less, rather than more, to put Freddy at his ease.

"You're asking me to beat Lord Darleigh while his hands are tied? So that he cannot defend himself?" He knew that the Lords of Anarchy were not the stuff honorable dreams were made of, but at least he thought they played in the vague vicinity of honorable. Not so.

"In God's name, why?" he demanded. "What has Darleigh done to deserve such treatment?"

"That's not important," Payne growled. "It won't make a difference. You're not the one who makes the decision, Sir Gerard is."

"Suffice it to say," Gerard interjected, "that Lord Darleigh has earned the displeasure of his fellow Anarchists. By trying to leave us. And you really must know, cousin, 'Once an Anarchist, always an Anarchist.'"

Freddy stared at his cousin, a sense of inevitability pressing down on him. One way or another, they would make him beat Darleigh, he knew it in his gut. But he would try to talk them out of it while he could.

"I will not do it, gentlemen," he said calmly. "And I think now I'll just go and inform Miss Craven that we should be on our way this afternoon. I apologize for leaving your party so soon, cousin, but I feel that it is necessary."

"How would you feel if something untoward were

to happen to your Miss Craven, cousin?" Gerard asked softly, his eyes narrowed as if he were sizing Freddy up to determine how far he could push him.

"What do you mean?" he asked silkily, his fists clenching against his thighs. "For I must warn you that if you are threatening Miss Craven, Sir Gerard, then I will be forced to demand satisfaction."

Rather than flinch as any other man in his right mind would do, Sir Gerard grinned. "Are you calling me out, by God? I vow, you are amusing, Freddy, make no mistake about it. But let me assure you that if you do not do as Lord Payne and I ask, that is, use those brutal fists of yours on Lord Darleigh, I shall be forced to see to it that Miss Craven makes the acquaintance of any number of the gentlemen at this party. To such a degree that she might not be willing or able to marry you afterward. You understand that, don't you, cousin?"

And before Freddy could smash his fist into his cousin's grinning jester's face, he found his arms pinned behind him by Lord Payne, who had moved more quietly than Freddy had guessed a man of his size could.

"I will kill you for this, Gerry," Freddy said through clenched teeth. "Kill. You."

"There, there, old boy," Gerard said, unmoved by his cousin's threat. "I will see to it that Miss Craven isn't touched, so long as you do as we ask."

"Come along, Lord Frederick," said Lord Payne as he gripped Freddy's arms. "We've got to get you ready for your fight." And as Freddie was led through a door in the wall he'd not even known was there, he sent up a silent prayer that Leonora would, as his cousin promised, remain safe.

Despite her exhaustion from lack of sleep, Leonora found herself unable to settle down long enough for a true nap. After tossing in her bed for three quarters of an hour, she finally cried defeat and got up and got dressed again.

During one of their after-dinner conversations, Lady Melisande had boasted about the quality of horseflesh in the Fincher stables, so, knowing she hadn't the concentration to read, Leonora decided to go investigate. Perhaps a few minutes with the animals would clear her mind.

And if Jonathan had been a frequent visitor to South Haven, perhaps he too had touched those same stalls, scratched the noses of those horses.

It was a fanciful notion, but after the memorial stone by the pond, she was caught in some place where the memories of the dead seemed to hover among the living.

Her shawl around her shoulders, she followed the path from the house to the stables, and was surprised to find them deserted. She was no expert, but weren't stables supposed to be in constant motion? With grooms and riders and the like taking care of . . . things? In truth she had little notion of what went into keeping stables since she spent most of her time in London where the mews to their town house was shamefully small. But surely things were much more stable-oriented in the country?

The quiet, however, meant that she could investigate without having watchful eyes on her, so she took advantage of it. The smell of fresh hay and clean dirt met her nose as she wandered into the shadowed recesses of the building. In the first stall she saw a pretty bay mare who knickered, and tossed her black mane when Leonora reached in to pet her nose.

"What a sweet girl," she crooned at the big animal, and when the mare pressed her snout into Leonora's hand in search of a treat, she regretted not coming prepared to bribe the horses with apples or lumps of sugar. "I'm sorry," she said, rubbing the spot between the horse's eyes—where the horse herself was unlikely to be able to reach for herself. "I promise next time, I'll bring a treat. Perhaps some hay?" She grabbed a handful from one of the bales stacked against the wall and that seemed to please the horse.

"Now," she said, speaking to the horse since there was no one else about to have this discussion with. "Do you suppose someone would be mad enough to hide something in here?" Her eyes scanned the interior of the stable, looking for someplace that would afford a nook or cranny in which to stow cut traces or a sawed-through bit of carriage siding.

Then, she saw them. Two wide doors, facing across the wide expanse of the center aisle. Wide enough to hide a coach?

Or maybe an unscathed curricle?

Her heart beating with excitement, she strode quickly to the one on the right and tried the door. It was unlocked, and when she opened the door, it was completely dark inside. Opening the door wider, so the sunlight could get in, she looked inside and was disappointed to find only saddles neatly stacked, and a wall of bridles, and other tack that seemed designed for riding and not driving.

Shutting the door behind her, she moved to the other side and realized just how wide this door was in comparison to the other. From the other end of the barn they'd seemed identical. But now seeing them close up, she noticed one was definitely much wider. Curious, she thought as she tried the handle of this door. It, however, was locked.

Cursing silently, she scanned the room for somewhere a key might be stored. And noted the little office on the other side of the stable. When she pushed into the door, there on the wall, neatly labeled no less, was a row of keys. Finding one labeled "carriage room" she removed the key and pocketed it lest someone wander in and ask what she was doing.

To her relief, the key worked when she tried it in the lock, and deciding this room needed a lantern, she carefully removed one from where it hung on a peg, already lit.

Barn fires were quite dangerous, so she was meticulous about not swinging the lamp or touching it to any surface.

Opening the door of the second room wider, she held up the lamp, which cast a semicircle of light onto the contents.

And gasped.

She remembered the red paint with gold trim from the day Jonny brought it home, the grin on his face as wide as the Thames and as bright as the sun.

Leonora had twitted him about how much of his allowance had gone toward paying for the vehicle that had been built for speed rather than for safety. And he'd assured her that it was as safe as the driver who handled her.

Brushing away a tear at the memory, she carefully shut the door behind her.

It was intact. This sporting carriage that Sir Gerard and his cronies had assured her more than once had been stolen by thieves was hidden in a dark corner of Sir Gerard's stables and was very much intact.

If she'd had any doubts about whether her host knew more than he was telling about her brother's demise, then this must surely put period to them.

Setting her jaw, she hung the lantern on a peg on the wall of the carriage room and methodically examined the curricle from top to bottom, tip to tail.

For this curricle was not only unblemished, it was in the same condition as it had been when her brother drove it home from the carriage builders that first day.

She wondered if he'd realized then that his enthusiasm for driving would one day get him killed. Even if he had known, she suspected, he wouldn't have stopped driving.

For the one-hundredth time she wished that despite their grief she and her father had investigated things more thoroughly. She'd not even had the heart to examine her brother's remains when they were brought back to London for burial. Nor had her father, who had declared he wished to remember his son as he had been while living. Not in death.

It could have been anything, she thought, suddenly feeling overwhelmed by the possibilities. It was even possible—though hardly likely—that Jonny was alive somewhere and they'd buried some poor stranger in the Craven plot. She leaned her head against the stable wall and took a deep breath. What a waste. What an awful waste of a good man.

When she had regained her composure, she took one last look around the room, and noticed a flash of white in the corner of the box beneath the driver's seat.

Curious. She stepped forward and lifted the seat to reveal the hidden compartment there where drivers stored personal items, like gloves, handkerchiefs, and she knew in her brother's case, a bottle of blue ruin he'd bought in his salad days to add authenticity to the game of pretend that he was a driver on the stage line. The scrap of white cloth she found, however, was far too small to be a man's handkerchief. And it was embroidered in the corner with the initial *C*.

Lady Darleigh's first name was Corinne. Might she have left this here during a ride? Or perhaps Leonora's brother had hidden it there. Either way, it was a clue, and one she needed to show Frederick immediately.

Carefully closing and locking the door to the carriage room behind her, she slipped back into the office to hang the key where she'd found it.

She was stepping out of the office when she looked up to see Lord Payne striding toward her.

"Miss Craven," the big man said, a bit of green shining from between his front teeth, "you shouldn't be wandering around by yourself. You're likely to run into trouble." He stepped closer, and if he intended to intimidate her, she thought, it was working. "I wouldn't like it if anything were to happen to you."

Swallowing, Leonora stepped back from the man. "I am always getting up to some mischief, Lord Payne. You must know that about me by now. But I will heed you for now. I think there might be a storm coming from the looks of those clouds." She gestured to the horizon, where a very few dark clouds had gathered. "If you'll excuse me, I think I'll go have a bit of a lie-down before supper."

Boldly she brushed past him and all but ran down the path and into the house.

She didn't stop until she reached her bedchamber, where she closed and locked the door behind her.

Twenty-two

"Where have you been?" Freddy asked from where he'd been sitting before Leonora's fire contemplating the dilemma he now faced. "You look as if you've seen a ghost."

She jumped at the sound of his voice, and turning to brace her back against the door, she scowled. "Do not frighten me like that! What on earth do you think you're doing hiding in the shadows of my bedchamber?"

"I was waiting for you," he said calmly. "And thinking. But I must ask again where you've been. Because I know the look of a lady who's gotten away with something and you definitely have that look."

Sighing, she walked farther into the room, and removing the pins from her hat, placed it on a side table along with her wrap. "I was in the stables, if you must know," she said, excitement making her eyes sparkle. "I found something there. Something important."

Reaching out, he pulled her unceremoniously onto his lap. She gave a little shriek, but soon settled against him, relaxing a bit, though he could feel the tension of excitement in her. "Something to do with your brother, I suppose," he said, threading his fingers into hers.

He'd received a bit of a reprieve regarding the busi-

ness with Lord Darleigh, for that man had been out on
a trip to town with a few other club members when he,
his cousin, and Lord Payne had left the study that afternoon. His cousin said that they would call him when the
time for his punishment of Darleigh came, but Freddy
hoped that he and Leonora would be long gone before
that.

"I found Jonny's carriage," she said, bringing him
back to the present, pressing her hands against his chest.
"Do you understand how important that is, Freddy?"

"What condition is it in?" he asked, excitement making him sit up straighter. "Was it damaged at all? Could
you tell what happened to your brother?"

"There's not a scratch on it," she said, oblivious to his
physical discomfort as she shifted in his lap. "It's in perfect condition. You were there when Sir Gerard told me
it was stolen."

"We've known it was a lie," he said. "Or at least we
suspected as much. But now we have confirmation. Your
brother didn't crash his carriage, or take a turn too fast.
He was set upon."

"Wouldn't there be blood on the carriage seats?" Leonora asked. "I saw nothing like that. Perhaps he was
killed elsewhere?"

"Or my cousin has a very good valet," Freddy coun-
tered. "I know my own can remove just about any stain
you put in front of him. He'd grumble about being asked
to clean a carriage, but I have no doubt Gerard has a man
who is loyal enough to keep secrets. Else he'd have been
brought to the authorities by now."

"And we've already seen," Leonora said, running her
fingers through his hair, "that your cousin has far-reaching
influence. People are frightened of him, and that means
they are afraid of crossing him, as well. When he asks
them to look the other way, they do it."

Freddy thought back to that afternoon and his cousin's words. "I suppose you're right, but it's disheartening to know he doesn't care about the difference between fear and loyalty."

"He's a bully," Leonora said firmly. "A bully who is capable of finding out what one loves most and using it against you."

The threats against Leonora rose in his mind and Freddy's jaw tightened. He was damned if he'd let himself be used in that way by his cousin. He'd already killed one man. Was he really willing to kill another just to keep that secret?

"I won't let him hurt you, Nora," Freddy said, pulling her hard against him. Kissing her with the ferocity that had been lurking beneath the surface all afternoon. "Even if you decide not to marry me when this is all over, I promise you that I will keep you safe."

Despite her misgivings about marriage, Leonora knew that she would never love another like she loved him. And suddenly she wanted to capture every bit of happiness she could before she had to say good-bye.

"I need you, Leonora," Freddy said hoarsely, beginning to rise from the chair.

"Stop," she said sharply. "Let's stay here. In the chair."

He looked into her eyes and saw desire and daring there. "All right," he said, taking her face in his hand and rubbing his thumb along her lower lip. "We'll stay here."

With a catlike smile, she rose up and unbuttoned the back of her gown, letting the bodice fall, then pushing the rest of it over her hips and down to the floor. His eyes went straight to where the tops of her breasts mounded above her stays, and unable to keep his hands off her, he unthreaded the laces and removed the constricting garment. Giving a little sigh at being freed from the tight stays, she bent a little and taking her shift by the hem she pulled it up and over her head until she was standing before him in nothing but her garters and stockings.

Freddy wasn't sure where he wanted to start as he took in every glorious exposed inch of her. When he reached out to touch her, she batted his hand away.

"Not yet," she said with a raised brow. "You don't touch until I tell you you can touch."

He swallowed. He was going to like this game. "Yes, ma'am."

The obedience made her happy, he could see it in the way her lush lips curved upward.

Moving closer, she leaned forward and slipped her fingers into the soft folds of his cravat, and finding the jeweled pin there, unfastened it and set it aside. Then taking the end of his carefully knotted neckcloth, she untied it, and slowly, carefully, unwound it from his neck. Moving to kneel on his lap, she leaned forward to kiss the hollow below his Adam's apple.

"Lovely," she whispered, running her finger down and over the exposed skin at the neck of his shirt. There was just enough room on either side of his hips in the large chair for her to place her knees there. Rising up on her knees, she brought her breasts up to the same level as his mouth, and when she lifted one plump globe to his lips, Freddy couldn't resist touching his tongue to the tip. Her sharp intake of breath let him know that despite her calling of the shots she was not unaffected by their little game.

Moving to her other side, to suckle it, he slid his hands over the silky skin of her torso and held her still for his ministrations. She gasped, but not to be outdone, she slid her hand down to where his hardness threatened to burst from his breeches, and rubbed a not quite steady hand over it. And Freddy lost the rhythm of his suckling.

"God, Freddy," she exhaled as he moved his hips out

a bit in the chair, so that his phallus was at just the right angle to brush against the apex of her thighs. Using her thigh muscles, she moved up and down, while he worshipped her breasts, and when the pressure became too great, he pushed her back a little and unfastened the fall of his breeches, allowing his cock to spring forth.

She moved forward and down a little to bring the head into contact with her core and they both gasped with the pleasure of it. Rubbing himself in her wetness, he stroked his thumb over her bud of pleasure and Leonora jerked, gasping.. When it became almost too much to bear, Freddy took her hips in his hands and thrust up a little, his cock poised at her entrance.

The tease of her slick heat threatened his weakening control.

"My God, that's good," he said against her breast. "I need to be all the way inside you, Nora. Now."

Her breath coming in short gasps, she lowered her weight on her knees, and while he slowly pressed upward, she took him into her body. When he was fully seated they stilled.

Savoring the feel of it.

Then, just when Freddy thought his control would snap, she rose up a little on her knees, every inch marked with delicious friction. She lowered again on a gasp and then up, setting a rhythm as old as time.

He strained to keep himself from letting go, determined to make it good for her.

But it was almost more than he could bear. The silk of her skin, the warm heat clasping his prick, the scents and sounds of their lovemaking were all pushing him toward the edge.

Finally, on a downstroke, Leonora broke rhythm and, with a sharp gasp, spasmed around him, her movements erratic as the ecstasy of the climax took over. Finally allowing himself to let go, Freddy thrust into her, gripping her hips in hands that trembled with desire. They moved together in a frenzy until, with a shout, he stiffened and emptied himself within her.

A few minutes later, feeling as if his legs were made of jelly, he rose from the chair with Leonora in his arms and carried her to the bed, where he somehow managed to pull back the counterpane and deposit her on the sheets. Keeping his gaze on her, he fastened the fall of his breeches

"That was interesting," she said with a kittenish grin. "I don't think I quite knew what I was starting there."

Moving to sit on the edge of the bed, he whistled softly. "If that was a first attempt, then you are a very good beginner, love."

A shadow moved into her eyes. "Of course it was a first attempt," she said with a frown. "I hardly go around seducing gentlemen every day."

A pang in the vicinity of his heart made him reach out to take her hand. "Of course not. I didn't mean that. Only that it was quite well done. That's all."

Her eyes still troubled, she nodded. "I saw something like it in a book once."

That was surprising. And fascinating. "Do you still have it?"

A blush crept into her cheeks. "Of course not," she said, her expression reminding him of a disapproving schoolmarm. "It was in a shop. I wandered into a section where ladies weren't allowed. But as you know, I never was much of a one for such restrictions."

He laughed softly. "No, you never were, were you?"

She reached out and stroked a lock of hair from his forehead. "I thought about demanding that the proprietor let me purchase it just like any other customer. But

I decided it wouldn't be worth the unhappiness it would cause my father. He did try to keep me on a tight leash in those days. Before he lost all illusions of reining me in, that is."

"Poor fellow," Freddy said, only half joking. "I think your father and your brother both worried far more about you than you can possibly have imagined."

Looking down at her hands, Leonora smiled sadly. "I did give my poor brother a difficult time of it, didn't I? I never meant to. Only to do what I thought I should be entitled to do as a human being. Not a lady or a gentleman. A person."

He touched her lightly on the cheek, and she turned into the caress like a cat seeking a stroke. "I know you did," he said softly. "And I feel sure that Jon did, too. He once lamented your pigheadedness, but in the same breath he expressed just how proud he was of you for never backing down from a fight you thought worth fighting."

She looked up, her eyes shrinking. "Truly?" she asked, sitting up to move closer to him. "Did he really say such a thing?"

"He did," Freddy said with a soft kiss. "He loved you. And I know he'd be bursting with pride to know how far you've come in the investigation into his death."

"I've found very little," she said with a sigh. "All we know for sure is that Jonathan is dead."

"Not all," he responded with seriousness. "You also know that my cousin had something to do with it, and that someone is keen to cover up the true nature of the death. I should say that's a great deal more than anyone else who's looked into this mess knows."

"I suppose," she said without any real enthusiasm. "And we found the carriage, which proves definitively that there was no accident. I wonder if Lord Payne knew the carriage was there."

At the mention of Payne, Freddy frowned. "What has Payne to do with it? Besides being my cousin's right-hand man?"

"He saw me leaving the stables this afternoon. Just after I found Jonny's carriage," she responded with a shrug. "I could see that he thought I was up to something, but I was able to evade him and get up here, thank goodness." She grimaced. "In a completely unrelated detail, he had a bit of spinach from lunch stuck between his teeth." She shuddered. "If he weren't already a frightening man based on his personality, that bit of spinach sealed his fate as completely ineligible for me."

Freddy was diverted by the spinach comment, but the real detail in Leonora's speech that caught his attention was Payne's appearance in the barn. "Do you think he suspected something? Or was he simply being his usual charming self?"

Her brow furrowed. "Perhaps I was simply feeling guilty because I'd been putting my nose where it didn't belong," she acceded, "but I do think there was more intimidation in his demeanor than he usually displays."

Debating whether to tell her about what Lord Payne and his cousin had told him that afternoon, Freddy finally decided against it.

Given her fright that afternoon, Leonora already had quite a bit to worry about.

"I think I'll have a bath before dinner," he said suddenly, rising from the bed with reluctance. "Perhaps you can sleep now?"

To his amusement, her eyes were already half closed. "Just for a few minutes," she said, her voice trailing off.

At least one of them could rest, Freddy thought wryly.

* * *

"I must speak with you, Miss Craven," hissed Lady Melisande to Leonora that evening as the ladies made their way to the drawing room after supper.

Leonora had spent the meal listening with half an ear to Lady Summerton's chatter while her mind was wrestling with what she'd found that afternoon in the stables. There had to be some way for her to confront Sir Gerard about Jonny's intact curricle without endangering her entire party. But she could think of no way to do it.

Lady Melisande's attempt to get her attention was a welcome diversion, to say the least. "Of course, Lady Melisande," she said in a low voice as they stepped into the drawing room behind the others. "Where?"

Her hostess laid a finger over her lips and indicated that Leonora should come with her to the small parlor across the hall where the lady of the house wrote letters. Or so she informed her guests their first night in South Haven.

"I must show Miss Craven the interesting letter I received from my mother this afternoon, ladies," Lady Melisande said to the room in general as she led Leonora across the hall and shut the door firmly behind them.

"Whatever is the matter?" Leonora asked, noting that the other woman was trembling. "What's happened?"

Unbidden, the thought of Freddy injured or hurt, or worse, dead, rose into her mind's eye. She schooled her features and tried not to demand that the other woman tell her at once.

"Miss Craven," Lady Melisande said hoarsely, "in one hour from now the gentlemen of the Lords of Anarchy are gathering in a large barn on our property so that your fiancé can beat one of the other members into a bloody pulp. I believe my husband means for your fiancé to kill him."

Leonora stiffened. "What? That's absurd. Freddy would never agree to such a thing, whether it was bidden by this ridiculous club or not. He is an honorable man and would not fight an unfair fight."

"Even if my husband and Lord Payne threatened you in order to coerce him into it?" Lady Melisande said sharply. "Because I can assure you my husband will use any means necessary to get his own way. And he long ago realized that you are Lord Frederick Lisle's weak spot. If you are to stop your fiancé from doing real damage to this other man then you must get him away from here at once."

It was too much to take in, but Leonora found her brain was working overtime. Perhaps because of the danger inherent in the situation. "Why are you helping me, Lady Melisande?" she demanded of the other woman. "You never showed any particular liking for me, but now you are offering me a way to escape your husband's machinations. Why?"

"Do you think I enjoy this way of life, Miss Craven?" the other lady demanded. "For I can assure you I do not. My husband likes to think he is the king of a tiny kingdom of men willing to do his bidding. But what he really is, is a madman. I intend to see to it that your brother is the last man to die at my husband's hands. But you must help me to do it."

"All right," Leonora said. And together, the ladies came up with a plan. Leonora would have Freddy's coachman and grooms ready his carriage for them to leave that night. And her aunt would be driven to one of her nearby friends' estates as soon as possible.

"I do not believe my husband will harm your aunt," Lady Melisande explained. "He will be angry, but as it's your aunt and not Lord Frederick's he will not see her as a valuable pawn in his game." Which was a relief, since Leonora was unsure whether her aunt would agree to leave on such short notice.

"Now," Lady Melisande said with authority. "You must go. Hurry. There isn't much time."

Mindful of her words, Leonora walked as quickly as she could without drawing attention to herself to the wing of the house where Aunt Hortense had been holding court. For someone who claimed to be at death's door, she looked fit as a fiddle when Leonora stepped into her bed-chamber.

Quickly, she outlined their need to leave at once, a plan which Hortense readily agreed to.

"I have been bored almost to death in this house, gel," she told Leonora. "I wish you'd asked me to leave sooner!"

Leonora wasn't sure she and her aunt had been at the same house party, but for the sake of expedience did not say so. "I will see you back in London after you've spent a few days resting at Lady Mumford's home. Will that be agreeable?"

The old woman gave what would in a younger person have been a shrug. "I suppose it will have to do. Clara is a bit of a hypochondriac, but I shall manage to endure it for a few days. Then when I hear from you that the coast is clear I will leave for London."

Relief washed over Leonora. "Thank you for agreeing so readily, aunt. I was afraid you'd be difficult."

"Never fear," Aunt Hortense said, hugging Leonora with surprising heartiness. "I will do as you wish. You just make sure that young man of yours is able to escape this serpent's nest unscathed."

Since Leonora had told her as little as possible about their true reasons for leaving, she could only imagine that

Hortense had supplied her own story to go with the dramatic exit.

Once that was settled, she was free to pack her own bags, and to instruct Freddy's valet to pack for him as well. At exactly nine o'clock Freddy's curricle would be waiting for them at the gates to South Haven. And Lady Melisande had promised Leonora that she would see to it that her husband's perimeter guards were otherwise occupied at that time.

All that was left was for Leonora to get Freddy out of the barn, where Sir Gerard and the others had assembled to watch Freddy pummel some poor soul into dust.

She sent up a silent prayer that they'd be able to escape unscathed.

When the ladies left the men to their port after dinner that evening, Freddy felt a frisson of excitement in the air. And as soon as the men began walking through the French doors toward the barn, he guessed why.

"Tonight?" he asked his cousin as the other man walked with surprising languor toward the outbuilding. "You might have told me."

"If I'd given you the exact time, old man," Sir Gerard said with a knowing grin, "then you would have known when to make your escape."

"Are you accusing me of reneging on a promise?" Freddy demanded, his temper rising. "I said I would do as you asked, and there's an end to it."

"No need to get your back up, cousin," Sir Gerard said with a chuckle. "You'll have your chance in the ring soon enough."

By this time they'd reached the inside of the barn, which was lit up with torches along every wall. It was a large open space, which had not seen a horse or cow in a great many years if Freddy knew anything about it. A ring had been marked off with a rope attached to stakes every few feet. The other members of the club had already begun to gather around the circular enclosure and Freddy found himself being propelled to one side of the ring, while Lord Darleigh was on the other side.

"Strip to the waist," Sir Gerard said sharply, when he and Freddy got to his designated side. "I hope you've recovered enough from your match with Lord Payne to do yourself justice tonight. I should hate to see a relation of mine bested without much of a fight."

Unwinding his cravat and unbuttoning his waistcoat, Freddy chose not to point out that if his cousin was really worried about the family honor he'd dispense with this nonsense altogether and call the whole thing off. But sensing that Gerard would not find such a tirade amusing, he shrugged out of his coat, and waistcoat, then began untucking the voluminous tails of his shirt from his breeches.

When he was finally naked to the waist, the barn was loud with the sound of men chattering. And if Freddy were not mistaken, there were more men here than guests at his cousin's house. Perhaps they'd advertised the event at the local pub, he thought, puzzled. Noting the quality of the gathering's attire, he thought it more likely that his cousin had sent word to London. If that were the case, it would mean that Gerard had been planning this since long before they left London. And a jolt of anger ran through him at the thought of being used like that.

He noticed Lord Colburn, a club member, was surreptitiously moving through the crowd with a large velvet bag, which the audience members were filling with pound notes.

Suddenly, Freddy knew exactly where his cousin's fortune came from.

"I think you'll do," Gerard said from beside him,

where to Freddy's surprise his cousin began to remove his own cravat.

"What are you doing?" he demanded. If he was supposed to fight his cousin then was it to be a fight to the death? Or perhaps there was to be some sort of initiation. Where he would find himself being beaten at the hands of each member of the club.

That supposition seemed more likely when he saw that Lord Darleigh and Lord Payne were also removing their clothing above the waist.

"It's an initiation of sorts, cousin," Gerard said with a barely disguised grin. "We do this with gentlemen who show a particular affinity for leadership. And you, being so commanding, cousin, will be the perfect candidate for a role as one of my lieutenants. If, that is, you survive your initiation."

Glaring at his cousin, Freddy turned to watch as Lord Payne, his body still bearing the bruises from their bout earlier in the week, stretched his arms across the ring. Lord Darleigh, on the other hand, looked nervous. And as he shrugged out of his coat, Freddy saw that the other man was favoring his left arm, as if he'd suffered some injury to it earlier in the week.

Before he could protest again, Gerard walked into the center of the ring, his muscled torso glistening in the torchlight. "Gentlemen," he said in a loud voice, and immediately the chatter ceased. "Gentlemen, you are here tonight to witness the initiation into the Lords of Anarchy of a new member. A man who has long been known amongst the *ton* for his legendary prowess in the bedroom, at the reins, and on the dueling field. My cousin Lord Frederick Lisle might hail from one of the most respected families in England, but he has more than enough black-sheep credentials to make him a valuable member of our illustrious company."

Freddy felt the eyes of the room upon him as his cousin spoke, sick that Gerard's jealousy of him had grown to such heights that he would publicly denigrate his own family.

"To prove himself worthy of membership in the Lords of Anarchy," Gerard continued, "my cousin will have to defeat not only Lord Payne, but also myself and Lord Darleigh. Only when he has overcome all three of us at once will my cousin be welcomed into the fold as a Lord of Anarchy."

All three of them? Gerard was mad, Freddy thought as he watched the other men move toward the center of the ring. He flexed his shoulders in an unconscious preparation for the fight, though he could not imagine it would do any good. Still, he'd need to be ready if he was going to survive this madness, he thought.

Moving onto the balls of his feet, he danced around a little. He was moving into the center of the ring toward the others when a cry sounded from the edges of the crowd. "Fire!"

"Fire!" another shouted. And soon the whole barn was filled with the scent of smoke and the bellows of alarm as a rush of men hurried to escape from the enclosure.

Twenty-three

$\mathcal{L}$eonora let Freddy's groom give her a hand up into the curricle as they waited in the shadows beside the fence of Gerard's paddock. She could hear the cry of fire rippling through the crowd inside the barn and she strained her eyes to see if Chester, Freddy's valet, had been able to get to his master yet. Then she saw a flash of gold in the firelight and was relieved to see Hanson followed by a shirtless Freddy running at full speed toward them.

In one swift leap he was in the vehicle and his valet was headed for where the coach and four had been hidden.

They were almost to the gates leading out of the estate when a shout went up behind them and Leonora looked back to see that Sir Gerard had spotted them. But as he was on foot, he was impotent to do anything to stop them. Especially since his stables had been evacuated because of the fire alarm.

"Spring 'em, Smitty," Freddy barked to his groom as they took off into the night and raced as fast as the curricle would take them.

Leonora dared not speak, but appreciated the warmth of Freddy's bare arm around her shoulders.

"How did you ever manage this?" he asked when they

were finally beyond the periphery of his cousin's estate. Leonora gave him the cloak she'd brought for him which Freddy took gratefully, before asking again. "How, Leonora?"

Shaking her head, she said, "I'm not even sure how I did it. Lady Melisande told me when the ladies left the gentlemen to their port what her husband was planning tonight. And I knew that there was no way we could remain in that house without further risking our necks. So, I told Aunt Hortense to prepare herself to go to her friend's house in the next county—that is where your coach and four are headed, by the way. Along with your valet and my maid."

"All right," he said with a grin. "I can last a few days without Chester, I think."

"Then I spoke to Smith about driving the curricle and had him ready it for a long journey. Fortunately your horses were rested from our journey out here so they were ready for another one. The last thing was to put a torch to one of the hay bales. It managed to make enough of a to-do that panic set in among the men in the barn and voilà!"

She felt him staring at her in the darkness, and Leonora found herself in the unusual position of feeling bashful.

"You are an amazing woman, Leonora Craven," he said finally, kissing the top of her head. "I don't think we'd have made it out of that house alive if you hadn't arranged this escape for us."

"I feel sure you would have come up with something," she said with a slight shrug. "If you weren't faced with having to fight for membership in a club you don't even want to be a member of."

"Yes," he said with a laugh. "There's that. Thank goodness you spared me from that fate."

"Anytime, sir," she said with a giggle.

"Leonora?" he asked after a few minutes had passed.

"Yes?" she asked, snuggling up to him beneath the cloak.

"Where are we going?"

"We can't go to London because if we were seen there in this condition it would cause the scandal of the season," she said with a sigh. "So, I remembered that your friend the Earl of Mainwaring has a house not far from here."

"He does," Freddy responded, sounding surprised. In the darkness she couldn't see his expression but she thought perhaps he was puzzled.

"It was your valet's suggestion," she explained a little defensively. "He said you'd been there before and that he thought the earl wouldn't mind. I hope that's all right?"

She heard him laugh softly before he pulled her close. "It's perfectly fine, my dear. I just hadn't realized before that your talents extended to large-scale escapes and capers."

"Just because I am a poet doesn't mean my mind is always in the ether communing with the muses," she replied with a laugh. "I am rather a managing sort of female. As you will recall from the last time we were betrothed."

There was a pause and, for a moment, Leonora could only hear the sounds of the road—the jingle of the horses' tack, the wheels on the road, and the wind whipping through the trees.

"I should like to speak about that," Freddy said into the darkness. "Soon. Not tonight. I think I should very much like to be fully dressed for that discussion."

She could hear the smile in his voice and knew that whatever the discussion entailed, it would not be a difficult one. At least on his side. She had some things to discuss that would perhaps make it difficult for Freddy to forgive her. For now, however, she was just glad they were alive.

"I can wait," she said softly, leaning up to kiss his cheek.

When he turned his head to kiss her properly, she did not protest.

They reached Mainwaring's little manor house a few hours later. By that time the wind had followed them from South Haven and turned into a rainstorm, and when Freddy approached the front entrance it was miserable out.

Fortunately the butler recalled Freddy from a previous visit and welcomed their ragtag party inside with no questions asked.

He gave orders that his curricle was to be hidden in the stables and that in the event someone should call looking for them, they had not been seen.

Only when he was sure the horses and the servants had been seen to and were comfortably situated did Freddy allow himself to relax. He'd learned from his father that servants—both equine and human—were to be treated fairly and with consideration and dignity. And theirs had proved themselves tonight to be the most loyal sorts.

Though he suspected Leonora might have already fallen asleep, when he'd finished looking in on the horses, he slipped silently into her bedchamber. Quietly, he undressed and climbed into bed beside her.

"Did you see to the servants?" she asked in a sleepy voice as he slipped his arms around her.

He might have known she would guess his task. "Yes," he said against her hair. "All right and tight. We can sleep here for several hours then set out tomorrow in Mainwaring's carriage."

"You're lucky to have a friend like that," she said quietly.

"Your brother was that sort of friend, too."

"I know," she said, turning so that they were face-to-face. "He told me. If ever he needed help, it didn't matter the time of day or the circumstance, he could call on one of you. The four horsemen."

He smiled in the darkness. "That was a silly name," he admitted, remembering the day they'd come up with it. The young men they'd been.

"Perhaps," she said, nestling against his chest. "But young men are often foolish. From that silliness however were born lifelong friendships. That cannot be counted as silly,"

"I miss him," he said, thinking how all this mess with his cousin had begun. "He would have loved the adventure tonight."

"He would," she said, and he guessed that she was smiling.

"I think we should be able to bring charges against my cousin now," he said. "The fact that the curricle was there on his estate should be more than enough to prove that your brother's death was suspicious."

"I hope so," Leonora said, her voice sounding sleepy. "I want this to be over. I am ready to get back to ordinary life."

He wondered how life with her could ever be anything like ordinary, but said nothing. There would be time enough for them to discuss such things.

With a sigh, he pulled her close against him and they slept.

The next afternoon, they arrived in London, exhausted. Though he was reluctant to do so, Freddy left Leonora at her father's house with an admonition for her to rest.

Given his own exhaustion, it wasn't until the next day that he presented himself in her private parlor.

"I missed you," Freddy said, reaching out to take Leonora's hand.

"We've only been apart a matter of hours," she responded, squeezing his hand.

"I believe there is still the matter of an engagement to see to," he said quietly. "A true engagement."

Looking up, she saw that his handsome face was serious. And deadly earnest.

"I love you, Leonora," he said, standing and pulling her up to face him. "I want you to be my wife. And I will not stop until that happens."

"When we parted five years ago," she said softly, "I thought I would die from the ache of losing you."

"Then why did you turn me away?" he asked, the pain of that rejection evident in his voice. "We might have been together all these years. We might already have a nursery full of children and another on the way."

At his wistful tone, Leonora's heart sank. It had been foolish of her to allow Freddy back into her life when she knew full well that they could never marry. And selfish.

Unable to face the confusion in his eyes, she dropped his hand and turned to compose herself.

Rather than pressing her, Freddy let her go. He'd always been good that way. Allowing her space to breathe. But it was time to tell him the truth, and she greatly feared that when they parted today, it would be forever.

"I regret not telling you the truth five years ago," she said finally. To her surprise, her voice didn't break as she spoke. "I thought it best to keep the matter to myself, though I can see now that it was unfair to you. Not to let you know my true reasons for breaking things off. Especially since I had known all along that a marriage could never happen between us. I suppose I was just selfish.

I wanted to know what it was I'd be missing, you see. And you were so terribly sweet to me."

"Leonora," he said, stepping up behind her—so close she could feel the heat from his body. "You are frightening me. What could possibly keep you from marrying me?"

Turning, she saw that he was serious. And suddenly she could keep her secret no longer.

"When I was fifteen," she said, "I met a young man at our local assembly. He was charming and handsome, and was the first man to show me any sort of attention. Certainly not the sort of attention a man pays a woman. And I was smitten.

"I was already writing verse, and I suspect part of me thought I had to experience romantic love before I could ever begin to truly understand the emotions necessary for fully expressing them in poetry."

She smiled ruefully at the foolishness of her younger self. "But I truly did believe myself to be in love with him. And he with me."

"Since you are not now married to the man," Freddy said tightly, "then I can only suppose something happened that prevented you from forming a lasting attachment."

"Yes," she said softly. "And by the time he was gone, I'd experienced enough emotion to last me a lifetime of emotional verse."

"What happened?"

"Anthony was a soldier who had come to town with his regiment for several months. And we made use of every moment we could spend together that summer. Father was often busy with his own work, and my governess had been gone for a year then. So it was possible to spend quite a bit of time to ourselves."

"You got with child," he said, his voice carefully

neutral. As if any hint of disapproval on his part would send her fleeing.

"It's such a cliché," she said, grateful she hadn't had to say the words out loud. "But we were only together that way a few times. And as soon as I realized about the baby, I told him at once. Foolishly, I thought we could simply move up the date of the wedding we'd talked about all summer. But it is remarkable how quickly a rake's promises dissolve in the face of true commitment."

"He refused to marry you?" Freddy asked, his tone a mix of disgust and disbelief. "To give your child his name? After he'd seduced you?"

"As I said," Lenora said with a sigh. "A cliché. Oh, he promised to do all the right things. He would speak to my father the very next day and we would be married within the month. And when he did not appear the next day, I feared he'd been in an accident. Or had taken ill. When he didn't come the third day, I went to the village, to make sure he was all right. But his rooms had been vacated and one of his friends told me that he'd been called to London."

She laughed bitterly. "Even then, I thought he'd come back to me. But when a month had passed with no word, I knew that what I'd feared was the truth. He wasn't coming back."

"What did you father say?" Freddy asked, his fists clenched. "I hope he put a bullet in the bastard."

"Papa searched for him, but by the time he found Anthony it was too late."

"He was gone?" Freddy asked.

"He was dead," Leonora said, flinching at the memory. "He'd gotten into a brawl in a tavern near the army barracks and was stabbed to death."

"That saves me the trouble of killing him myself,"

Freddy said, stepping forward to lay a hand on her shoulder. "For there's no doubt he deserved it."

"Perhaps so," she agreed. "But at the time, I thought my world was over. And that my child would have no father."

It was obvious since she had no child now that something had happened, but to Leonora's relief Freddy didn't press her. Even so, she would have to tell him the truth of it now.

"Not long after that," she went on, "I lost the child."

He made as if to take her in his arms, but Leonora placed a staying hand on Freddy's chest. "There were complications," she said, hating the words even as she spoke them. "And the end result was that I can no longer bear children."

She watched his eyes change as the meaning of her confession sank in. And her heart clenched as he took a step back.

"Why didn't you tell me?" he demanded. "It would have made no difference to me."

"But what of the children you just mourned, that you thought we might have had if I'd not broken our engagement the first time?"

"You cannot blame me for weaving castles in the air when you hadn't told me how things stood," Freddy said sharply. "It was a logical hope that we would have children. Had I known the truth I'd have changed my expectations."

"You say that now," Leonora said, "because it is what you hope you'd have done."

"We'll never know," he said with a frown. "It's clear you didn't trust me enough to tell me the truth. Then or now."

"Can you blame me?" she asked. "The only other man

I'd loved abandoned me when I told him I was carrying
his child. Was it really so foolish for me to expect the
same thing when you were so clearly looking forward to
fatherhood?"

"You didn't give me the chance to do the right thing,"
he said quickly. "That you placed me in the same cate-
gory as that bastard who left you before shows how little
you thought of my sense of honor."

His words hurt. Because they were true. And Leonora
let the shame wash over her. "It was wrong," she said at
last. "I was a fool not to tell you. It was selfish and that
is why I had to let you go. I was too cowardly to face you
and tell you the truth, but I could make sure that you were
free to fall in love with someone else. To have the family you wanted."

"Do you know how much your rejection hurt me, Leonora?" Freddy demanded, his anguish visible in his
face. "I had expected to live the rest of my life with you
and you turned me away with no good reason. No explanation. I could only imagine I'd hurt you somehow."

He laughed bitterly. "But it would seem that it was you
who wronged me. For no good reason other than a fear
of telling me the truth."

"Do you deny that most men wish to marry in order
to father children?" Leonora asked. "Is it not what the
church says marriage was created for?"

"The church, perhaps, but we are hardly the picture
of piety, my dear. It's my brother who is the vicar in the
family. Not me."

"I wanted to save you," she said, knowing her words
were not recompense enough. "I wanted you to have the
children you'd wished for. And I suspected you'd forget about me before long."

"You should have given me the choice," Freddy said
softly. "By refusing to tell me the truth you did the same

thing you're always railing about when it comes to men's treatment of women. You made the decision for me. As if I didn't know my own mind and hadn't the sense to make the right choice. You robbed me of agency in the matter. If I'd done anything like that to you, you'd have rightly ripped me up over it."

It had never occurred to her to look at her actions in that context, and Leonora knew that if their roles were reversed she would have dismissed him as a paternalistic typical male. If she hadn't already been ashamed of her actions, she would certainly be now.

Suddenly, she was exhausted and overwhelmed. And she wanted him to go so that she could cry in peace.

"Freddy, I have wronged you," she said. "And now that you know the truth, you'll see that the only rational thing for us to do is to dissolve this betrothal. It was never meant to be real anyway."

"I see nothing of the sort," he said firmly. "And what if that physician of yours was wrong? You might even now be carrying my child."

"That is wishful thinking on your part," she said mournfully. "He was quite certain that the damage was permanent. And aside from that, you are not thinking clearly. When you've had a moment to think things over you'll see that parting now is the best decision for you."

"And what of you?" He stepped forward and stroked a finger down her cheek. Leonora closed her eyes at the caress. "What about what's best for you? Surely a life of solitary reflection is not the way for you to live life to the fullest."

"I am trying to do right by you," she said, reaching up to take his hand in hers. "Perhaps you are a younger son, but you deserve to have a family of your own. I want that for you."

"I am not convinced." He squeezed her hand.

Knowing that if she let him he would persuade her out of her decision, Leonora pulled away and walked toward the door.

"It is for the best," she repeated, then fled the room.

Twenty-four

$\mathcal{H}$ours later, Freddy was halfway through another decanter of brandy when his butler arrived to announce that he had visitors.

"Tell them to bugger off," Freddy said, hunching deeper into his armchair. "Don't want to see 'em."

"Afraid not, old fellow," Mainwaring said with a meaningful look at the butler, who took himself away with a nod. "There's news, and though from the look of things you are in no state to do anything about it, it's important."

"Don't give a damn," Freddy said morosely. "Not unless someone has figured out how to raise the dead. 'Cause I'd bloody well kill him again."

"Kill who?" the Duke of Trent asked conversationally, dropping into a chair across from his drunken friend. "Not like you to be so bloodthirsty without reason."

"Oh, I've got reason," Freddy said with a laugh. "If ever a man deserved killing again it's Anthony."

"Don't know any Anthony," Mainwaring said, pulling up another chair for himself. "Though if you think he's worth killing, I have little doubt he is."

The butler returned then with a tray of coffee and

sandwiches, and when he was gone, Trent set about pouring Freddy a cup of the steaming drink.

But Freddy would have none of it. "What the devil are you about trying to sober me up, man? I'm not half drunk enough."

"Which is not usual for you since you got back from France," Mainwaring said meaningfully. "What's happened to put you in such a mood?"

"Normally I'd guess it's a woman," Trent said thoughtfully, "but I cannot imagine the lovely Leonora doing anything to jeopardize things a second time around."

Freddy gulped down his glass of brandy, then frowned as he began to search for the decanter that Mainwaring had hidden from him. "There's where you're wrong, friend," he said absently while he patted the chair around him. "For Leonora has ended our engagement. Again."

"What?" Mainwaring exchanged a look with Trent. "That's impossible. I've seen you together. You were like a pair of bloody lovebirds."

"A lot can change in a day," Freddy said, staring into his now empty brandy glass. "She's doing it for my own good. Which would be hilarious if it weren't so damned infuriating."

"How so?" Trent asked, getting to the heart of the matter. "How could not marrying her be for your own good?"

Freddy sighed. "It's complicated," he said, thrusting a hand through his already mussed hair. "But the gist is that she cannot have children and thinks to protect me from myself by forcing me to marry some other woman who can."

"But I thought one of the benefits of being a younger son was not having to worry about getting heirs and all that?" It was a subject Trent had often teased his friend about. Mostly because as a duke, Trent had no such freedom.

"One would think," Freddy said, resting his head against the back of the chair. "But it is clear that Leonora doesn't think so. And I did not help matters by mentioning children at some point. But dammit, that was just daydreaming. It didn't mean I had my heart set on a dozen children."

"And she won't take you at your word?" Mainwaring asked. "Or am I wrong and it does matter to you?"

"It matters," Freddy said, "but not enough to give up the woman I love. Especially after what that bastard Anthony did to her."

"Ah yes," Trent said, "who is this Anthony? Since he is not happily married to Leonora I suspect the answer is angry-making."

Quickly, Freddy told the story of what Anthony had done to Leonora. Both Trent and Mainwaring swore when he was finished.

"And you're sure he's dead?" Mainwaring asked, flexing his hand as if anticipating a fight.

"According to Leonora he is." Freddy leaned forward and clasped his hands between his knees. "Though I suppose it's not impossible that she only said that to protect me. I can't imagine her father allowed the man to get away without doing the right thing, though."

"True enough." Trent nodded. "Likely Craven was as angry at being denied a chance to bloody the fellow's nose as you are."

"That's not all I'd have bloodied," Freddy growled. "When I think about Nora abandoned and alone. Suffering a miscarriage that likely frightened her to death. I just want to carry her off and wrap her in cotton wool. She is strong, of course she is, but that doesn't mean she should go through things alone. Unfortunately, she won't bloody let me take care of her. For my own good."

"It's not like you to take no for an answer, man," Mainwaring said, shaking his head. "In fact, I'm rather surprised you didn't persuade her that you're capable of making your own decisions."

At his friend's words, Freddy straightened up in his chair. "What did you say?" he asked aghast.

Mainwaring shrugged. "It's just that I think you might have found a way to convince her that you want her whether she can have children or not."

"She ran away, Mainwaring," Freddy bit out. "Was I supposed to chase after her and take her by force?"

"Of course he doesn't mean that," Trent said hurriedly, glaring at Mainwaring who looked unrepentant. "I think perhaps what he means is that it is unlike you to back away so easily. Especially when Leonora has done this to you before. An imbecile could see that the two of you are meant to be together. But you cannot let her fears keep you apart."

"Unless, that is," Mainwaring said unrepentantly, "you truly would prefer to marry someone who can give you a nursery full of ankle-biters."

"Don't be an arse, Mainwaring," Freddy said sharply. "I love her. I don't give a damn that she cannot have children. Except for her own sake, because I know she would make an excellent mother."

"Ah, good," Trent said with a nod. "Then I believe we have some information that might assist you in persuading her. Or at least will get your foot in the door in the event that she refuses to see you."

Freddy frowned. "What?"

"Not good news, I'm afraid," Mainwaring said apologetically. "I followed up on the information you sent me on your return to London. It seems that the Darleighs were found murdered on the Great North Road just outside of London. And Jonny's curricle wasn't with them."

"Gerard." All traces of his earlier inebriation fled as the import of Mainwaring's announcement hit him. "It had to be. My cousin had them killed. Because they fled."

"It's very likely," Trent agreed. "And it also means that Gerard is tying up loose ends. He didn't follow you to London, but that's not because he doesn't wish to make sure neither you nor Leonora is able to report your suspicions to the authorities."

"Damn it," Freddy burst out. "I was supposed to stay with the Cravens until this died down. I was so angry when I left their house, I forgot about it. Leonora and her father must be protected." He rose and began unwrapping his cravat as he stalked to the door.

Mainwaring grabbed his arm. "Wait a minute, old fellow. There's more."

"What?" Freddy demanded impatiently.

"We need to figure out a way to stop Gerard once and for all," Trent said. "And I think perhaps you and Leonora might be able to do it. If you work together."

"I don't want her put in harm's way." Freddy was not going to let anyone hurt Leonora ever again.

"We won't," Mainwaring assured her. "In fact, if the plan goes right, you'll have plenty of time to persuade her to marry you."

"Let's hear it, then," Freddy said impatiently.

"Are you sure that you don't want a nice cuppa tea, miss?" Leonora's maid asked again as she tidied her mistress's bedchamber.

Leonora had wept herself to sleep almost as soon as she heard the front door close when Freddy left. She'd hoped to stay by Freddy's side at least until they'd managed to close the net around Gerard, but it seemed that had been too much to hope for. She wasn't sure why she'd felt so compelled to tell Freddy the truth this afternoon, but something about the sincerity of his proposal had made her own mendacity cut like a knife. It had been physically impossible for her to go another minute without telling him the truth of what had happened between them five years before. And indeed, why she could not marry him now, either.

Instead of the relief she'd hoped for, however, all she'd felt on seeing the betrayal in his eyes was a degree of hopelessness she'd not experienced since all those years ago when she'd lost both her child and Anthony in one fell swoop. Now, of course, she was glad not to be tied to a man like Anthony, but her heartbreak at the time had been genuine.

Turning over the lavender-water-soaked cloth on her forehead to capture the coolness of the other side, Leonora tried and failed to erase the memory of the hurt in Freddy's eyes just before she left him that afternoon. She'd done so much harm to him at this point, she could never hope to atone for it.

And he'd been right when he said she was patronizing him not to let him make the decision for himself. But she knew him so well. He would do the right thing no matter how much it hurt him. If she could, by some miracle, conceive, then perhaps things would be different. But she would not let that insidious hope flourish in her breast. Her courses were due in a few days, which would put a rest to such wishful thinking. And the sooner that happened, the better.

A brisk knock on her bedchamber door broke her from her reverie.

"I told them you weren't to be disturbed," her maid grumbled. Leonora didn't move, but she could hear Peggy's skirts rustle as she crossed the room to the door.

When she heard Freddy's voice, however, she sat bolt upright, flinging the cold compress aside.

"Miss," Peggy said, aggrieved, "I told him you weren't to be disturbed, but he won't take no for an answer."

"It's important, Leonora." Freddy pushed past Peggy into the room and stood watching her. "I'd not have disturbed you otherwise."

Searching his face for some other explanation, she saw only fatigue and determination.

"It's all right, Peggy," she told the maid. "Leave us alone. We are betrothed after all."

At the lie, Freddy's brow quirked. But Leonora refused to feel bad about the obfuscation. He was the one who'd barged into her bedchamber. A little white lie was the least he could give her.

"All right, miss," Peggy said with a frown. "But you just call out if you need me."

When the door had closed behind the maid, Leonora was suddenly aware that she was alone in her bedchamber with him. A glance at Freddy told her he was thinking much the same thing.

Swallowing, Leonora climbed down from the bed and walked in stocking feet to the door that led into her sitting room. She heard Freddy following behind her.

When they were seated across from one another, she indicated with a hand that he should state his business.

"Lord and Lady Darleigh were found murdered on the Great North Road this morning," he said without preamble. "Jonathan's carriage was missing. I've sent a man to search South Haven but haven't heard back yet."

"Dear God," Leonora said, pressing a hand to her chest. "It's what they both feared from the moment Lord Darleigh decided to leave the club, but now it's happened, I can hardly believe it."

"My cousin has shown no compunction about killing anyone who dares to leave the club, or anyone who tries to uncover his illicit dealings as Jonathan did," Freddy said. "Or as you and I have."

"If this is about finding someone to protect my father and me—" Leonora began.

But Freddy raised a hand. "We can discuss that later. What we need now is to find some way to trap Gerard once and for all. And to do that I need your help."

Leonora was ashamed to admit that in the aftermath of their confrontation that afternoon, she'd not spared more than a moment's thought for Gerard. Or her brother for that matter. "Of course I'll do whatever you need," she said firmly. "He should be punished for Jonathan's death as well as those of Lord and Lady Darleigh."

"Well, since we no longer have the curricle to offer as evidence against him," Freddy said, "it will be more difficult to prove his guilt. Which means we'll need to lure him into killing someone else."

Leonora's eyes widened. She understood the need to catch Gerard in the act, but was it really necessary to use someone as bait? She had little doubt of who the proposed victim would be.

"Surely there is another way," she said, shaking her head. "You do not need to risk your life again to catch him."

But Freddy gave an elegant shrug. "I don't mean to let him succeed.

"I have too much to live for," he added, his eyes intent.

She held his gaze and felt her heart quicken. "I do not want to see you hurt," she said finally. Looking away.

Whatever he'd seen in her look must have satisfied him, for he moved on, saying, "I mean to make him an offer he cannot refuse. I'll invite my cousin to race our curricles from the Cumberland Gate of Hyde Park to the Golden Hind in Greenwich. A shorter route than your brother's race but enough, I believe, to catch out Gerard."

Gasping, Leonora shook her head. "Why in God's name would you wish to do that? Hasn't Jonathan's death been enough?"

She was surprised to see that her hands were trembling. Closing her eyes, she tried to block the image of Freddy's broken body on the roadside, just like Jonathan's.

Freddy moved to her side, took her hands in his large ones and rubbed some feeling back into them. "If there were any other way, Nora, you know I'd consider it. But my cousin is just cocksure enough to suppose he'll be able to commit the same crime in the same place twice. And I have every intention of turning the tables on him."

"Will you have help from Mainwaring and Trent?" she asked, staring at their joined hands. If she dared look up she knew the tears that threatened would spill. And she wanted to appear strong even if she did not feel it.

"Of course," Freddy replied, rubbing the back of her hand with his thumb. "They insist upon it."

At least someone was thinking sensibly about the matter, she thought.

"What do you need me for?" she said aloud, hearing the querulous tone in her own voice, but preferring it to the naked fear she felt on his behalf. "It sounds as if you and your friends will be able to take care of things."

"Oh, we will," he assured her. "But I have a sneaking suspicion that his wife will attend the race in some fashion. She might claim to find his lifestyle revolting but she won't miss an opportunity to see him defeated. Perhaps she will confide her knowledge of his crimes to you. I think you have proven yourself quite capable of handling her."

"But if we are no longer betrothed—" Leonora began.

"That won't necessarily mean that we no longer have feelings for one another," Freddy said patiently. "Nor does it mean you are no longer Jonathan's sister. You have just as much reason to fight back against them as I have. Perhaps more. And my cousin has made it clear that he is willing to kill to keep from having their secrets exposed. Hopefully, he'll make some mistake that will lead to his downfall."

"So we are both to serve as bait to them, then," Leonora said.

"I do not think you'll be in danger," Freddy said. "But, yes, in our different ways we are meant to lure these two into revealing themselves in public. And I think it might be a good idea if you invite your friends Lady Hermione and Miss Dantry along. If only so that you will have reinforcements if needed."

She didn't like it. But neither of them had been able to come up with a better plan. And Leonora was not sure she could bear to let her brother's killer escape with no punishment at all. It would be the height of injustice. And she had made a vow to see that Jonathan's death was avenged. This might be the only chance she'd ever have to do it.

"All right," she said, "I will write to Ophelia and Hermione at once. I feel sure both of them will not wish to miss such an opportunity for excitement. And I believe Lady Fincher cut Ophelia once so she will be glad to return the favor."

Freddy nodded, and now that their business was settled, an awkward silence fell upon the sitting room.

Finally, Leonora said, "If that's all you needed, I'd best go send those letters. And I'll need to find someone to watch the house this evening."

"You cannot possibly think I'm going to leave you and

your father to the mercy of some hired hand, do you?" Freddy shook his head in disbelief. "I will stay here just as we agreed before our row this afternoon."

"But Lord Frederick," she protested. "It's not necessary."

"It's Freddy to you," he said sharply. "And it is absolutely necessary. Leonora, I have no intention of letting you go without a fight. I will not press you on the matter yet, but know that I have every intention of wedding you before this year is done."

Leonora closed her eyes. "Why do you insist upon this? I have already let you go. Why can't you let me go, too?"

"Because I'm in love with you," Freddy said, rising to stand before her. "I know you think your decision was what's best for me, but I am a man grown. I know my own mind. And I won't give you up again."

Before she could respond, he took her hand and pulled her to her feet. They stood facing one another for barely a moment before he turned and strode to the door leading into the hallway.

"I have a few things to take care of this afternoon, but I will be back in time for dinner," he said as he walked. "In the meantime, do not go out unescorted. I have two guards watching the house to make sure no one attempts to break in."

Knowing that protest would be useless, Leonora said simply, "Very well."

Turning before he opened the door, Freddy said, "It will all work out, Nora. I promise you. We will avenge Jonathan's death, and find some bit of happiness for ourselves."

When he was gone, she dropped back into her chair.

Though part of her was frustrated at his insistence upon the match between them, a larger part rejoiced at his passion for her. Though she knew it would be better for him if they parted ways, she was quickly coming to realize that losing him again would mean something more than simple sadness for her.

It would be the end of any chance she had at happiness.

Twenty-five

*A*fter determining that his cousin and his wife had indeed returned to London from the country, Freddy next set out to arrange a private meeting with Gerard.

While he waited for a reply to his note, he paid a visit to the mews behind his town house to ensure that Archer's grays were none the worse for wear after the harrowing escape from the Fincher country house. Fortunately, both horses seemed well rested and Ulysses' strained fetlock had healed perfectly. Odysseus, the other gelding, not wishing to be ignored, stuck his head out of his adjoining stall as Freddy stepped out, and sniffed at any part of his master he could reach, in search of the carrots Freddy sometimes brought them.

"Good afternoon to you too, Ody," Freddy said with a grin as he dug the treat from his pocket. "I haven't forgotten you, old fellow. Just needed to make sure your counterpart is recovered."

The sound of the horse's chomping was loud, but not loud enough to mask the sound of someone's booted feet crossing the cobblestone floor. Turning, he saw his cousin stroking Ulysses' snout.

Straightening, Freddy crossed his arms and leaned against the stall door, the picture of calm.

"Your grays are as fine a pair as I've seen in years," Gerard said conversationally, looking up from the horse, who as if sensing some unrest in the air, tossed his head a bit. "I am glad to see that your precipitate flight from my country home didn't leave any lasting damage."

"If you think to shame me for removing my lady from a situation that endangered her," Freddy said, brows raised, "then I fear that dog won't hunt."

Stepping away from the stall, Gerard brushed his hands together before replying. "I do not believe Miss Craven was put in danger at any point during her visit to my home. My wife saw to her every comfort, I feel sure."

"Perhaps we have different definitions of danger, then," Freddy said with a grin that didn't reach his eyes. "For I consider threatening to leave her without a protector in your unconventional household is quite dangerous. What would have happened to her if I'd died during your private fight in the stables? I have a strong feeling that some of your guests would have seen her lack of protection as a challenge. Perhaps even you would have done—if Melisande were not the sort to cut off your bollocks herself and feed them to the pigs."

Rather than argue, Gerard shrugged. "My wife is a strong woman. And she does not tolerate my wandering eye. So, your little poetess would have been perfectly safe."

"We will simply have to agree to disagree, Gerry," Freddy said with a shrug. "I assume your presence in my mews indicates that you've received my challenge?"

Gerard sucked his teeth. "Indeed it does, cousin," he said coolly. "Though I had always assumed the gentleman being challenged had the choice of weapons. It seems that you have usurped my own agency by inviting me to a competition of your choosing."

Raising his brows in mock surprise, Freddy shook his head. "How melodramatic you are, Gerry. I meant only to issue a friendly challenge between friends. My new curricle against yours. Since you are the leader of a curricle racing club, it seems like something you would be especially suited for. Plus there is the whole matter of Jonathan's death along the same route."

A furrow appeared between Gerard's brows. He did not like this line of questioning, it would appear. "What has Jonathan's death to do with anything? I have already assured you it was an accident. And sadly, his own vehicle was stolen from my carriage house the same evening that you fled. I assume that was a coincidence. Wasn't it?"

At the mention of Jonathan's curricle, Freddy stiffened. He wasn't sure what he'd expected from his cousin, but a bold allusion to the murders Gerard had only recently taken part in was not it. "Come now, Gerry. Do not try to convince me that you have no knowledge of exactly what happened to Craven's curricle. I have little doubt that you oversaw the burning of it yourself. After you made sure that Lord and Lady Darleigh were taken care of."

If he was hoping for Gerard to protest his innocence, then Freddy was doomed to disappointment. As unruffled as ever, he said, "Now who is being melodramatic? I vow, cousin, you must think me a veritable monster to ascribe three murders in the space of a month to me. What happened to Lord and Lady Darleigh was shocking, but I certainly had no hand in it."

"That is because you are adept at delegating unpleasant tasks to those who serve under you in your club," Freddy retorted. "But I do think there are some things you like to do yourself. Whether it's getting rid of evidence, or taking special charge of your victims' property,

I know in my gut that you enjoy getting your hands dirty. Otherwise you cannot claim the deed for your own."

The two men stared at one another for a moment, and Freddy saw the clench of his cousin's jaw as confirmation that one of his accusations had hit its target.

"If you believe I am capable of such crimes," Gerard said finally, "then I suggest you take your suspicions to Bow Street. Or is there perhaps some reason you haven't yet? Could it be because you have no real proof besides your own delusions that I have committed these murders? For I vow, I cannot think of any other reason for you to hang back."

Freddy clenched his fists. "You know very well lack of proof is my reason," he said through his teeth. "But it's no delusion. I will find it eventually. And you will be punished."

"Your threats have grown tedious, cousin," the other man drawled. "I will answer your challenge with one of my own. Then we can be done with one another."

This was an interesting development. "What is your counterchallenge then?"

"If you win, I turn myself in to the authorities," Gerard said smugly. "But if I win—and really, I am so much your superior behind the reins that there is no doubt I will best you—then you will agree to be the . . . let us call it the enforcer, for the Lords of Anarchy for the coming year."

It was a canny offer. And one that Gerard must know Freddy could not refuse. Letting his cousin walk away from what he'd done without punishment was unthinkable. And Freddy was willing to risk himself for the next year in order to ensure that Gerard's victims had justice. That Leonora had justice for her brother.

"It's a deal," he said before he could dither over the matter further. "We will begin at Hyde Park and drive the route from London to Bedford, ending at the White Hart."

Gerard offered his hand, and reluctantly Freddy took it.

"I do hope you achieve the outcome you so richly deserve tomorrow, cousin," Gerard said with a nasty smile.

"The same to you, Gerry," Frederick said with a confident grin. "Until tomorrow."

He only wished he were as sure of his cousin's defeat as he seemed.

When Freddy still hadn't arrived by ten that evening Leonora, desperate for something, *anything,* to get her mind off his words before he left her earlier, found herself wandering down the upstairs hall toward the door of Jonathan's rooms.

Stepping inside, she set down the lamp she carried and surveyed the room. This disarray caused by Sir Gerard's henchmen when they'd searched the room last week had been tidied. And objectively, Leonora could find no fault with the job the servants had done.

It was just that she knew now.

Knew that Jonny would never be there to arrange his papers just so. Or place his pastel crayons in the order he preferred.

There was no life in the room now. And Leonora could not pretend he might come bounding in at any minute to quiz her over some political issue they disagreed over.

And when they found a way to catch Sir Gerard, it would be time to move on.

"It's dreadfully empty, isn't it, my dear?" her father asked, from the doorway. He was in his wheeled chair and maneuvered himself farther into the room and rolled to a stop beside her.

Leonora put her hand on his shoulder. "It is, Papa. And I'm not sure we'll be able to prove that he was killed by Sir Gerard. There is simply no proof to be had. And tomorrow, Freddy is going to risk his life . . ."

Mr. Craven patted her hand. "There must be another way."

Moving farther into the room, he turned the chair so he was facing her. Leonora sat in the chair near the bookshelf, watching him.

"There is something we are missing. It might not even be something necessary to prove the man's guilt to the authorities," Mr. Craven said. "A man like Sir Gerard has his fingers in many pies."

That was certainly true. Apart from murder and kidnapping, which is what one had to call their detaining of Lord Darleigh against his will, there were the underground fights that provided his income.

She wasn't sure what it was that made a man like Gerard need a steady stream of violence in his life. Most men were perfectly happy with the sorts of prizefights she remembered her brother attending in his youth. There were tales of spectators coming from miles away to watch Gentleman Jackson in his heyday.

She'd heard rumors that many of the fights in London were run by men in the rookeries who were—if the rumors were correct—more violent and dangerous than even Sir Gerard. What would those men think if they knew Sir Gerard had been selling seats to his underground no-rules fights?

"Papa!" she shouted. "You are a genius!"

Her father shook his head. "I'm not sure that's true, my dear. I only asked a logical question."

"But you are," she said, jumping up from her chair to kiss him on the cheek. "You asked what other crimes Gerard was involved in. The only profitable one I could think of was his underground no-rules fights. I saw the purse his crony Lord Payne held the night of the fire, and it was overflowing."

Mr. Craven smiled slowly. "I should think someone like Irish Jack O'Dowd would be very interested to hear that someone is making a profit off fights that are being conducted just miles from his territory."

"I should imagine he'd be quite upset, given that he too makes his living from selling tickets to prizefights," Leonora said. "Papa, I'll bet anything that the papers Jonny had hidden in his safe were something to do with those fights. Maybe some kind of record of how much Sir Gerard has been earning from the bouts."

"What papers?" Mr. Craven asked, surprised. "You never asked me about any papers."

The note from Jonathan had been so upsetting that Leonora had thought of nothing but searching her brother's room as soon as she got home that day.

Quickly she relayed what the note had said. Especially the mention of how he'd hidden some papers that would harm Sir Gerard in some way in his safe.

"My dear girl," Mr. Craven said when she'd finished. "Your brother has been storing his important papers in the safe in my library for years now. The small one in his bedchamber was hardly worth keeping a five pence in. I believe Moppet, my spaniel, could break into it."

She gaped. "There's another safe?"

"Let's go look," he said, rolling his chair across the well-worn carpet. "I am suddenly quite eager to see the look on Sir Gerard's face when he learns that Jack O'Dowd is coming after him."

Turning to shut the door behind them, Leonora took one last look at her brother's empty room.

"We did it, Jonny," she said quietly. "We're going to end Sir Gerard Fincher."

As she turned, a draft—for what else could it be?—skimmed across her cheeks, as gentle as a kiss.

It was quite late by the time Freddy returned to the Craven town house that evening.

In addition to making sure that Archer's curricle was in top condition, he'd also seen his man of business about making sure that if by some twist of fate his cousin managed to fatally injure him in the course of tomorrow's race, Leonora would be well cared for.

He knew she had a sizable dowry coming to her for when she married, but if she wished never to wed, she could depend on Freddy's bequest.

It was a sobering meeting. In large part because despite her insistence that she would never be able to have children, he couldn't shake the feeling that even now she might be carrying their child.

Her revelation earlier had sent all his hopes for the future crashing down around him.

It wasn't that she had lain with another man. Though given the chance he'd cross oceans to find the blackguard who tempted Leonora into giving him her virginity then ran off when she told him about the child he'd fathered.

How could a man do such a thing? It was unfathomable to Freddie who, for all his rakish reputation, had wanted only one woman in the last half decade. And the idea of leaving her frightened and alone with a baby on the way was simply not possible.

Stretching his shoulders, he climbed the stairs up to the bedchamber he'd been given, on the other end of the hall from Leonora's, and was relieved to see his valet had taken him at his word and gone to bed.

He unwound his neckcloth as he crossed to the writing table near the window. He could have sworn it was empty when he left that afternoon, but in the dim light of the lamp, he saw a few papers scattered over it.

Sure enough, there on the gleaming mahogany surface were three ledger pages. At the top of each page were names Freddy recognized: Gerard, Lord Payne, Lord Darleigh, and others from the rolls of the Lords of Anarchy.

Scanning the columns, he saw that the bottom of each of the three pages there boasted an eye-poppingly large positive number. And across the top of the first page, a name which any *Times* reader would recognize.

It was all here. And maybe the best and most permanent way to remove Sir Gerard Fincher from their lives forever.

"I realized what his plan must have been tonight," Leonora said from behind him. "When Father and I were going over the things we'd learned about Sir Gerard, I said something about the safe that had been stolen and Papa reminded me that Jonny had been keeping his important papers in the safe in the study."

"And there they were?" Freddy asked, tossing his neckcloth to the side.

"There they were."

Her hair was down, and she wore a perfectly sensible cotton nightdress. And to Freddy's eyes she'd never been more beautiful.

Wordlessly he pulled her into his arms. And they stood together, heat against heat.

"It is a clever plan," she said against his lawn shirt. "But he was too much the gentleman to go through with it."

"I think it's highly likely my cousin threatened to hurt

you," Freddy said, breathing in the sweet lilac scent of her. "Or someone else he cared about."

"But he might have been able to destroy Gerard before he had the chance to hurt me," she said, sounding sad but resigned.

"It was a gamble." Freddy smoothed a hand over her hair. "And I have a feeling your brother wasn't willing to risk your life in exchange for his."

"I certainly hope you don't plan to make the same mistake," she said with a sharp look.

"No." He brushed a thumb over her cheek. "I plan on sending those papers to Irish Jack first thing in the morning. And another note to my cousin. I thought it would be only cricket to give him a running start."

Leonora nodded. "What do you think your cousin will do?" she asked.

"I imagine he'll get himself on the first ship bound for India, or the Americas. Really, anywhere out of Irish Jack's reach. Which can be quite far, I'm told, when he's got his back up."

"All that death," she said. "I wonder if Lord and Lady Darleigh might have been saved if I'd spoken to Father earlier." He could see in her eyes that she blamed herself.

"I think it is safe to tell you this now," Freddy said gravely, "because my cousin will be leaving town soon. But please keep this information to yourself for right now."

He reached into his pocket and pulled out a crumpled letter.

She unfolded it, and as her eyes scanned the page, she squealed. "They're alive? But how?"

"It's in the letter," he said, "but the long and the short of it is that Darleigh had been planning his own getaway for weeks. His wife was rightly worried that he might succeed in bringing Gerard's wrath down on them, and so asked you for help. What she didn't know was that on the night of the fire, when they drove off in your brother's curricle, it was in order to fake their deaths."

"How did they manage it? The curricle was supposedly stolen, again, and there were bodies."

"They didn't kill anyone." Freddy smiled. "Lord Darleigh just relied on one of the timeworn traditions of running away. He bribed the magistrate to send notice of his death to my cousin."

Leonora gaped. "And by the time Gerard figured out the truth, they would be long gone."

"Exactly."

"You cannot know how relieved I am. When I found those papers tonight, all I could think of was how I'd let Corinne down."

"You are a kindhearted lady," he said with a grin.

"Now." He stepped back and without warning lifted her up in his arms and carried her to the sofa, where he pulled her onto his lap. "I hope you will show me how kindhearted you can be."

"That all depends on what you tell me, sir," she said pertly.

He wanted more than anything to make light of this thing between them. But it was too serious for that now.

"I am in love with you, Nora," he said, gazing down at the face that had grown so familiar he could see it even when she wasn't in the room. "And have been since the first time we met."

If it were possible for her to grow lovelier, she did. "Me, too," she said, her eyes shining. "I've just been too stubborn to realize that love sometimes means allowing the beloved to make his own decisions."

"Managing female," he said without heat. "In some things, I am quite capable of knowing my own mind."

"And," he continued before she could speak, "I want to marry you, Nora. And there are any number of ways to have children without bearing them yourself. One of the luxuries of being a younger son is not worrying about producing an heir. And I'm dashed if I'll waste that very valuable bounty on some other lady as fertile as the day is long, but who isn't you."

As he continued to speak, he saw her smile grow wider but her eyes fill with more tears.

"I'm so sorry, my love, for ever doubting you," she said, throwing her arms around his neck and kissing him.

When she was breathless, she tucked her head under his chin. "Of course I will marry you. You sweet, stubborn, infuriating man. It's all I've wanted since the first time you asked me."

"We've both grown up a great deal since that first betrothal," Freddy said once he'd kissed her breathless again. With his free hand, he reached into his coat pocket and took out a jeweler's box.

At the sight of it Leonora's eyes went wide. "It cannot possibly be the same one," she whispered. As if using too loud a voice would frighten it away.

"Open it and find out," Freddy said, revealing nothing.

Her hands shaking, Leonora lifted the lid of the blue velvet box and inside was the very same ring. Only whereas before it had been a square-cut sapphire, now the blue stone was surrounded by a circlet of diamonds.

"For every year we were apart," Freddy said, his voice hoarse with emotion. "To remind you that no matter what separates us, I'll always come back."

Leonora, who had been fashioning words into ideas for more years than she could count, found herself speechless.

So she thanked him without words.

And Freddy liked that quite well, indeed.

Epilogue

One month later

I cannot believe the Lords of Anarchy have been disbanded," Hermione said for the third time in as many minutes. "The entire scope of London driving clubs will be changed forever."

In the weeks since the discovery of the pages from Sir Gerard's fighting ledgers, many things that had once loomed large in Leonora's world had been blown away like so many dandelion petals.

The most important was that, thanks to Jonathan's work, the information that his corner of London had been infiltrated by a poacher had been conveyed to Irish Jack O'Dowd, and he had wasted no time in giving Sir Gerard a choice: leave England and live, or remain in England and die.

Like most bullies when faced with an opponent bigger and stronger than them, Sir Gerard chose to live. He and Lady Melisande had departed for Paris later that week.

Of course, Paris wasn't nearly as far away as it might be, but for now, the man responsible for Jonny's death was gone, and for that Leonora was grateful.

With the loss of its founder and most influential leader, the Lords of Anarchy had publicly declared themselves disbanded.

Now, in celebration of their marriage and the club's demise, Leonora and Freddy had invited their friends to join them for a small gathering. Since their wedding by special license the same week Sir Gerard left town, Freddy had moved into the Craven town house. Which is where they now entertained their guests, with tea for the ladies and something a bit stronger for the gentlemen.

"Perhaps now that the Anarchists are no longer there to set a poor example for the other clubs, Hermione, they will make some changes themselves." Now that she no longer spent every moment fearing what Gerard would do next, Leonora had turned her mind to helping her friend fulfill her wish to be a member of a driving club. "Allowing more ladies to become club members, for instance."

"Why don't you start your own club, Lady Hermione," Mainwaring offered from his position near the fire. "Then you won't have to worry about crackbrained presidents using the club to reap ill-gotten gains. Because the crackbrained president will be you!"

Leonora almost bit her tongue when she saw the expression on Hermione's face. It didn't matter what poor Mainwaring said, Hermione would find a way to misunderstand—or in this case, perfectly understand—and get angry.

"It's not a bad idea, my lady," Freddy said after exchanging a speaking look with his wife. "If you can't beat them, join them."

Hermione sighed. "I have no desire to be the president of a driving club," she said, pushing a blond curl from her forehead. "I wanted to join a club mostly because I want to compete. With the best. And at the moment, that simply is not possible."

"Well," Ophelia said loyally, "I have the utmost faith in you, Hermione. And I have little doubt you'll be racing with the best of them one day soon."

Leonora had no trouble at all understanding why her friend wanted to take her rightful place among the driving elite of London. She'd felt the same way about her poems being relegated to ladies' magazines, when it seemed as if the male writers all ended up in the prestigious journals. It was frustrating to be kept out of the most competitive circles.

Before she could say anything, however, the Duke of Trent said, "I am afraid that our celebration of the demise of the Anarchists may be a bit premature."

Everyone in the room stared at the duke.

"Well, don't keep us in suspense, man," Freddy said, sitting on the arm of Leonora's chair. "We are all agog to hear this tidbit of yours."

"I hardly think Trent would use the term 'tidbit,'" Mainwaring said under his breath.

"When I was at Jackson's this morning, minding my own business," the duke said, "I was approached by none other than the loathsome Lord Payne."

"Oh no," Leonora said. "I am sorry, your grace. That cannot have been pleasant."

"I feel sure Trent has mixed with much worse fellows than Payne, my dear," said Freddy. "Though I do agree that any meeting with Payne must necessarily be unpleasant."

"He informed me, as if I would be delighted to hear it," the duke continued, "that he and some of the other former Anarchists have decided to reopen the club, only not to the public. They will race and do whatever it is they did—presumably *not* conducting boxing matches that will get them on the first packet to India."

"I might have known they would spring up again," Leonora said with a grimace. "Like an illness that cannot be completely cured."

But Hermione was clearly tired of the subject of driving clubs.

"I think instead of focusing on the misdeeds of the Anarchists, we should instead celebrate the man who made it possible to put an end to Sir Gerard Fincher's reign."

Lifting her teacup, she offered it in toast. "To Jonathan, who was an exceptional driver, and a better friend."

"Hear hear!" Freddy said with a solemn nod, raising his own glass.

And one by one the others did so as well.

Leonora, who once thought she grieved in solitude for her brother, was touched to see how much they all missed him. When Freddy reached for her hand, as if guessing her thoughts, her heart swelled with the knowledge that she would no longer have to face life's difficulties without a partner to share the burden.

When the conversation had reverted back to males on one side of the room and ladies on the other, Leonora turned to Hermione, who had been quiet since her toast.

"I hope that you will consider what Lord Mainwaring suggested, dearest," she said, "for I think you are a good enough whip to manage your own club."

"It's not that I haven't thought of it," Hermione said with a shrug. "It's simply that there aren't that many ladies who like to drive. And those who are really good are already members of other clubs."

"Why is it that you cannot manage to get even one of them to accept you?" Ophelia asked with a frown. "You *are* a good driver. It's odd."

"I wasn't going to tell you," Hermione said in a low voice, "but the reason I can't get into a club is that my father has threatened every club in town that if they accept my application, he'll have them blackballed from White's and Brooks's."

"Oh, Hermione," Leonora said, squeezing the other girl's hand, "I am so sorry."

"What will you do?" Ophelia asked. She was always thinking ahead.

"I sincerely do not want to tell you," their friend said, her eyes downcast. "But I have to tell someone, or I'll burst."

Looking up, she said, "I too was approached by Lord Payne this week. It would seem that as the new club president, he wishes to make some changes in the eligibility rules."

"Please, no!" Leonora gasped.

"You didn't." Ophelia clapped a hand over her mouth.

"I did, I'm afraid," Hermione said apologetically. "I told Lord Payne that I would join the Lords of Anarchy."